Advance Praise

"Paul Yarbrough brings readers deep into the sweet, endless bliss of a southern childhood. On the bridge between boyhood and manhood, his characters deliver delight, inspiration, and humor in every scene." —*Julie Cantrell, New York Times and USA TODAY bestselling author of* Into the Free *and* When Mountains Move

"…the reader is drawn page-by-page into the past…a sampling of the South in an engaging coming-of-age tale." —*Denise Weimer, author of The Georgia Gold Series*

"*A Mississippi Whisper* transports the reader to a time and place cherished in every heart that recalls childhood with fondness. A superb read." —*Fred Miller, author of short stories appearing in* Front Porch Review *and numerous other publications*

"Paul Yarbrough's novels are delightful tributes to the life and culture of Mississippi. The stories, characters, and feel of his work will ring true to every Southerner, no matter where you call home." —*J. Steven Wilkins, author of* Call of Duty: The Sterling Nobility of Robert E. Lee *and* All Things for Good: The Steadfast Nobility of Stonewall Jackson

"The South is a place loved by those who know her as a mother loves a child, faults included. Many have noted that Southerners have a long memory, where the past is not dead or really past.... *A Mississippi Whisper* caresses the memory like the smell of fresh plowed fields, the calling of a bobwhite, or the taste of fresh home-grown tomatoes caresses the senses of a man reflecting on his youth." —*Walter Donald Kennedy, author of* The South Was Right

"Paul Yarbrough beautifully catches the cadence and rhythm and humor of pre-adolescent Mississippi boys in the early 1950s. Anyone growing up in the South at that time will recognize familiar sights and sounds." —*Lynda Lee Meade Shea, Former Miss Mississippi and Miss America*

"There's a lot of Tom Sawyer or Harper Lee's Scout in this tale. And it's worth re-visiting that innocent time, even if a murder mystery is the vehicle for the ride." —*Noel Workman,* Delta Magazine

A
Mississippi
Whisper

Also by Paul H. Yarbrough
Mississippi Cotton

A
Mississippi
Whisper

Paul H. Yarbrough

WiDō Publishing
Salt Lake City • Houston

WiDō Publishing
Salt Lake City, Utah
www.widopublishing.com

Cover Design by Steven Novak
Book Design by Marny K. Parkin

Print ISBN: 978-1-937178-58-1
Library of Congress Control Number: 2014950454
Printed in the United States of America

To
Margaret Faith Yarbrough: a daughter of Mississippi

"A human life, I think, should be well rooted in some spot of native land, where it may get the love of tender kinship for the face of the earth, for the labours of men go forth to, for the sounds and accents that haunt it, for whatever will give that early home a familiar unmistakable difference among the future widening of knowledge: a spot where the definiteness of early memories may be inwrought with affection, and kindly acquaintance with all neighbors, even to the dogs and donkeys, may spread not by sentimental effort and reflection, but as a sweet habit of the blood."

—George Eliot

"It happened that several persons were conversing of a certain battle, and one of them remarked that the Mississippians did not run. 'Oh no!' said another, 'Mississippians never run.'"

—Jefferson Davis,
speech at Old Capitol, Jackson, Mississippi, 1862

Prologue

I REMEMBER THE FIRE; AND THE HIDDEN GRAVE, AND THE shock at what turned up. I remember bobcats. I remember a Negro baseball player.

It's funny how we remember things a long time ago better than things right now. Somebody told me once when we are younger our minds are more fertile and better able to absorb; how fruitful soil husbands seeds better than dry, windswept, old and hardened ground that rejects new life. I remember when I became ten-years old. It was almost as if it were a book I had read a hundred times.

News about the Supreme Court and a judgment changing schools around the country.

Everyone seemed to talk about Ethel and Julius Rosenberg.

And General Eisenhower becoming president; and Stalin, the big leader of the Communists in Russia, dying. Everybody seemed pretty happy about him dying. My daddy said Stalin was a murdering screwball. But it made me wonder why a murdering screwball was on our side in WWII. I figured I didn't know why, because of my age.

The Korean War ended in 1953 before school had started, but I never understood the reason for a war there. Daddy and my grandfather, Big Daddy, and lots of other men said it would have ended a lot sooner if we had listened to General MacArthur instead of those knuckleheads in Washington. Big Daddy said MacArthur's talent stood next to Robert E. Lee's or Stonewall Jackson's, and nobody could ask more. He had low regard for Truman, even if he was a Baptist. He said if he had been a Methodist they probably would have impeached him. My grandmother said they should have impeached him for being a Methodist if he had been one. She didn't realize I was in the room until after she had said it, so I think she regretted saying it. She had a lot of Methodist friends who she taught piano to and played bridge with. I didn't ask what "impeached" meant, but it didn't sound like it was something you wanted done to you—like being impaled while picking blackberries.

We all dreaded one thing the most. We lived in terror of it. It seemed to be talked about more, and feared more, than spies and wars and communists, and anything else. It didn't break bodies alone, it broke hearts and souls and families too, my mother said: poliomyelitia—infantile paralysis—polio.

There seemed to be a lot of other things people would end up talking about, like the Yankees winning the pennant in the American League and the usual thing of the Dodgers winning the National League pennant, which meant a Dodger-Yankee World Series. They would play in October and everybody who had a transistor radio tried to sneak it into school; or tried to come up with some strange ailment so he could stay home and listen. Or, for a few lucky ones, to watch on TV, something brand new.

In 1953, some guy named Hugh Heffner came out with a magazine called *Playboy*. And it would be in some of the stores. My brother, Henry, said it would be a magazine with some pictures of naked girls. I wondered where he heard about it, but I assumed it was true because my mother said if she weren't a lady she would write Mr. Hefner a letter and tell him where he could put his magazine.

But things in my home in Jackson were important because they were right there so close you could almost touch them. And you knew most everybody and who they belonged to.

My daddy's name was Randolph McCoy, but most everybody called him Randy. My grandfather, also named Randolph, though he had a different middle name. But everyone called him Mr. Randy except Henry and me. We called him Big Daddy. My mother's maiden name was Linda Everette. She had become a McCoy before my daddy sailed to Burma in WWII. Her mother, who we called Minnie, wrote verse and song, and played and taught the piano; and though she played many selections and requests, her soothing, gentle, efforts of *Moonlight Sonata* were etched on my childhood soul. Her husband, my other grandfather, Charles Everette, my namesake, had died in the great influenza epidemic of 1919 shortly after my mother's birth.

I remember my mother had an expression she used about almost any excitable situation. We called it her Mississippi statement: "In a Mississippi Minute"; or "You're making a Mississippi Mess"; or "You're as filthy as Mississippi Mud." She usually directed them at Henry or me.

My sister, Katy Jean was twenty. She struggled. These are things I remember, and an old colored man named Joe Washington who had played baseball in the Negro Leagues, who had a build more like a boxer than a ballplayer.

With will and memory I often go back to a time, to a place. And like an eddy drawing events to it, often it is the fire and the ashes drawing my mind to the memories.

Chapter 1

WE HAD MOVED INTO OUR NEW NEIGHBORHOOD A YEAR
before, and Henry and I had made friends with some
boys up the street: Ronny Erl and his brother Buck—the
McGinnis boys. Buck had one of the greatest talents of any
of us. He could put three golf balls and half a pickle in his
mouth at one time. I always thought he could get a job in the
fall at the fair in one of those sideshows, if his mother would
allow it. We kept telling him to ask her but he never would.
He said she would start screaming at him about ruining his
teeth if she found out.

I never learned Buck's real name, but Ronny Erl was
Ronny Erl's real name. There had been a misspelling on his
birth certificate and instead of being "Earl" it came out "Erl."
His daddy said just leave it and it would be a special name
for him, and it still sounded the same. Ronny Erl and Buck
told me the name Earl had come from some old great uncle
or something on their momma's side of the family. The story
passed that he had been caught for stealing chickens up in
Arkansas during the Depression and some farmer shot him
in the behind (I heard his daddy say "ass" when he didn't
realize we were listening). Since they couldn't get all the
pellets out he had to kind of sit on the side of his hip when

he sat down at the table. The reminder of what he had done became a family blot, everybody said; and Mr.McGinnis had just as soon not keep the name spreading through the family tree. Ronny Erl's mother called it a terrible old rumor started by some scalawag rednecks back a long time ago. Earl had arthritis in his hip or some such she had said. Anyway the McGinnis' lived up the street, and we became friends. And Ronny *Earl* remained Ronny Erl.

In 1953, you could stay out until way after dark in the summer as long as you didn't disturb the neighbors too much. Of course, if you played in the street you had to watch for cars, and when you ran out to get lost in the fog of the DDT truck you had to be careful not to get run over. Daddy had said if it weren't for the DDT truck we would be inundated with mosquitoes, so a few boys getting run over was a small price to pay. My mother told him he shouldn't make jokes. He would say, "Who's joking?"

In the fourth grade, we started long division and my guess was it would only get worse in the fifth grade. Ronny Erl said we would probably start doing *real* long division. Big Daddy had once told me that in the old days, the most important things in school had been readin', writin' and 'rithmitic, as everyone used to say. I asked him if he used those things a lot. He said the most important thing a man could learn to read was the baseball box scores, the most important thing he could learn to write was a letter to his girlfriend, and the most important arithmetic was how much money you had in the bank.

My mother said, "Charlie, honey, there is more to life than box scores and money. And you must never forget to write your mother first."

Henry and some of the other guys in the neighborhood were beginning junior high school, where you moved from class to class every hour, and you had a locker where you could stockpile things like baseball cards and gum. In elementary school stuff like that could easily be spotted since you didn't have a locker, and you had it taken away. The guys starting in junior high also started seeing girls in a different way. Billy Cohen cut out some pictures from the Sears and Roebuck catalogue in the women's lingerie section and kept them inside his locker. Henry said it was pretty exciting stuff.

Most seventh-graders were twelve and almost teenagers. The way people talked about teenagers it seemed they were monsters that couldn't legally be shot but deserved to be. I still had over three years to get there. Henry and Buck were knocking on the door of *deserving to get shot.*

We had moved to our new house on Stonewall Drive the summer before. But I was just now getting full use out of a summer because last summer, before we had a chance to really meet everybody in the neighborhood, we drove the car to New Mexico for six weeks, a long vacation as far as Henry and I were concerned. Katy Jean wasn't strong enough for the trip, but she was happy staying with Minnie. Her piano music and stories were as satisfying to Katy Jean as any trip would have been, but I wished she could have seen the mountains.

At twenty, Katy Jean had been born ten years before me. But I seemed to gain faster and faster on her until now I thought of myself as her big brother.

It seemed like Mother and Daddy had a distinct voice whenever they were talking about a different subject. When they talked about going to the picture show they had one voice; when we were in trouble they had another voice; when they talked about *traditions* yet another. But when speaking to Katy Jean they were more gentle. I just made her smile, a laughing smile, like how Streety made her smile when he put his paws in her lap and tried to lick her face. Next to me, I wondered if she didn't love Streety more than anybody.

Streety, a Collie, was the first dog we ever had. Not a hunter, just a friend. Daddy had taken him in when Katy Jean was six or seven, and it was love at first sight Mother had said. We all loved Streety, even Mary Hester, although she would fuss about him tracking dirt into the house. Mother frowned on dogs in the house, but Streety liked to cuddle up to Katy Jean and make her laugh, so allowances were made.

To Daddy the trip to the mountains was mostly work because he and my grandfather, Big Daddy, had some business interest in a lumber mill up in Chama, and Daddy took us all out there while he worked on some business.

We had a small lumber company in Jackson, McCoy Lumber and Supply. I don't think it was a million-dollar company or anything. If so, Daddy didn't spend money as such. He talked about saving money, not spending it. Most grownups talked about money as something to save. My mother had to help out as bookkeeper, secretary, and a bunch of other jobs which had been all put together; so she functioned, as Big Daddy called her, a Girl-Friday of the company.

For Mother, going to New Mexico was vacation for ten minutes, and then work for ten minutes, though she enjoyed herself. She mostly was happy anyway, except when I did something bad like set the back yard on fire or empty the neighbors' mailboxes into the creek which ran through our old neighborhood. Before I was five I had done both of these. The fire, an accident because my friend Deedee and I had been playing with matches; the mail dumping, because we didn't think those papers in the metal boxes at the end of the street were important to anyone. Henry thought it funny that before the first grade he had a brother who was both a mail robber and an arsonist. I got a switching for both crimes. Henry said I was lucky because, most of the time, the punishment for those things was twenty years in prison.

I had finished the fourth grade last May and wouldn't be just nine years old anymore. In September I would finally be ten, a magic age, Henry had told me. Being almost two years older than me, he said it would put me in double digits; and it would be a long time before it changed, if it ever did. I also would be in the fifth grade, which would be important because it made you one year away from "graduating" from elementary school. Anyway, for some reason, the fifth grade loomed as a big move. Of course, you still couldn't do most of the things a teen-ager could do and almost none of the things grownups did. But life changed.

A hot morning with white clouds piling up in the summer-blue sky was a sign thunderstorms might break in the afternoon. It wasn't the heat, not even the humidity, people frequently talked about like a fear plague. Hot weather meant summer and summer meant swimming, and people believed there existed a connection to polio and the heat and public swimming areas. Last night the word had spread phone-to-phone, friend-to-friend; someone we knew had been taken to the doctor with symptoms.

Stonewall Drive existed as the main street of our world. We lived in a subdivision like many people in towns were doing now. Daddy said people were moving in from the farms. To him it seemed sad. Henry and Katy Jean and I were the first ones in the family not to be born in a small town or on a farm. Before we moved to Stonewall Drive, we had lived on the other side of town, outside the city limits. My first memories, however, were of a small frame duplex so close to downtown we could walk there from our house. Unless it rained, we even walked to church on Sunday down by the Capitol building. And if the wind were blowing the right way you could smell the aroma from the cottonseed oil plant down by the railroad tracks. But now, out as far as we lived, we had to ride in the car, or catch the city bus to get downtown, and the wind didn't bring those smells out to our house.

An old house stood a couple of miles from us, outside the city limits, elevated on a slight ridge and along Old Canton Road. Once far out in the country, but now with the city limits being moved farther out than they ever had been, the old house property encroached on the city. When we first moved to our neighborhood, we started calling it the Big House. It's gray boards and windows appeared odd, like they were eyes set in an odd sized head; the kind set in a multi-headed monster in a picture show.

It struck me as a figure of somebody. Everyone said it had been built over a hundred years ago. Most people thought it an old farm that had had slaves on it, as there were three smaller houses, shotgun houses, lined along the dirt road leading away from the house down toward Bobcat Creek and the Pearl River. Slave quarters, people generally called them. Since the Big House still stood, it must have been one of the few places Sherman or Grant hadn't burned. They had been such lovers of fire, they burned everything in their way: homes, farms, buildings. And it didn't matter whether the owners were black or white. The Republican Army had made war on people, not on armies, Big Daddy said.

Whatever the history of the Big House, two nights ago one of the three shotgun houses burned to the ground after an afternoon thunderstorm, heavy with lightning, sent it up in flames. Toward the end of July thunderstorms were common in the heat, but in the summer of 1953 I doubt something so normal had ever uncovered something so alarming. It was not the fire but the discovery in the ashes that stirred everyone. And it stirred the past.

Chapter 2

FOUR OR FIVE BLOCKS FROM OUR HOUSE WAS A VACANT LOT. A single lot no one had ever built a house on was, as far as we were concerned, land for baseball, football or any-thing else we decided to play. We claimed it by "adverse possession," Grover had said, whatever that meant. Today it meant a baseball game between two sides of whoever showed up.

The winner would be whoever had the most runs when time to quit, and the base paths were marked by the eye-ball method. The street provided a boundary for a home run. If you hit one out into the street in the air it was an automatic homer. On the ground, a ground-rule double.

Today a bunch of us, including Billy Cohen, had showed up, although his daddy usually had him working at the family jewelry store downtown. Billy said any work the rest of us did would be hot and sweaty, but he had a white-col-lar job. He said his daddy had him appraise diamonds and stuff. His daddy probably had him sweep out the store and the white-collar part was probably a white T-shirt, but Billy was too tough to argue with.

Billy often talked about his favorite player in the big leagues, Al Rosen, a third baseman for the Cleveland Indians.

It so happened the Indians had started pretty good against the Yankees, who had won four straight world championships starting in 1949. Cleveland had some pretty good players, Rosen being one of them. Billy said Rosen could hit better than any Jew anybody ever saw. Being Jewish, Billy liked to talk about things Jews did well. He always talked about Maurice Silverman, who had joined the First Mississippi Rifles shortly after Mississippi's secession.

Maurice had fought for four years and come home broke, out of bullets and money, like most other Confederates. Maurice had worked his way into prosperity by buying land after the war, and he didn't steal or deal with Carpetbaggers or Scalawags to get it. Like most of us, Billy had as much pride in his ancestors who wore the Gray as he had in those who lit the Minorah. Next to his daddy and Al Rosen, his favorite Jew was Judah Benjamin, the Secretary of War of the Confederate States of America.

But Daddy disputed Billy about baseball players. Daddy said Hank Greenberg was the best Jewish ballplayer. The "Hammerin' Hebrew" they called him, Daddy said. I think Billy claimed Rosen because Billy hadn't been around when Greenberg played. Daddy had said he thought maybe even Sid Gordon hit better than Al Rosen, so it didn't matter.

The Indians also had a player by the name of Larry Doby, the first colored guy to play in the American league. Doby could hit pretty good and a good home run hitter, too, but the idea of colored players playing for the Jackson Senators didn't seem like something ever happening. There were a bunch of colored players in the major leagues now, but Big Daddy said he didn't think any colored players would ever play in Jackson.

After we'd been playing awhile, a truck drove up and parked across the street. A small trail of white smoke puffed from the tailpipe as the driver shut off the engine; the tailgate was up and closed, with a wound length of wire to hold it in place. The driver stepped out of the truck just in time to snag a fly ball. His big black hand reached out and caught it on the first bounce, the second of which would have carried the ball into the side of his truck.

It was Joe Washington. Henry and I thought he looked like Jersey Joe Walcott, the former Negro heavyweight champion who lost the year before to Rocky Marciano. Joe Washington worked at different jobs around town, including delivering ice for the Jackson Ice Company, and Daddy sometimes hired him for jobs around the McCoy warehouse.

He took one step and threw the ball back to us. "You boys better watch fo' cars out here in dis street. Dere ain't many comin' by, but it only take one to knock you dead."

"Thanks," someone yelled. Joe waved. Actually we weren't worried, being skilled in car-dodging in the DDT fogs. But he was just being a nice guy.

Somebody called time out to go pee behind the wisteria bushes. The rest of us sat around under the shade of a pin oak and watched Joe as he strolled down the driveway to the back yard across the street, soon coming back out to his truck with an old washtub slung over his back. He took a moment and unwound the wire holding the tailgate in place, then after lowering it he slung the washtub up into the bed with various other items. As if in response to the clanging of the washtub, an old canvas began moving in the bed as if it had lungs. Squinting, we could see the nose, the head, and finally the full form of a huge dog appear from underneath the canvas shade.

Joe moved to the side of the truck and patted him on the head. "Go back to sleep, Gumbo," he said. "You can't get out here. Too many cars."

Joe made a couple more trips to the back yard, bringing an old mantle clock and a croker sack full of things we couldn't see. After he made his last trip, he crossed the street to the lot. He turned toward his truck, put up his hand and said, "Stay, Gumbo. Stay, boy." Gumbo whined and wiggled, champing at the air to leap from the bed. "Stay, boy."

Joe ambled up, smiling. Big drops of sweat rolled down his carbon- black face, and I was certain I saw little rainbows in the drops as the sunrays hit him. He had a hand-painted sign on the door of his truck: Joe Washington's Junk and Scrap.

"Y'all got a nice lot here to play but dat street pretty close. Be careful." He took out a bandanna and wiped his face. "And y'all better be careful 'bout any dese folks liv 'long here see y'all peeing in the bushes."

"You can see us?" someone asked.

He wiped his face with a blue bandanna. The big grin reappeared. "I believe when I see boys *stop* playin' baseball to go into some bushes, dey ain't squirrel huntin'."

"I told you somebody was gonna see y'all," Henry said. Of course, he had probably peed there more times than at home.

"So I jus' tellin' y'all. Y'all watch out or some police man'll arrest y'all. It's against the law to pee in somebody else's bushes. I don't spec nobody would bail y'all out. And I believe Mr. Charlie McCoy right here better be careful yo momma don't find out." He laughed. "You neither, Mr. Henry." He glanced at the house next to the lot. "You boys think dere's a water faucet at dat house I could use? It's hot out here today." He probably had seen it and didn't really need our permission.

Almost everybody pointed at it.

Joe removed his hat and bent to his knees. He turned the hose on the back of his neck and over his head and showered himself holding his head back, opening his mouth wide, allowing the flow into his mouth. Standing, he shook his head, water drops slinging about, then put his hat back on and with his bandanna again wiped his face. Within seconds, sweat drops returned.

"Say Joe, do you buy junk?" I asked. "I mean good junk?"

"Well, maybe. If'n I can make some money resellin' it." He stood erect, hands on hips. "Why? You got some *good* junk?"

"Well, maybe. I might."

"Now don't start pokin' around in my room for stuff to sell," Henry barked.

Joe laughed. "Mr. Charlie jus' let me know what you got, and we'll see. But I don't wanna start no family feud." He wiped his face one more time. "Well, you young-uns don't play too hard. I need to git back to work." He climbed into his truck, and waved. The white smoke trailed behind the sounds from the well-used muffler.

"I bet he could've beaten Joe Louis," Grover said.

"Yeah, maybe..." Billy said. "But not Max Baer."

We played some more and were about to quit with our side losing 23–7. Billy smashed one into the flowerbed across the street. Grover Butts, chasing it down and hustling all the way, cut through a flowerbed. A home run. We collapsed under the shade tree, our side defeated, 24–7.

The clouds were still building, though not darkened, and the heat held. One by one we strolled over to the water faucet. The people who lived there never seemed to mind as long as we didn't leave the water running; the same house with the wisteria bushes. It worked like our own outdoor bathroom.

We had all been lying on the ground and were about to leave for the food store when a motorcycle policeman pulled off the street and *motored* over to us. We glanced at one another, then stood.

"Hello, boys. How're y'all doin' today." He turned off his motorcycle's engine and put the kickstand down. He removed his patrol cap then wiped his brow. "Boy, I could use something cold to drink," he said. "This heat's murder."

"Yes, sir. We were jus' fixin' to go down to get a Co-Cola at the store," someone said.

We waited for him to say something about whatever we had done wrong, because we were pretty sure he didn't come by just to tell us he was hot and thirsty. Everyone kept glancing across the street at the flowerbed. It was probably a good bet it would be the subject.

A tall man, he wore dark blue trousers and a light blue shirt, a leather strap crossing his shirt, which supported the pistol on his belt. He had a shiny silver badge on both his chest and patrol cap. He wore black boots reaching his knees. He removed a pair of dark glasses. Now, we could see his eyes. Serious ones.

"Well, boys, I need to talk to y'all for a minute. Whooo, is it hot," he said again, wiping his brow again. "We received a complaint about y'all, or at least about some boys playing baseball in this lot. I don't guess anybody else been playin'?"

"We didn't do nothin'." Grover would deny something even if he wasn't there. Henry had said he'd probably be a lawyer someday.

"Now, jus' hold on, young man. Apparently somebody did something or I wouldn't have gotten a call. Now, the lady across the street says y'all were trampling her flowers, runnin' into them to chase your baseballs." He paused, his eyes scanned each of us.

Billy peered at his tennis shoes, shifting back and forth since he had actually done the hitting, and Grover moved behind Billy in an effort to hide, since his fielding caused the flowerbed incident. I think the policeman knew somebody had to be guilty. "Now, what's the story? Is she tellin' the truth? I don't think she'd jus' make something like that up. Now, what about it, boys?"

Finally, Billy spoke. "Well, once, somebody, I think, may have hit one that rolled up in her yard. Maybe it landed on the edge of her flowers; may have rolled into those kinda pink ones." He pointed to the pink flowerbed. "And he...," pointing at Grover, "might have stepped on one, accidentally."

Grover's eyes rolled, thrilled at being singled out. He came from behind Billy, ready to make some excuse. Grover's daddy owned part of the Ford dealership in town. Grover could talk if he had the chance. He wouldn't get it.

Just then the old lady, probably about eighty-something, came swishing across the street, waving a cane and pointing at everybody. She wore an apron, tied at the back, and her eyes peered over the top of her skinny, wire-rimmed glasses, the kind mostly old people wore.

"Those are the ones. Those are the boys who were *stomping* my chrysanthemums. I jus' don't know...I work so hard to keep them pretty and watered and these boys jus' go crashin' into them like a bunch of feral hogs."

I thought she was a bit harsh, calling it "stomping." Grover may have flattened one or two of her flowers with his Keds, but he really wasn't *stomping* them. I saw him stomp a jelly sandwich one time in the fourth grade, trying to see how far the jelly would squirt. He actually had the distance record for it, everybody proclaimed. Anyway, he didn't really stomp her flowers, in my opinion.

The patrolman took her by the arm when she came up. I think he worried she might fall down, as rickety as she moved. "Yes, ma'am. I'm talkin' to them now." She yanked her arm away from him as if he had attacked her.

"Well, officer, I'm tellin' you, my late husband worked so hard puttin' those flowerbeds in for me, and I jus' can't stand to see them torn up. It jus' breaks my heart. It jus' breaks my heart, I tell you, officer. Why the way he cared for those beds, bless his heart, I just don't know what to say. And, by the way, they almost hit that colored boy with their baseball. Almost hit him *and* his truck. He buys just about everything I throw out, and I don't want him killed in some wild baseball game."

I think her name was Mrs. Nettleton. We weren't supposed to say bad things about adults, but one time Henry told me she was a loon. The rumor circulated she had driven her husband mad by always demanding he water, fertilize, and weed her flower beds. Finally, one day she sent him to the store for mulch or something and he never came back. It had been almost ten years ago. That's what everybody said anyhow. I guess she assumed him to be dead by now. When I asked my mother about the story, she said she had no idea about its truth, but I shouldn't repeat such things. I think

Mother believed the story, but she never said so. I asked Daddy, one time about Mrs. Nettleton being a loon, but he just told me to not say things about grownups. He didn't say she wasn't. Instead he told me to go clean up my room.

"Yes, ma'am, I understand," the policeman said. "Let me see if I can get this straightened out."

I couldn't tell if he really understood or not. He probably said it to be polite. It didn't seem to me a guy who had a job riding around on a motorcycle would really care about a bunch of flowers. Just something he had to say, probably.

Both of my grandmothers and my mother had flowers in the yard and around the house, and they tended and cared for them as if they were children. They knew where every bed looked best and grew best, and they would worry if they weren't cared for properly with the right amount of water and the constant chore of weed pulling. They could sing out the names from memory: Geranium, Azalea, Impatien, Vinca, Chrysantheum, as if they were musical notes put together for a great score of nature.

On the other hand, we thought of them as something taking up good space for baseball and football. And we called them pink ones and blue ones and yellow ones. We had little interest in the beauty of nature. But you had to be careful about stepping on them or ripping them up with the lawn mower. Ladies were real emotional about their flowers. It was like a great crime to harm them. Of course, our opinion wasn't asked for much, and probably Mrs. Nettleton really did like her flowers. And I guess, when you're eighty-something, about all you want to do is fool around with flowers, since your husband never came home from the store one day with the mulch you needed.

The policeman kept trying to calm her down while at the same time talk to us, and I did feel pretty bad for her because we had upset her, and her having a lost husband and everything made me sad, even if she was very old and probably would be dead one day. He assured her he'd be sure we were more careful, and he had made us promise we'd work out some system so we didn't knock the ball over in her flower beds. He told us if we couldn't work out something, he'd have to tell our parents we couldn't play on the lot.

We were pretty sure by now we weren't going to get arrested, but our parents finding out we had smashed somebody's flowers and had had the police called might have been worse than jail. Nobody's parents wanted the police called about their children.

My parents had always told us to remember who we were. Remember your name. It didn't matter how famous you were, you should never bring shame to your name. And wrong-doing wasn't simply wrong of itself, but it could give you a bad name. I wondered if Grover had been the first one in the Butts family to ruin someone's flowers.

Finally, the policeman asked, "Are y'all gonna be playing anymore today?"

"No, sir. We jus' finished. We were fixin' to leave and go get a Co-Cola," I said.

He grinned, probably relieved. He didn't have to worry about getting called back today, I guess. "Well, when y'all come here again, remember what I told you. Like I said, if you can't stay out of this lady's flowers, y'all can't play here anymore. You fellows don't need to be upsettin' her. And I've got other things to do."

"Yes, sir."

I think he meant because of her age she might have a heart attack or something. Also, I'm sure he meant we shouldn't bother old people.

She turned back toward her house and her flowers and started talking to him as she left. "Now you make them behave the way they suppose to, officer," she said as she wobbled away. "I don't wanna have to call your chief of police."

I think she wanted him to think she had great influence. But he didn't seem to care.

"Yes, ma'am." He had taken out his handkerchief again and wiped the band of his patrol cap and seemed like he just wanted to get away. He probably had some criminals to check on, and this crime was boring anyhow. "Let me walk you across the street," he said. He gently took her arm, which she immediately yanked away again.

"I can get across by myself. I don't need your arm. What I need is that husband of mine back here standing guard like he oughta be doin'. If he weren't dead I wouldn't have to worry so much about my chrysanthemums. Bless his heart." She paused for a moment. "Well, I guess he's dead by now. That's another thing: the police never found him." She scowled at him.

She stormed off, crossing the street without checking the traffic. A truck full of cotton bales blew its horn at her as it passed. She hissed and waved her cane. Billy leaned over and whispered it surprised him she hadn't shot the bird.

The motorcycle policeman turned to us. "Now y'all stay out of that lady's flower garden. In fact, try not to hit the ball in her yard. Y'all hear me? I don't wanna have to come back.

I want y'all to be able to keep playin' ball here, but y'all can't be damaging other folks' property. Why don't y'all go up to the school ground or somewhere where there're not any flowers?"

"Yes, sir."

"Sir?" Ronny Erl asked.

"Yes, son?"

"Has anybody told you how the fire started up there off Old Canton?"

"Lightning. One of them little houses away from the main house. Place's pretty much deserted, as I hear. Don't think anyone's lived up there for years, anyhow." He put his dark glasses back on, hiding his eyes. "Heard on my call-radio a while ago they found some human remains. Anyway, the place is outside the city limits so the sheriff is mostly in charge of anything they found."

"Remains?" Billy said.

"That's what they said. Y'all stay away from there for the next few days. Y'all'll jus' get in the way." He gave the starter a hard push with his boot, then a second thrust, the motorcycle booming to life. Over the roar he shouted, "Now y'all watch out for those flowerbeds."

He turned into the street and roared away.

It was no longer a rumor. Someone had burned.

Chapter 3

WE RODE DOWN TO BROADMOOR FOOD STORE, A NEIGH-borhood grocery store. It first opened before the war. Everything seemed to be measured before or after the war, World War II. The Korean War was called the Korean War; WWII was referred to as *the war.*

Broadmoor Food Store, like most things out this far, still operated as a country store. Next to it stood a filling station where Daddy gassed up the car every once in a while. It was a Texaco station, with the sign of a big red star mounted on the overhang, that had been there for years. I guess over time the weather had rotted a couple of holes in it because you would see sparrows nesting inside. And the red star had turned dark brown.

Mr. and Mrs. Payne owned the grocery store and ran it themselves. At the Texaco station, there was a man who ran out and wiped the windshields and opened the hood checking for oil and batteries and spark plugs and other engine gadgets. He always had a cigarette dangling from his lips, even while pumping the gas or checking under the hood. Henry said one day he might blow himself up, and Texaco would fire him if he were still alive.

The Paynes were probably older than Daddy but not as old as Big Daddy. Mr. Payne's hair had whitened, but it was still there to comb. Their children were gone from home but still lived in Mississippi, except for their daughter, who had got married and moved to Charleston, South Carolina. The Paynes had five boys and one girl, but two of the boys were killed in WWII, one at Anzio and the other at Tarawa. He had told Daddy one time he had started the war with six children and ended it with four. He said he was glad the war didn't go on any longer, said it about killed Mrs. Payne. My mother said Mrs. Payne hadn't been the *only one* it about killed.

My mother told us she had prayed every night my daddy spent overseas. And she had told Henry and me for the last three years to remember to pray for our boys in Korea. Every night we prayed, right up until the armistice last month.

Mr. Payne sometimes snapped out personal editorials when the subject of the Korean War came up. "More of our boys getting killed for politicians, and that *sorry* Truman wouldn't listen to MacArthur," we heard him say.

The store didn't get real busy except sometimes on Saturday. And, of course, it closed on Sunday. The small grocery store was going the same way of the family farm. The big food chains were like the corporate farmers, Daddy had said. But Mr. Payne took time for every customer and he still had some regulars; enough, I guess, to keep the store going. He also allowed the newspaper, *The Clarion Ledger*, to use the store as a drop off point for the paperboys to pick up their papers in the mornings. He would offer us credit if we didn't have a nickel for a Coke. Something Henry and I had been told not to ask for. If we didn't have the money we didn't need to be buying it. Anyway, spending money was a sin, almost, and spending money you didn't have was as bad as not tithing.

"That's a nickel, Mr. Charlie," Mr. Payne said, acknowledging the cost of my Orange Crush. He often attached the honorific to our first names. He then repeated it four more times each for Ronny Erl, Grover, Billy, and Henry.

We sat out on the sidewalk in front of the store and talked about who might have burned up. Being told by the policeman to stay away made us want to go more, but we didn't. We didn't want to ride our bikes all the way out there and get run off.

Mr. Payne had told us the morning newspaper said one of the shotgun houses had burned, and the fire department kept the fire from spreading. And the rain keeping the grass damp helped. He also mentioned a county inquest by the medical examiner.

Opinions among ourselves varied on who the remains might be, the consensus being we wanted it to be some War Between the States casualty, though as someone pointed out, the body would have to be almost a hundred years old. Billy said it might be a gangland killing, although we had never heard of a gang let alone a gangland killing, in Jackson.

"Bet there's a bunch of junk up there at that house you could sell," Billy said. "Inside the Big House, I mean. If you can't sell it to Joe, you could sell it door-to-door. Or there are a bunch of places over in Rankin County around Pearl where you could sell it."

I wasn't sure why people would buy junk for their house, but Billy's enthusiasm excited me about door-to-door junk. Instead of only selling to Joe, I'd sell it to everybody. And making money always seemed like a good idea. Henry said when it came to making money you needed to listen to Jews, and Billy was a Jew.

"And rabbit tobacco. Bet there's a ton of it down close to the river," Billy kept on. "That's what I'm gonna sell. I'll be the next American Tobacco Company, sellin' rabbit tobacco."

"What're you gonna do with rabbit tobacco?" I asked. He said *rabbit tobacco* very fast, like one word.

Billy stuck his thumb in the top of his drink, shook it up real fast and fired it at a wasp. He missed, and the wasp buzzed us.

"Cut that shit out, Cohen, you gonna get me stung," Henry yelled.

Billy laughed.

Henry had yelled so loud Mr. Payne heard. "Now, boys, I don't wanna hear that kind of language or y'all'll have to leave."

Henry bowed his head, "Yes, sir."

"What is rabbit tobacco?" Grover asked. "Is it like crossvine?" Crossvine being the smoke of choice to most guys in elementary school who smoked.

"Sell it. I bet we can sell it to Bob's Tobacco House," Billy said. "Rabbit tobacco's something that grows out in the woods. It's not planted like tobacco in North Carolina and Virginia and places like that. Rabbit Tobacco grows for free. If it's free, we can make a lot more money. It takes money to grow stuff like cotton and peas and regular tobacco, because you gonna need some money, first of all, to plant it. And land, too—land belonging to you. Rabbit tobacco is like plums and blackberries; it's free."

"Ahh, c'mon, Billy," Henry said. "It had to get planted sometime by somebody. We learned that last year in sixth grade. There isn't any such thing as *spontaneous generation*. Mrs. Flowers told us about some science stuff and some French guy named Pasteur had proved it."

"Oh, it got planted for free a long time ago. It's like manna—the stuff God dropped for the Jews—like a present. Things like manna and blackberries and rabbit tobacco were originally for the Jews, because it's free. It's in the Old Testament."

"Oh," Grover said. His interest had weakened. He believed his future was in cars. He cupped his hands around the neck of his Co Cola while he poured some peanuts into it, then held the bottle above his head to see what town the bottle came from. It must have been from Jackson, since he said nothing. If it were from Iuka or Vicksburg or Memphis or someplace he probably would have shouted as if he had bottled it himself. It was really something to get an alien Coke bottle. "Jackson." A brief dejection we had all experienced.

"Where'd you get that about stuff being free?" I glanced at Henry.

"That's cause y'all are Baptists," Billy said. "Y'all mostly study the New Testament. That's why Jews can drink wine. Plums and blackberries are free. And they can let them ferment. Baptists have to eat them right away 'cause they think of them only as food. If fruit gets too ripe, Baptists aren't allowed to eat it, or drink it."

"Methodists can eat and drink anything they want," Grover said.

Billy kept on. "And they got manna because Moses led them, and he was a pretty important guy, so God wanted him well-fed. When they had to cross the Red Sea, Moses just parted the waters."

"Jesus would've just walked across," I said. "That's in the New Testament."

"Yeah, but none of his friends could or they would've drowned. Moses knew the guys he led were in a hurry. So he just parted the sea."

"What about junk?" Ronny Erl said. "Is it free?"

"Sure," Billy said. "Junk is like manna and plums. If it belongs to somebody, it's property, like cotton and butter-beans. But junk is free. If there is any good junk up there, you oughta get up there before the whole place burns down."

Billy had finished his drink and started pounding his glove, deepening the leather pocket. Billy was friendly but if he had to, he'd fight anybody, anytime. Some of the guys called him *Jew-Tough*. I had asked Henry what that meant. He said some of the guys had made up the expression because Jews had been picked on a lot and some of them tended to fight back more than others, and Billy could fight when he had to. I thought he was plenty tough, Jew or not. He was a good friend, but I never understood if he pounded his glove to toughen the leather or to toughen his fist.

"We ought to go up there some time," Billy said. "Some of those old country houses have graves too. Maybe even some old coins or something else buried with them. You have a future in junk, Charlie McCoy. I'm tellin you. You really do."

Henry leaned back against the building, his legs out-stretched across the walk. He turned up his R.C. and swallowed most of it then cut a giant belch, an art form dis-allowed at home. "I don't think you're supposed to dig up graves. It's against the law. Besides, we don't know if there are any graves. Not even sure if the people who used to own the place are white or colored. Besides, if anybody died up there, they prob'ly ended up dumped in the river."

"Aw c'mon, people dig up graves all the time. Sometimes they have to move 'em. Sometimes they get the sheriff to do it if they suspect foul play," Billy said. "And you never know what you'll find at some house as old as that one, no matter how rich they were. And nobody gets buried in the river, unless they're murdered or accidentally drowned, white or colored."

"I mean it's not as if you can dig 'em up like you're on some kind of a treasure hunt," Henry said.

"If they've been abandoned, it's okay," Billy said.

"All graves are abandoned," Grover said.

"I mean the ones not looked after or nothin' like that." Billy pounded his glove some more. "There gotta be graves all over the world people ain't found. I mean there are dead people everywhere. My daddy says some of those fine antique shops in New Orleans have a lot of stuff that prob'ly came from old cemeteries, but nobody claims it. And some of the stuff they find is worth a lot. It's a big opportunity, I'm tellin' you. Might be some antiques up there."

"You mean people jus' go out diggin' up graves and sell the stuff to whoever they want?" I said.

"Even if that's so, I don't think they're free for the takin' and jus' anybody can dig 'em up first-come-first-serve," Henry insisted. "I mean, it's not like at the ballpark and looking for dropped money under the bleachers."

"Well, people can get money and stuff from abandoned sunken ships," I said.

"Yeah, but it's not on private property. The ocean is anybody's property," Henry said.

"I think in New Orleans they're all the time finding stuff floating around or washed up after storms," Billy said. "If it's jus' lying around, it's anybody's."

Henry kept on. "I jus' think there's some kind of law about rootin' around in graves."

Before long we were all grave-robbing experts. Mrs. Payne came out to sweep the sidewalk and I noticed a smile, overhearing our talk.

"Y'all remember the picture show called *The Body Snatcher*?" Grover being first to reveal his in-depth research on the subject. "Well, Boris Karloff, or whoever he was, ran around robbin' graves for money. He was all the time sneakin' around at night."

"That's why it was illegal," Ronny Erl said. "He was sneakin' around. You don't see people in broad daylight rootin' around in cemeteries unless they're droppin' off flowers or buryin' brand new dead people. And anyway, that's jus' an old picture show."

"Well, I didn't say it wasn't illegal, I just said it was like that," Grover said. "And he wasn't robbin' them for the money they might've had in their pockets. He was gettin' paid for the bodies. They were using the bodies for doctors to do stuff to, and the doctors were paying them. I think it was to figure out how to surgery on live people, maybe."

"Surgery? What's that mean? You're crazy," Billy said. "That sounds stupid," as we all laughed. "You mean *operate*. Operate is when they do surgery. There ain't no such thing as surgery on people."

"That's what I meant," Grover said. I think he was a little embarrassed, and I changed the subject before we could ridicule him anymore. Everybody liked Grover, but he almost failed the second grade. Henry said the reason he hadn't was because Grover's daddy gave the principal a new Ford at a big discount. I sometimes wondered if Henry hadn't made it up. But we all kind of believed him.

"Y'all remember in *Frankenstein* the guy who kept skulking around robbin' all the graves so Dr. Frankenstein could make a new guy? " I said. "Well, he had this little screwball helper named Felix or something like that, who ran around digging up guys for their brains and other parts. Finally, he had to steal a brain and picked out a bad one. That's why his new guy became a monster. Felix swiped a bad brain." My academic brilliance ended the subject.

Billy stood up and finished his drink, capped with a louder belch than Henry's. "Well, anyway, the real money's in rabbit tobacco."

"I gotta go," I said.

"Where to?" Henry said.

"Jus' somewhere."

I was going over to Minnie's. As long as she had lived, she probably had a lot of junk around. Minnie had told me she would pay me twenty-five cents an hour to clean out her garage and the old chicken house. And she told me I could have anything she didn't need. Like most grownups, she didn't waste, so I knew whatever she discarded wouldn't be worth a whole lot. I figured Joe could give me an idea of its worth. But in any event I would at least get twenty-five cents an hour for moving stuff out.

An old house, it had a chicken house behind the garage. Long before I was born, her house had been in the country.

They raised chickens and even had a milk cow, although the house only occupied about ten or twelve acres, I had been told. Now, it sat as a red brick home in town with a large porch on one side where we often sat and talked, or listened to those older than us talk.

My cousins in Canton always called me a city boy since I had never milked a cow. It didn't seem hard, really. It seemed to me you sat on a stool and grabbed a hold of the little tit things and yanked up and down. But it didn't look like fun either. Besides, in kindergarten somebody told me cows would bite you. Henry had told me I was an idiot. He said cows didn't use their teeth like tigers or bobcats. He said they might kick you but they didn't bite.

Although the land around Minnie's house had been sold off for houses, and the fences for livestock long since removed, the old chicken house remained at the back of the garage, useful as a storeroom full of junk.

"Now when we clean this out, you haul what you don't want out to the street and tie it up with this old rope." Minnie pulled up an old frayed length that might have been around as long as the house had. "I keep these pieces of rope for things like this, so don't keep the rope to resell." She smiled at me when she said it. "For the stuff you want to try to resell, just put it out by the back porch—BY the porch, not on it—and maybe your Daddy will send a truck from his warehouse and let you take it home until you can sell it to somebody. But you watch out for my shrubs and flowerbeds when you're moving it out by the porch. I don't want you stompin' around in my beds, now."

"Yes, ma'am. I think I might have someone who I might sell most of it to. Even if he doesn't want it all, maybe he can find somebody who will." I had never met anybody but Joe who dealt in junk, but by saying it, it made me sound like I knew what I was doing. Besides, I couldn't be sure Daddy would let me bring a bunch of junk home just to sit in his yard. I could hear him saying, "You're not going to pile a bunch of junk up in my yard!"

She poked around in the few items I had piled up. "Once I get this old chicken house cleared out, I might have it taken down. I might pay you and your brother to take it down without tearing up the boards. They probably have some salvage value."

"Yes, ma'am."

"Might even pay you fifty cents an hour for such a job."

"Yes, ma'am." The thought of getting fifty cents an hour was almost too much for me. Riches in my future.

"But let me think about it," she added. "Don't go counting your money yet."

"Minnie, did you ever hear about who owned that house out off Old Canton? The one where the house burned up and they found the skeleton?"

"No, honey. Just an old farmhouse is all I ever heard. It seems I remember some colored folks lived out there a long time ago, maybe. If your granddaddy were still alive he might recall. You might ask Mr. Randy. He's older than I am."

"I jus' wondered who might've been buried. That's what everybody says: the skeleton was somebody buried a long time ago. Maybe under the house."

"Who is *everybody*?"

"Mr. Payne up at the store." I didn't mention the policeman.

"Oh, well, darling,' I don't have any idea except there was a lot of talk when I was a little girl about some big whiskey still buried out there. If it's true, the place is cursed. That's what my mother said. I just don't have any idea. But you collect this stuff as soon as you can."

"Yes, ma'am."

Chapter 4

I HAD FINISHED DEALING FOR JUNK AT MINNIE'S AND JUMPED on my bike to run by the Tote –Sum before I pedaled home for supper.

The entire front of the Tote-Sum opened, but at closing time, ten o'clock, someone pulled the three doors down. At seven o'clock in the morning, they went up. All the cold drinks were in three coolers under the opening, and the coolers were kept full with crushed ice poured throughout the day. The Tote-Sum operated like an old general store in a small town, where people not only bought stuff, but also gathered around an old cracker barrel and talked about most anything from baseball and farming to politics. The drink coolers in the Tote-Sum were like the old cracker barrels: a gathering place. They sold so much ice some people called it an ice house.

The Tote-Sum, located at a three-way intersection with a view down one of the streets, allowed you to see the Western Auto Store and the ice cream shop. Off to the left of the store, facing in the other direction, a supermarket, a hair dresser, and a furniture store. The railroad crossing a block away often carried the Panama Limited or City of New Orleans screaming past, up toward Memphis or down toward New Orleans. It crossed the street right behind the McGinnis Hardware store.

Ronny Erl had been stacking some inventory for his daddy, and I waited at the Tote-Sum for him so we could ride home together before supper. Grover sat on the curb of the parking lot eating some jellybeans. I plopped down next to him and begged for a couple. He reluctantly gave me two licorice ones. Like Jesus said, *asking for bread and getting a stone.*

"I hate licorice," I said. "Gimme a green one or a red one."

He spoke, exposing a mouthful of red and green goo. "I have it on good information that the licorice plant is a legume related to beans and peas native to southern Europe and parts of Asia."

I stared at him.

"I read it on a bubble gum wrapper," he said. "The ones that give information along with the gum. I read one time about a two-headed pig born in China."

"I don't care if you read it on the bathroom wall of the filling station. Licorice stinks. It tastes like medicine."

"I don't have any more except them," he said, gobbling the last colored one.

"Now, you boys don't get in the way of the customers," Gifford said. "I don't mind y'all sittin' on the curb, but don't get in the way. Okay? We're gonna get busy in a bit."

"We won't, Gifford." Gifford worked as the manager, but we were allowed to call him by his first name, since he wasn't very old. And he probably didn't want to be called Mr. Stockman anyway, having finished high school just two or three years ago.

"And don't y'all be spittin' if any ladies step up. Some of 'em don't like it."

We would spit at bugs or roaches crawling by in their caravans, in search of cookie crumbs or bits of chocolate in a discarded wrapper, or the sticky syrup in an old bottle cap. We didn't bet money on it or anything, just enjoyed the reward of beating everybody else. Lewis chewed tobacco, which would have been the best ammunition. One day he nailed a cockroach from about five feet away, probably a state record, but today he was in the back working. Grover and I spit with standard mouth spit.

"Y'all been working all day, I guess," Gifford said. "Or been playin' ball? I'd go fishin' if I had as much free time as y'all have. Y'all need to be workin'somewhere. Makin' some money."

Gifford had a high school boy working at the ice house. A pretty hard job anyway, crushing ice and lifting cases of bottles and things, so guys our age didn't get offered much to do at the ice house. Lewis had the job this summer. Since he was sixteen and a teenager, we didn't hang around him much, but he played football for the single white high school in town, the Central High Tigers, the best team in the state. They hardly ever lost a game. Lewis played end and was pretty strong, so he could chop ice and move cases of bottles around. And when chewing Beechnut, in my opinion, he could spit tobacco as far as anybody who dipped or chewed. He said Beechnut had some special aerodynamic features grown into the leaves. Daddy shook his head and smiled when I told him. My mother would have screamed if I told her I had acquainted myself with somebody who chewed tobacco.

Gifford came from a small town somewhere close to Pelahachi, about forty miles from Jackson, but since he hadn't gone to college, and because his family farm didn't make enough to make a living, he came up to Jackson to get a job. Daddy said that had happened to a lot of farmers.

Big Daddy said once people fooled themselves into pass-ing the income tax amendment back about the time Daddy came along, life changed for everybody. And the national government would forever be worse than the boll weevil—chewing up profits and leaving a trail of waste. He said the twentieth century would be the end of family farms in the South. Big Daddy often told me old stuff like that.

Gifford seemed out of place behind a cash register. He belonged on a tractor or behind a plow, like Gary Cooper playing Sergeant York. Gifford was strong. You could tell it came from farm work, not from lifting weights or play-ing football. From hard work. He was tanned and his hands were tough and beefy from effort, not from paper work, either. I had the feeling if he tried to use a typewriter he would crush the keys like they were noodles. He had become the store manager.

Daddy said corporate farming and industry had tried to make city-slickers out of farm boys the same as it had crushed local stores. Big Daddy said he guessed he could live with it as long as it didn't make Yankees out of them, because the *memory* was important if things were to ever change.

Gifford lit up a Camel. I watched him as he tilted his head back, inhaled, and let the smoke pour from his nose and mouth. "Ahhh, that's better. 'Bout to have a nicotine fit."

"What's a nicotine fit?" I asked. It sounded like some-thing a rabid dog would do.

"Oh, it's kinda jus' something we say when we don't get a cigarette when we want one, or hadn't had one in a long time."

"You don't go crazy or nothin' like that, do you?" I asked. "You don't go foamin' or spittin'around, do you?"

"No, I don't guess so," Gifford said. "It ain't like a real fit. Y'all watch out, we're gettin' some traffic in here now."

Two cars pulled into the lot; at the same time a policeman rode up on a motorcycle, though not the same one who had lectured us at the lot. Policemen often came by to get a drink. The drink boxes were close enough to the curb so they could still hear their radios, if something happened and they had to rush off. He pulled out a Coca Cola.

"Howdy, Gifford. Still hot out here."

"Yeah. I believe so. And I got the drink." Meaning the ice house gave the policeman a free drink. Whoever managed the store mostly paid for policemen drinks.

I think they were just being friendly and not trying to bribe them or anything. But they only bought them drinks. I don't think a policeman could get something like a case of beer and four or five loaves of bread for free. There happened to be one policeman named Burly something-or-the-other. He was always snarling and mean as a yellow jacket, I had heard a man say down at Daddy's warehouse one time. He acted like the free drink was his inalienable right. His meanness had no limits, but it especially focused on colored people. He would call them niggers out loud where they could hear him.

One time Lewis told Ronny Erl and me the ice house ought to give Burly free toilet paper since he was so full of *you-know-what*. Some people said the word nigger devoted a special cruelty to Negroes. But most people who said it had just grown up hearing it.

"Y'all find out who was in the fire?" Gifford asked. He had returned to work the cash register with customers coming in. Grover and I had gotten off the curb and were leaning on the other side of the U- shaped counter to listen. We could hear Lewis rattling bottles in the back and uttering some cuss words he probably thought no one heard. Grover and I grinned.

The policeman turned up his Co Cola and almost finished it. "If they have, they haven't told me. We aren't gettin' a lot of information since it's out of the city limits. Sherriff's gettin' filled in mostly."

Lewis came from the bottle room. He could hear the conversation and came out most likely in case the policeman dropped some interesting information. Gifford had been wiping the counter with a rag and had spun it into a tight rope-like shape. He held one end and snapped the other, catching Lewis on the forearm.

"OW!" Lewis squealed.

"Stop cussin' back there," Gifford said. "Mighta been a lady up here."

The policeman smiled. We giggled.

"Go get the milk pushed up," Gifford said, chasing Lewis into the cooler.

"Aw c'mon, I wanna hear what's goin' on," Lewis whined. It sounded funny, a big guy like him whining.

"You've heard as much as I have, son," the policeman said. "Which ain't much."

Gifford popped the rag in Lewis' direction again. "You see? Nothin' to hear. Now get that milk pushed up before we get real busy."

Lewis mumbled something, probably a cuss-word as he opened the cooler door.

"Anybody live up there?" Gifford asked.

"I don't think anybody lives up there anymore," the policeman said. "I heard some colored folks owned some of the property at some time or other, maybe a long time ago. But I don't believe anyone lives there now. All that area is pretty much deserted with a right of way planned for the new four-lane highway.

Red nodded to Gifford and the policeman, then moved over to the drink cooler and rummaged in the ice for a drink. He picked out a Barq's Orange. They were all a nickel no matter the size. Then he put the drink back in for a second and put his hands down in the ice and water.

"Cold feels good on these old hands," he said. He smiled at Grover and me. "Hello, boys. What y'all being busy 'bout today?"

I saw his hands. They were huge, tanned except for the palms, which were as light as mine but calloused; both were craggy and gnarled, and you could tell he had spent his life working with them. The end of one of his fingers was missing but I never would ask how he lost it. Ronny Erl told me one time he had asked and Red said he didn't know. He said he had just got up one morning and he didn't have it no more. He worked in the hardware store now but had worked part-time in the cotton seed plant downtown when he was a boy. I told Ronny Erl I'd bet a nickel that's where he lost it, really. But I never asked. Besides there wasn't but about an inch missing.

Red worked for Mr. McGinnis. What he didn't have time to do Buck and Ronny Erl did. He kept an enormous set of keys hanging on his belt. He could have had a key to every lock in Hinds County. I wondered what they all were used for because they made him appear so important. He looked like a jailer. I didn't know his age but I'm sure he was older than Daddy. Most of the time he wore a khaki shirt and trousers and the back of his shirt always seemed like it had a patch of sweat in the back. Sometimes, when Joe had an ice delivery, Red would come over and talk to Joe. They were always talking about baseball while they had a drink. If he wasn't talking baseball with Joe, he was talking farming with Gifford.

Once in a while he would come across the street to get some pipe tobacco. And I think he liked talking with us boys anytime he came. A lot of old people did that. They seemed like they wanted to talk with younger people. Red seemed about fifty, as near as I could tell.

He told us one time he came from Alabama "a skip and a hop" across the line from Meridian, but his daddy moved the family over to Jackson soon after he "stopped being dressed in diapers." After he finished high school he had moved around, even up north for a bit, until he tasted the cold and came back South.

"Hey Red. We're jus' talkin' 'bout the fire up off Old Canton," I said.

"Oh, my, yeah," he said. "We was bettin' them firemen was 'fraid the fire would spread from the shack to the grass. Then there would've been really a bad fire. Not much but woods and dry grass all the way to Madison. The grass's dry all over, down to the river. We ain't had a good shower since early in July before the thunderstorm. A fire mighta burned half the county up if it was to have its way. I guess the thunderstorm wetted the grass jus' enough."

Red struck a match and tried to light his pipe.

The policeman moved up next to the drink cooler to put his empty bottle in the wooden drink case. "Does anybody lives up around there now?" he asked Red. "Where the fire started up off Old Canton?"

"No, sir, not for sure, but I think it's deserted all 'round up there. I don't think anybody lived there for years and years. Could be there's an old family cemetery up there, maybe. Might be the fire uncovered part of it. Maybe that's what them bones were. "

"What about those old stories about a slave-girl poisoning the folks who owned the house, and the slaves hanging her? I've heard that story somewhere down home," Gifford said.

"Aww, Gifford that's a story people make up 'bout any house that's old and deserted. That story is 'bout a plantation down in Louisiana at St. Francisville. I don't believe the old house out yonder got anything like that. I think some of them Cajun folks passed that story up here. People still say after Annandale burned up above Madison, ghosts moved in all 'round Madison county. All jus' a bunch of stories though." Red finally managed to get his pipe lighted while he laughed.

"Maybe so. I jus' heard the story," Gifford said. He flipped his cigarette butt into the parking lot.

"Where is St. Francisville?" Grover asked.

"Down in Louisiana by the river—the Mississippi River," Gifford said. "Only way to get across down there is on a ferry. Ain't no bridge."

"Well, what 'bout the slave hanging?" Grover asked. "What'd she get hanged for?"

"She poisoned her master. But the other slaves was afraid of her and they decided to get rid of her. So they hanged her." Red glanced at Gifford and smiled. "They say her ghost still haunts the place." His pipe had gone out again so he struck a match and held it over the bowl of his pipe and inhaled, drawing a large cloud of white smoke. He shook the match out and flipped it in the driveway. He grinned. "But they's so many stories that go 'round, you can't never tell what's true and what ain't. Lord knows the old house off Old Canton'll git people makin' up all sorts of tales."

"You think it's haunted, maybe? Maybe by something else?" Grover asked.

Red pulled up his Barq's and opened it on the side of the drink box. His pipe had gone out again. He banged it on the end of the box, scattering the burnt tobacco, then put it in his shirt pocket, stem first. He tilted his head back and guzzled down almost half the contents in one gulp.

"That's what I mean. Any old house that's abandoned gonna have some rumors attached to it 'bout it being haunted. If it ain't haunted 'bout one thing, then another. Jus' gotta be haunted. Jus' the way people imagine things." He rubbed Grover's hair and laughed. He took another slug, then stifled a belch. "I think in the old days it mighta been a cotton farm. Took the crop up to a big gin in Canton. But like I said, I'm not sure 'bout the place and sure don't have no idea who owned it. Some folks say them little shotgun houses mighta been slave quarters before the war. But I don't remember any white people livin' up there. Not ever, as near as I can recall."

He pushed a new can of Prince Albert into his back pocket. We often asked him for his empty tobacco cans of Prince Albert, useful for collecting things: marbles or nickels or little stones we thought valuable. Occasionally we would blow one of the cans up with a cherry bomb at Christmas. Also we played an old joke sometimes by calling up a grocery store and asking: *"Do you have Prince Albert in a can?"* Usually, they did, and when they said, *"Yes, we do,"* we would say: *"Well you better let him out before he suffocates."* You would laugh the first time you heard it.

The parking lot had pretty much emptied. It kind of came in spurts. The policeman had finished and gave a heavy stomp on his pedal, revved the engine, and took off. There had been a voice coming from his radio, largely covered by static, then he called back *"ten-four"* and took off.

Gifford slowly wiped the counter with his rag. "How big a place was it when you was a boy, Red? Around the old house up there, I mean?"

"Well, I s'pose it was a farm of some 300 or 400 acres, I b'lieve. It was rich soil being close to the river and all. Folks would go huntin' up around there like it was public land or somethin'. Part of it would flood sometimes and the soil would get fed from the river. So it could grow mos' anything. I imagine it growed its share of cotton or anything else someone had a mind to grow. And I'm sure a lot of seeds got sold to the cotton seed plant downtown, too. They'd git oil from 'em. You boys be careful if you go up there," Red said, probably thinking we'd go up there as soon as we had the chance.

"Who all's buried there, you think?" I asked

"Well," he said, "I couldn't say anybody is. I'm jus' wonderin' like y'all are. Might or might not be a cemetery. Jus' wonderin'."

"You don't think there's a slave buried up there like Gifford said?"

He didn't answer right away. "I don't b'lieve so. Like I jus' said, I think that's jus' a Louisiana story. But what y'all oughta do, is ask Joe. The ice man. The same one who works down at your daddy's warehouse sometimes—Joe Washington. I think maybe he grew up out there toward Madison County. He the man to ask. There was quite a few colored people living out there."

Chapter 5

Yo momma gonna find out you and Li'l Mr. Ronny Erl done bin up ta summin' bad at dat Bobcat Creek. Dat why you is late." Mary Hester liked to pretend she could scold.

Mary Hester seemed around twenty I guessed, but she looked older. She worked hard and Mother could keep her busy four days a week in the summer; three during school. We thought of her as family, though late in the afternoon she would return to her small frame house in a colored section of town where she lived with what we were told was an "uncle." I had never seen him except through her screen door.

"Who says it was Ronny Erl? And who says I was doing anything, anyway. And anyway she's not gonna find out unless somebody tells her, Mary Hester. And besides, that was way last week. Nobody cares now."

"Y'all's momma'll care if'n y'all done somethin' reckless."

Even if you'd done something wrong, if you went a week without getting caught it was like a statute of limitations. All was forgotten in a week if you hadn't been caught. It was something Mary Hester would do: she would say something to get my attention then chuckle because she wouldn't *really* get me in trouble. Although if it was serious enough, she wouldn't lie to Mother or Daddy. But this wasn't *serious,* so the two of us would squabble back and forth.

"And anyway all we were doin' was throwin' cinder blocks in the creek. There ain't nothing wrong with that." I didn't tell her we were making a dam to flood the road.

Billy had briefly convinced Ronny Erl and me to go into the tobacco business. Ronny Erl came up with an idea for damming up Bobcat Creek down by the railroad trestle where it crossed a gravel road. He thought if we dammed up the creek, and it rained hard enough, the water would back up and we'd have a water supply to increase the growth of rabbit tobacco. He said we would have the biggest supply of rabbit tobacco in the state.

We finally gave up the idea as stupid, mainly because the cinder blocks wouldn't hold back enough water and the creek would recede to no more than a couple of inches of standing water in a few days anyway. But we kept making a dam for fun. Billy told us he had thought it was a bad idea from the beginning. I shrugged. I really didn't care since I had my eye on the junk business, and not the tobacco business anyway.

"And I'm not real late. Supper ain't ready."

"Yeah, but y'all not s'pose to be climbin' up on dat railroad trestle. And dem cinder blocks might b'long to somebody. Might be private prop'ty. And dat little boy fell off'n dat trestle last year and broke his arm. So I don't spec yo momma wants you up ther' fallin' off neither. And I's gonna tell her." She chuckled. "I am." Another chuckle. "Now I got to git dem clothes in off'n the line. So you don't git in here and mess up de kitchen, you hear me. You can't eat nothing this close to supper. An' yo momma don't want you sayin' *ain't*. I heard her correct you a hundurd times. And you s'pose to be home before supper, not when it start. And if you git here after it start you might git yo daddy's attention. Y'all s'pose to be on time for supper, he all de time sayin'."

Mary Hester had to finish her work so she didn't miss the bus. Since we lived on the outskirts of town, and the buses didn't run except every hour after suppertime, if she missed her bus, Daddy had to drive her home to almost downtown; and it put him in a bad mood having to drive back into town. And we didn't want him in a bad mood with a recent discussion of buying a television going on.

About half the people in the neighborhood had a television, and my mother and daddy had been talking about it all summer. Henry and I had already missed the All-Star game on television in July, and every day brought us closer to the fall shows our friends had talked about last year. We were just about the only ones in school who weren't sure if Lucy and Ricky and Fred and Ethel had moved to California or not.

"I don't wannta be standin' at dat bus stop wid crazy people bein' around," she mumbled, stumbling to the back yard with the clothes basket.

I stopped for a second. I had been checking the kitchen to see what she had made for supper. I banged open the back screen door and followed her to the clothesline. *Crazy people*? "What are you talkin' about, Mary Hester? Whaddayamean, crazy people?"

"Dem people settin' fires runnin' 'round. I be 'fraid dey gonna set me on fire maybe."

"Whada you talkin' about?"

She had begun taking clothespins off the sheets, dropping each into the basket on the ground. Pulling the sheet
down the line, she pulled more pins, then folding the sheet
over until she reached the end. "Dey be talkin about it all
de time." She folded a sheet four ways and placed it in the
basket. Within a few minutes she had all the clean sheets
folded and placed in a neat stack in the basket.

"What do you mean 'all the time'?"

"Well, I done heard 'bout it on de radio this afternoon;
right after *Stella Dallas,* and den all de rest of de day at some
time 'nother. Dey jus' keep talkin' 'bout it. Ain't you been
hearin' de radio? Now, see, if'n you hadn't been stealin'
and chunkin' dem cinder blocks off dat trestle you mighta
known 'bout it. De fireman found a human head."

"It was jus' an old skeleton about fifty years old. And
nobody *set a fire*. Lightning started it. And anyway, we
weren't stealin' the cinder blocks."

"Didn't b'long to y'all."

"Didn't b'long to nobody," I said.

"B'longed to somebody. An' dat somebody weren't y'all."

"How can you be so sure they b'longed to somebody?"

"Everything b'longs to somebody. Dere ain't no free stuff
'round," she said, taking a clothespin out of her mouth and
dropping it in the clothes basket. "And skeleton is a skeleton, don't matter how old it be. It wuz somebody one time
or 'nother. An' if it wuz *somebody* dat somebody had a head.
An' they jes *said* lightning started it. Dat's jus' what dey say.
Dey ain't got no proof of dat. Dey jus' makin'up dat lightning bidness."

"Oh, never mind. Where-abouts is Henry? And we were building a dam, not jus' chunkin' them."

"He prob'ly got hisself lost. But I think he gone up the street still cutting somebody's yard." She laughed and laughed some more. "Buldin' a dam; wooee! Y'all think y'all a little pack o' beavers? Hee, hee."

"And what makes you think somebody'll set you on fire?" I asked.

"I jus' 'fraid dey will is what I said."

"Same thing."

"Is not."

"Is too."

She giggled. Mary Hester treated us like we were her own, and she would worry about most anything, most anytime.

Right after Daddy came back from the war, one time a mad dog was running around somewhere in our old neighborhood. Daddy stayed with us at home while my mother went to the store. He took off down the street with a pistol in his hand, searching for the dog or the police maybe, but told us children to stay inside. After he left, Henry and I ran outside and climbed a large white trellis so we could watch for the dog.

Anyhow, a deputy sheriff shot the dog before Daddy came back, and we shimmied down the trellis and back into the house before he found out we had been gone. I'm sure if he knew we had left the house we would have both gotten a switching. Henry had told Mary Hester the story, and she worried *forever* about mad dogs in our new neighborhood. She told me dogs went mad because people fed them biscuits. When I asked my mother, she rolled her eyes. Then she said, "Just don't feed the dog at the table."

I really don't think Mary Hester feared mad dogs any more than lightning bugs. I think she thought it was her job to worry. She had her gentle ways.

"Pick up dat basket o'clothes and bring 'em into the house. Bout time you did something to earn yo supper."

"I always earn my supper," I protested.

"Buildin' dams ain't earnin' no money," she said.

"Well, it's what engineers do. And what're you sayin' ain't for?"

"I said yo momma told *you* not to say it. She didn't tell me not to say it. And too much o' dat engineerin' get you engineered into mischief." She pushed me gently in the back, moving me through the screen door, the clothes basket pressed against me. Then she stopped and peeked into the living room to be sure only I heard. She whispered: "I b'lieve somebody done laid down dere trick out at dat house. An' dey don't want nobody to find out."

"What? Laid down..."

She put her fingers to her lips, "Shh."

I whispered: "What do you mean, *laid down their trick*?"

"It's what I heard 'round at my neighborhood. Ever'body think so in my neighborhood."

"Well, what...who is ever'body?"

"I got to finish my work now. You better get warshed up 'fore yo momma get home."

"Tricks laid down. What's it mean?"

"Sumin' colored folks set 'demselves 'bout. It's hoodoo. You go on now. I'm busy with supper."

"Hoodoo? Wha...? You mean voodoo?"

"No. Hoodoo. Hoodoo and voodoo ain't de same."

"Wha…"

"You go on now. I got to do supper."

She had to finish putting the clothes and sheets away so she could have supper ready to put on the table when my mother and daddy came home. She mostly tried to finish so she would have everything done and could catch the six-thirty bus. Almost six o'clock, she had set the table when Mother and Daddy arrived. Katy Jean sat on the sofa by the radio where she sometimes listened to Mary Hester's radio programs early in the day: *Stella Dallas, Just Plain Bill, Ma Perkins, The Brighter day.* Mary Hester worked through the house while she listened.

Mother kissed Katy Jean on the forehead. Then she pointed her finger at me. "Charlie, help Mary Hester, and lay out the silverware and napkins."

"Yes, ma'am."

"Isn't Henry home yet?"

Henry opened the front door.

"Henry, you are filthy." She didn't get mad when she saw his dirty tee-shirt covered with stained sweat and grass stains from working. Getting dirty from working and getting dirty from sloppiness were two different events; one was excused, the other was a crisis. But in either case she would point it out. "You need to get cleaned up before we sit down to eat."

"Yes, ma'am."

Daddy had dropped down in his favorite chair and had opened the afternoon newspaper before supper. "Been cutting yards, son?"

"Yes, sir," Henry said.

"Nothing much in the paper about the fire except what the morning paper said. Must not have been much more to it. I'll bet that skeleton was in some old grave from way back, whenever. Probably jus' some old private grave."

I turned toward Mary Hester and pulled my index finger under my throat from ear to ear signifying a blade cutting across it. She restrained a giggle, I could tell. *Hoodoo.*

We sat around the supper table passing and scooping and passing until the actual eating began. The food had been blessed, so getting it on the plate and eating it came next. The supper table presented a time of conversation. Our parents used the opportunity to encourage us to converse, develop *social skills* and remind us we were a family. I didn't think about all of this at the supper table, because all I could think about was eating. I thought my entire function was to enjoy eating, socially or not. Meatloaf and conversation was okay, as long as I didn't talk while I ate. Another potential crisis.

I mentioned how a policeman at the Tote-Sum said they didn't think anybody died in the fire. I didn't mention the other policeman while we were playing ball, because Mrs. Nettleton's precious flowers might have come up. Bringing up things at the supper table about things you did you weren't supposed to do wasn't the best thing for your social skills. My mother would just about have a heart attack if she thought we were bothering an old lady. And she dang sure would have had a heart attack if she thought we had violated someone's flowers.

Daddy said there would probably be some reasonable explanation sooner or later about what they found. "No great mystery to get worked up about," he said. "But we still should stay away for a few days and not get in the way of any cleanup."

"What explanation?" I asked.

"Just eat," he said.

I changed the subject to junk. "Daddy, would it be okay if I stored some stuff down at the warehouse? Stuff I'm gonna get from Minnie's. Just to keep it there for a little bit?"

"Is that some stuff she was paying you to clean out?" He was focused on cutting a tomato slice.

"Some of it. She said I could keep anything I thought I could sell. But she didn't want it at her house forever. That's why she wanted me to clean out the garage and chicken house. So it's gone from her house."

"Well, I don't want it down there for long. What makes you think you can sell it?"

Katy Jean smiled at my business dealings. Mother didn't smile; she listened to see how the process would go. Henry wanted to make some wise remark, I could tell, but more than likely he would get the *just tend to your own knitting* instruction from my mother. Henry had a paper route and earned more than I did with odd jobs. I wasn't old enough for a route and had to scramble for any work I could get. Minnie knew I could use the money and the work.

"Well, I jus' figured I can start some kind of little junk business and sell stuff door to door." I didn't tell him I wanted to gather junk from other places, too. "She's gonna pay me twenty-five cents an hour, and I can keep anything I want. But whatever I keep I have to take away pretty quick. She doesn't want it left there long. And she said maybe she'd pay me to take down the chicken house, if she decided to take it down."

"She finally gonna have the old chick—" Mother started.

"A door-to-door junk business? Brilliant," Henry said.

Daddy turned and abruptly pointed his finger at him, not saying a word. It meant *shut up and mind your own business and don't interrupt.*

Katy Jean tried to smile. Henry slumped, then leaned forward.

"Take your elbows off the table," Mother said.

"Well, why not just leave it over at Minnie's for a few days?" Daddy said, one eye still locked on Henry.

"I'm afraid she'll get tired of waitin' and have it hauled off."

"Pass the mashed potatoes, please," Henry asked.

"Just a second," Mother said. She leaned over Katy Jean's plate while she cut a piece of country-fried steak for her.

"Well, did she tell you how long she wants it left over there?" Daddy asked.

"She prob'ly said right away," Henry said, as if it was any of his business.

Mother handed him the potatoes and added, "Just stick to your own knittin'," she said. "Your mouth's about to get you in trouble." She held up her hand to Daddy who looked as if he was about to hit Henry on the head with the mashed potatoes spoon.

"I was jus' tryin' to be helpful," Henry said. It sounded more like he was begging for his life.

Daddy turned toward him again. Dangerous ground making Daddy tell you something twice. Katy Jean's attempt to smile disappeared completely. She didn't like either of us in trouble.

"She told me to take my time, but not to take the rest of the summer. She said she was paying me to get it out of there, not store it there," I said. My getting back to the subject saved Henry, at least temporarily.

"Well, maybe y'all can store some of it down at the warehouse for a bit. Maybe I can get Joe Washington to run by her house with the truck, and y'all can load it up. But I don't want it down there forever—pass the gravy, please—so y'all figure out what you wanna do with it pretty quick, junk business or not. You're aware Joe buys old junk and salvageable stuff, aren't you?"

"Yes, sir. I've already asked him if he wanted to buy some of my stuff." I handed him the gravy bowl. He paused while he dipped the spoon into the gravy then poured it into a cradle in his potatoes.

"So c'mon down to the warehouse in the morning and we'll see if we can figure out something, like where we can put it without it being in the way. And I think Joe will be by for a little bit so we can see when it will be okay for him to load up a truck with y'all. I think tomorrow is an off day for him at the ice house."

"Randy." Mother changed the junk business topic. "Katy Jean asked me earlier during the week if we were going to the coast before the end of the summer."

The Mississippi Gulf Coast was *the* place to go if your parents had the time or money. Everybody called it *the coast*. The entire Gulf of Mexico was available to swim in and some of the motels even had their own swimming pools. And some of them had air conditioning. We fished from a pier and there were miniature golf courses where we could be young Ben Hogans. The coast ran through three counties and several towns, from Pascagoula on the east to Waveland on the west. And from there it turned southwest to New Orleans.

The times Henry and I had been to the coast, we had stayed in what they called a tourist court made up of little cottages. They reminded me of little houses in the old nursery fables, with Rumpelstiltskin and other odd people. There was something special about not sleeping in your own bed, and although we weren't allowed to *destroy* our room, we didn't have to worry about making the beds.

And on the coast there were restaurants that served fried shrimp and even oysters when they were in season. They really were good fried, although some people like my daddy would eat the oysters raw. I couldn't do it though. They looked like snot when they were raw, a comment for which I had to leave the table one time; and though my mother didn't care for my description, she also thought raw oysters had a nasty appearance.

Katy Jean would smile and shake her head and communicate a soft "No, thank you" when Daddy offered one to her. Daddy loved to tease her into a smile.

But, it seemed, Biloxi stood as the center of everything on the coast. And there was as much to do for grownups as for children: whiskey and gambling, both illegal, but available courtesy of black market taxes and local sheriffs.

Daddy smiled at Katy Jean. "No, honey, we'll be too busy. We'll get down there in the spring. No later than April so we don't miss the oysters, maybe."

Summer would be running out soon, and we still hadn't gone over to Canton to visit some of Daddy's family. Of course, we would go fishing. But going to the coast wasn't something you could do a lot, considering the expense. If we were going this summer the subject would have come up before now. If there was one word we had learned at an early age it was the word *expensive.*

I had predicted the answer to myself but hadn't said anything. Katy Jean had been to the coast once before. Four years ago we had gone, a couple of years after one of the most destructive hurricanes ever had hit, and one of the few trips she could go on with us. I remember she seemed so happy sitting on the veranda of the hotel, her green eyes scanning the Mississippi Sound. I would sit next to her sometimes and watch sea gulls, and we gave each one names. Sometimes she extended her hands, trying to entice them to land.

At home sometimes she sat on the front porch and watched and listened to the birds. She recognized all of the sounds: the "peep" of the cardinal, always paired with his life mate; the melodious mockingbird who could change tunes like a chameleon changed colors; robins with their *cheerio, cheeriup.* Even grackles, lining the telephone lines along the street, with their harsh racket were a song for her. As she watched the seagulls and thrust her palms forward, it was as if one landed in her hands, she could lift with it and sail above the gulf waters.

Maybe next year we would go back.

Chapter 6

YOU BOYS COMIN' DOWN TO THE WAREHOUSE? SUMMER IS running out on you. You're not gonna have as many chances to earn some money," Daddy hollered from the living room. It didn't make him too happy to see me lying in bed at seven-thirty in the morning. "And Charlie, you want to come and see where we might put your junk?"

Henry began moving around under the covers. My bumping around had awakened him. He and I shared a bedroom while Katy Jean had her own room. He had awakened at four o'clock to deliver his papers but collapsed back in bed when he returned at six. Delivering morning papers was a hard job, but he made almost fifty dollars a month. Billy had said I could double that selling junk, and he could more than triple it selling rabbit tobacco. And we wouldn't lose any sleep.

Henry rolled over and sat on the edge of the bed, pulling his pajama top over his head. "Yaaa." He jumped up and mooned me.

"Oh, beautiful. A full one. You know what Mother would say if I told her you did that? She's say 'gentlemen don't do that.' Then she'd slap the snot out of you."

"Well, I'm in junior high now. My days of being a gentleman are behind me." He laughed.

"Did y'all hear me?" Daddy hollered louder.

"Yes, sir."

"Well, just don't stay in bed all day. And I've got plenty to do for a couple of you boys if you want to earn some extra money." His comment, "…if you want to earn…" didn't mean I really had a choice. And if you remained in bed you had to be sick or dead.

He didn't push Henry as much since he had regular work with his paper route. But the work I mostly did, odds and ends here and there, had no regularity. Daddy didn't want me falling into something called *sloth*. At the time I wasn't sure what *sloth* meant, but Henry told me it meant you were a lazy slob. Actually, being a lazy slob didn't bother me, but I couldn't say so. Until you were old enough to vote or hop a freight, you had to accept certain things.

"And tell Ronny Erl I've got enough for him if he wants to earn some money."

The work down at Daddy's warehouse didn't require enough time to hire somebody full-time. Besides nobody worked as cheap as we did. We would pick up, clean up, and do most anything not requiring *mental effort,* as Daddy put it. But we were paid, no matter how low-skilled. And my family saw no work as unimportant. I never learned who first said, "Any job worth doing is worth doing well," but you would have thought our family invented it. Of course, we were paid at ten-year-old rates of thirty cents an hour. Daddy told us not to forget our free meals and a roof over our heads.

"Your mother can bring you down in a little bit. I'm leaving now and going straight to the warehouse instead of the office." He threw down the last swallow of coffee then jumped in the family Oldsmobile.

The McCoy Lumber and Supply had its offices in the Standard Life Building, but rented a warehouse and yard down by the railroad tracks close to downtown. Same as the cottonseed oil plant, the warehouse had been built close to the tracks where lumber and lumber supplies were shipped. Every once in a while we'd see a hobo wandering around waiting to get a free ride in a boxcar. One time we heard about an old man trying to jump on while the train was moving, and he fell. The paper said he fell under the wheels and it decapitated him. Later Daddy told me what that meant.

Today Joe took off from his ice deliveries, and Daddy could use the help. Daddy frequently hired Joe part-time when he wasn't hauling ice or working at his junk business. Joe worked hard and Daddy paid him a dollar and a quarter an hour, which made him rich as far as we were concerned.

When we arrived, he was sawing some special board lengths Daddy had ordered. He stood under the tin shed built against the side of the warehouse and was working the band saw. You could hear the grinding, screeching, cutting of the wood, throughout the lumberyard. Sawdust flew like brown sleet. You could smell the burned wood.

Every time I saw it, I hoped anybody working the band saw was real careful, ever since a man cut off two of his fingers one day. I had started kindergarten and went with

Henry to the warehouse one Saturday morning. I didn't actually see it, but heard him scream, and when Henry and I got over to the shed, a couple of men had helped him get his undershirt wrapped around his hand as they took him to a car for the hospital. But there was blood all over the place, and Henry saw some bloody pulp laying in the sawdust on the ground which he told me later were the man's fingers.

Katy Jean stayed in the car and had not seen it. Daddy shooed me away immediately. But I'll never forgot the sight. Henry told me it might make me high-strung one day and I would have to see a psychiatrist at Whitfield, and I would have nightmares and wake up in a cold sweat. He said that had happened to a guy in the picture show one time. Humphrey Bogart or somebody.

Daddy had given us a job of untangling a big batch of baling wire strung out and entangled with some two-by-fours when Joe finally came over. Sawdust powdered his face. "Hello young-uns."

"Hey, Joe," almost in unison.

"Mr. Charlie, we'll clean out that spot yo daddy selected for you to store some stuff after dinner. I bes' be finish cuttin' some boards. He said y'all got plenty to do before then. Dat okay?"

"Sure," I said. "Thanks."

"Said y'all goin' into the junk business. Y'all gonna be my competitors?"

"This is the stuff you said you'd look at," I said.

"Tell you what. When we go to yo grandmomma's I'll pay you for anything I want. The rest we'll bring down here."

"Say Joe, how is Gumbo doin'?" Ronny Erl asked. "Are you working him?"

"Aw, he's doin' fine. I taken him down to the river a few times lately. He acted like he wanted to scent up some bobcats."

"You find any?"

"Naw. Bobcats is a hard animal to find even with the best dog. I jus' let Gumbo try for the workout he gits. Gotta be careful too, tracking bobcats. He's out here right now on your daddy's lot somewhere. Yo granddaddy said it's okay for him to run around with it fenced in. He prob'ly scared up a rabbit down by dat fence line. He's still puppy- frisky."

"What kind of a dog is he?" I asked.

"He's a red. A redbone coonhound some folks calls 'em. He'll scent up jus' 'bout anything. Or anybody. But you need more'n one if you serious 'bout huntin' bobcats."

By noon, Joe had finished sawing and we had untangled and removed most of the wire and other odds and ends lying around needing picking up or untangling. Mother had given the three of us some sandwiches and an apple each for our dinner, that she put in three brown paper sacks. Daddy bought each of us a Coca Cola out of the Coke machine.

Henry, Ronny Erl and I were squatting in the sawdust on the concrete floor under the shed when Joe walked over. "I'm jus' gonna eat my dinner wid y'all here in dis shade if y'all don't mind. Dis sawdust looks nice and soft."

His muscles were like a man of thirty, hard and rounded, sharp-edged when he flexed, like a man who worked at rough jobs, heavy jobs. I had heard Ronny Erl's daddy say one time Red Grange, the famous football player from Illinois, worked his way into terrific physical shape in the summer by loading and unloading ice. And it made me think of Joe as the iceman, chopping and lifting heavy blocks of ice.

It seemed funny to watch him peel an apple with his pocket-knife with little use for huge muscles or great strength; it was almost delicate, like my mother in the kitchen. I tried to visualize Joe shelling butterbeans.

"Do you get a lot of old junk from Mrs. Nettleton?" I asked. It really wasn't my business, but I blurted it out. Besides I thought I might get a few tips on junk dealing, especially if I was going to go door-to-door with it.

"Oh she jus' wants some ol' things she don't use anymore taken away. Most of it she gives on account I bring her ice from time to time. Some of the stuff I can resell, some I take down to the landfill."

"You take her ice?" Ronny Erl said.

"Well, she owns herself a 'frigerator. But she keeps her old icebox on the back porch jus' cause she had it for mor'n forty years, I s'ppose. She kinda old, and sometimes old folks don't like to change all-de-way. Anyway, she gets one block, once a week and de company tells me to go on and deliver it."

He took the remaining contents of the sack out, which included part of a newspaper and spread it on the bed of sawdust. He put each item down as if he were setting a table: a sandwich, a fried chicken drumstick, a hardboiled egg, and a banana to go with his apple. Next to the napkin he set a Mason jar full of iced tea.

"Have you been deliverin' ice to her for forty years?" I asked.

"Well, not me, I ain't quite been haulin' ice dat long, but somebody has," he said. "She's bound to keep dat ice box, I can say."

"Is she the only house you take ice to?" I asked.

"Only house," he said. "I jus' do her a favor since she lets me have first chance at stuff she gittin' rid of. Naw. I jus' deliever to stores dat sell ice to folks. If anybody around here got an icebox, dey don't use it no more; at least I ain't been tol' 'bout it. Most folks as old as she is, is dead or in de old folks home."

He sat with his back against the wall and his legs straddling his dinner. He had taken a big slug from the Mason jar, then wiped his mouth with his forearm.

"You know Red who works at my daddy's hardware store?" Ronny Erl said.

"Aw, yeah, I been knowin' Red a long time now," Joe answered. He cracked his egg on his knuckles, then began peeling it with his hands.

"Well, anyway he said you grew up somewhere around Madison County. He said you might of heard something about the house burning. The one out off Old Canton Road close to the county line. Not so far from our house. About who lived there in the old days and things like that. He said you might could tell us something."

"I lived up closer to Madison, some miles from dat house. But I guess I have a little familiarity wid it, I do. My daddy owned some land 'round dere once. But, old Red known me since my ball playin' days. Back 'for de war. His daddy wuz a scout for the White Sox. Told me once if they'd let coloreds play he mighta signed a contract. Course I wuz getting too old by the time we met. I wuz almost thirty-five years old. And his daddy died 'bout a year later."

I glanced at Henry and Ronny Erl. "You were a ballplayer? Baseball player?" Red had never mentioned his daddy being a baseball scout.

"Oh I played a lotta ball when I wuz a young fella. Played up in Nashville, for the Nashville Giants mostly."

"What league were they in?" I asked. I had never heard of them.

"Dat wuz one of de teams in de Negro Southern League. We wuz a semi pro team at first but we took pay on a regular basis soon after we got to be full professionals. Not a lot, but we shore took dat pay."

"You weren't born in Nashville though?" Henry asked.

"Oh no. I'm from right here in Mississippi. Born way back in de other century, 1899, not far from right where I'm sittin'." He chuckled, then took a bite of the egg. "I wuz just a boy when my daddy took us up to Chicago though. I wuz 'bout ten years old, right after the Panic. Dat's what dey called it when folks go broke. A Panic. But Daddy wuz trying to get work so we left home down here; wuzn't much older than you boys."

"Were you born in Jackson?" I asked.

"I wuz born in Madison county out in the country; between Canton and Jackson. Like jus' 'bout everybody else, we wuz farmers. And poor. We only set on 'bout twenty acres. Cotton growed up to one side of de house and beans to de other. Chickens kept the front yard clean o' bugs wid dere peckin'. We ate 'bout as much from huntin' as from farmin,' I 'magine. And Daddy really worked dem trot lines."

"How big is twenty acres?" I said. "Pretty big?" I couldn't remember if I had ever calculated the size of an acre. I had heard about acres as long as I could remember but never thought about the size of one.

"Bout fifteen or twenty baseball fields, I imagine. But dere wuz more'n jus'twenty acres. But we jus' set on twenty 'round the house, bes' I recollect. Me and my daddy did anyway. I b'lieve my granddaddy had more acres down toward the river, maybe. He had dat land since before the War between the States. He wuz a free black man and had property. Scalawags tried to get it after de War, but he kept it. Twenty acres anyhow, I guess. He'd drive a wagon down there and work the plot of ground down close to the river, then go back home and work his place. He worked some land up closer at Canton, too. Course he had a couple of workers with him. But he and my daddy hunted dat swamp area down by the river. Some of them places around Bobcat Creek and some of the sloughs is made up from the Pearl River. But I wuzn't around yet. But dat wuz a long way outta the city back den, like I say. It wuz a long way from downtown Jackson."

"Who took y'all's land after y'all moved away to Chicago?" Ronny Erl asked.

He started peeling the rest of his apple. "I don't know, child. All I recollect is we left. I couldn't tell you for a certainty if my daddy even got paid for the land." He ran his forefinger and thumb up the blade of the knife, wiping the apple juice away, then licked his fingers. His head swayed side to side as if he were recalling something he didn't want to.

I wanted to ask him if people ever told him he could have been Jersey Joe Walcott, but I didn't. He put down his knife and took a bite from his sandwich and almost half of it disappeared.

"How long were y'all in Chicago?" I asked. "Chicago's big and cold, isn't it? And a real lot of people, too."

"Oh dey's a lot of people all right. A lot more now than dey wuz back when I wuz dere. And it wuzn't like home, I c'n tell y'all dat."

"I don't think anybody lives in that house up off Old Canton now. The whole place is run down and grown over. At least from the road, that's what it seems like," Ronny Erl said.

"Oh, I'm sure it's not lived in. I never lived up dere. I been up dere many times since I come back to Mississippi, and I been up dere sometimes jus' to peck around. I just take Gumbo up dere to snoop and sniff out some coons down in the swamp below de house and scare up a rabbit ever once in a while. Jus' like to get Gumbo some work, so he don't get as lazy as me. I think one of dem little houses is what burned. Lightning is what dey say caused it. But I b'lieve dey say a big highway coming through dere one day. Calls it a interstate highway of some kind. Worries some."

"Worries? Who does it worry?"

"Jus' some...jus' some folks." He stood up and with his wadded sack in one hand he tilted his head and guzzled down the rest of his tea with the other, then shook out the remaining drops. He looked strong fully erect, and he didn't look lazy, like he said he was. I had heard Minnie say one time, "Some men, jus' looked lazy." But the way Joe handled ice and lumber, he didn't have that look.

"Wonder who was found in the fire?" Henry said.

"Maybe de Lord can tell you child...maybe he can." He rubbed his eyes when he answered.

"You think it's haunted or anything?" Ronny Erl asked. "The old house, I mean."

"Well, I ain't seed no spooks up there when I take Gumbo. But I recall some ol' stories my daddy told me when I wuz barely old enough to walk. But I think dey wuz jus' old stories he'd been told from way before..." He paused.

"Way before what?" I said.

He smiled. "Jus' way before *anything*, I guess, but y'all be careful if y'all git to playing' up dere. Lots o' moccasins. And you git stuck on a rusty nail, you'll be needing a tetanus shot, unless y'all want lockjaw." He screwed the cap on the Mason jar and stuffed the sack in his pocket. "Well, boys, I enjoyed my dinner time wid y'all. I'm jus' workin' 'til noon today over here. So, Mister Charlie, git wid me when we're to git dat load at your grandma's house. He turned toward the street and headed for his truck, but before he stepped into the street, he turned. "Like I say, y'all be careful if'n y'all go up dere."

Chapter 7

I CAUGHT THE BUS DOWNTOWN BEFORE NOON. I WAS GOING to meet Ronny Erl and see *Tarzan and the Amazons* at the picture show. Ronny Erl had some work to do at his daddy's hardware store and his daddy would bring him down later and drop him off. It gave me a chance to go by Bob's Tobacco House.

Often when downtown, I would go by Daddy's office. If I told him I was going to the picture show, sometimes, if he had his mind on something else, he would say, "Do you have enough money?" If I gave the right *look* I might get an extra fifteen cents for something *extra*. Other times he would say, "You boys are going to too many picture shows. You don't need to be spending money like it grows on trees."

I walked over to the Standard Life Building, not only the tallest building in Jackson, but also the tallest building in Mississippi—eighteen stories. Daddy's office was on the twelfth floor. I acknowledged a smile and a hello from the elevator operator. She was old but had a pretty easy job, although it must have been a dull doing nothing but going up and down all day. With a job like that, you couldn't even tell if it was raining, unless people were dripping wet when they stepped in, or had umbrellas or raincoats.

As we rode up to the twelfth floor I wondered the same thing I always did: what would happen if the elevator cable broke. If you jumped out of the twelfth-story window you obviously would splatter. But Ronny Erl said if you were in an elevator and it fell, what you needed to do was, just before it hit the bottom, *jump up* and you would actually be falling only a few inches. It would be the thing that saved your life.

"Hello, Mrs. Goldman," I said when I walked into Daddy's office. Mrs. Goldman acted as kind of a secretary and clerk-bookkeeper combination. A nice little Jewish lady, she had a pleasant way. She wasn't much taller than me, but she must have weighed about 250 pounds. Billy said she ate a lot of candy and butter, but she couldn't eat fried catfish because of Leviticus. I figured he knew.

"Hello, Charlie. How are you today?" She beamed at me.

"Fine."

"How is Henry doing? And Katy Jean? How is she doing these days?"

"Fine. Henry's starting junior high in September. And Katy Jean's doing okay, I guess."

She tilted her head and smiled a bit tiny. "Well, what are you up to today?"

"Oh, Ronny Erl and I are going to the picture show. Going to see *Tarzan and the Amazons.*"

"Well, where is Ronny Erl? You leave him outside?" Before I could answer she asked another question. She did that a lot—ask consecutive questions without waiting for an answer. "What in the world is Tarzan doing in Brazil?"

I wasn't sure what she meant. "I don't know. Where is Brazil?"

"That's where the Amazon is. It's down in the Brazilian jungle. Aren't you boys learning any geography in school?"

"Yes, ma'am," I said. I didn't want to say I hated geography. Then I would get a lecture on school and what a great thing it was and how I'd appreciate it one day. So I gave the best answer I could come up with. "I get those countries that are real big on the map mixed up sometimes."

"Real big on the map?" She put her papers down in her lap and peered over the top of her glasses.

She had sounded like a quiz master on a TV show. "Yes, ma'am. Like Africa and South America and Canada and all that."

"*And all that?*" she said. I thought she was going to choke.

The hole was getting deeper. Grownups liked to trap you sometimes when it came to talking about school. They were insistent school existed as the greatest thing since The Ten Commandments, and if you didn't remember every answer to every question, they would speak to you as if you didn't really appreciate the great chance you had to be locked up all day *learning.* All I had wanted to do was tell her about the dang Tarzan picture show and all of a sudden I am fighting for my intellectual life.

"I mean I get the places where they are on the map mixed up," I said.

She pulled her papers back up and turned toward her typewriter. "I see," she said, which of course meant she didn't but had become weary of the conversation. I was glad. I was tired of it, too.

Fortunately Miss Dolly entered and saved me. "Why, hello, Mr. Charlie. How are you doing today?"

"Fine," I said. She was a secretary who did a lot of typing and answering phones and stuff. She was real nice, too.

"Your daddy'll be off the phone in a minute if you want to see him. I heard y'all talking about Brazil out here. Who's

going to Brazil? It's hot enough right here in Mississippi."
She glanced at the ceiling fan going full speed.

Mrs. Goldman turned back from her typewriter. "Charlie gets mixed up about places like Brazil," she said with a smile. *Here we go again*, I thought.

"Well, Brazil's down there," Miss Dolly said, pointing toward the window, located on the south side of the building. "What do you get it mixed up with, Charlie?"

Mrs. Goldman had to answer for me, of course. "He gets it mixed up with Canada and *all that*."

Big Daddy came in from his office. "Well, what are you doing down here, Charlie? Your daddy's on the phone. Did you wanna see him?"

"Yes, sir. I'm gonna meet Ronny Erl and go to the picture show. *Tarzan and the Amazons* is on."

"And the Amazons?" he said. "What in the world is he doin' down in South America?"

I had started to feel like *Alice in Wonderland*. No subject ended. It just kept restarting. Before I could reply, Dolly spoke. "I just told him where South America was."

I was beginning to wish the elevator had crashed.

Finally Daddy hung up the phone; same question. "What are you doin' down here? Where is Henry?" Consecutive questions.

"I caught the bus. I'm goin' to the picture show with Ronny Erl. Mr. McGinnis is bringin' him down later after Ronny Erl's finished with his work. Henry is cuttin' sombody's yard. Gonna get three dollars."

Daddy lit a Chesterfield and took a big draw, then let the smoke flow from his nose. "Well, good for Henry. Sounds like you're the only one not workin'. You retired?"

"No, sir." I wanted to laugh but I didn't. He liked to joke around sometimes. He would frequently find some work for me if he thought I had too much free time.

"Big Daddy's got some things y'all can do down at the warehouse. And when are you gettin' Joe to bring your junk over there? I saw y'all got that space cleared out."

"We're gonna do it tomorrow afternoon."

"Okay. By the way, where you gettin' all this picture show money? It cost almost fifteen cents now, doesn't it?"

"Well, the New Joy still is just a dime, if you're under twelve," I said. The New Joy mostly had picture shows we liked. "That's jus' to get in. You don't get any candy or popcorn." I dropped a low-level hint so he might ask, "Do you have enough money?"

He reached into his pocket, I thought to pull out some change. Instead, he pulled out his pocket watch. "It's almost dinner time. I'd get you something to eat for dinner, but I'm gonna eat over at the Mayflower with a guy in town from the saw mill." He reached back in his pocket. "When does the picture show start?"

"One-fifteen," I said. "I'm gonna meet Ronny Erl there."

"Well, here's fifty cents. Get yourself a couple of Crystal hamburgers and something to drink, and try not to spend all you have left on candy or popcorn." He handed me a half dollar.

"Yes, sir. Thank you."

"Y'all gonna catch the bus home? Or y'all wanna wait around and ride with me after work? "

"We'll catch the bus." I calculated in my head at ten cents per hamburger and a nickel for a Coke, I had gained about a quarter since I had arrived. I started for the door.

"Charlie."

"Yes, sir?"

He smushed out his Chesterfield in the ashtray. "When did they start havin' Tarzan in South America instead of Africa?"

I had to walk about three blocks to the Crystal. The side-walks downtown were about fifteen feet wide on Capitol Street, and when they were first put down a long time ago, they were clean, almost white concrete most probably. And even though the street cleaners cleaned them every once in a while, they were still spotted with snuff-spit stains and squashed bugs and ground-in chewing gum and brownish coloring, making them un-white. But mostly they seemed to have their own smell; a sidewalk smell. I thought it funny that the sidewalks were so *filthy,* as my mother would say— she would have a heart attack if Henry or I sat down on the curb waiting for the bus. "Get up from there. You'll get filthy!" she would yell. But if we stayed out in the woods or the yard all day where everything grew in tons of dirt and *filth*, when we came in, she would simply say, "Go wash up for supper." Every time after playing outside in the grass and dirt we had to wash up, but sitting on a public sidewalk was like being un-baptized.

And certain blocks downtown carried the familiar smell from the cottonseed oil plant. The scent made me hungry whether or not I had an appetite. The smell of oil extracted an aroma like a bakery and I wished the air could hold it forever. My mother said it reminded her of her days in the Delta because, she said, "It is the embodiment of cotton;

it smells like home." Cotton came by train from the Delta down to Jackson, so the plant had been built right next to the tracks. And although the huge metal building with pipe outlets and flanges supported an industrial and city-fied life, it related to the land, like a giant barn.

I headed toward Bob's Tobacco House, two or three blocks away, and since I still had about a half hour before I met Ronny Erl I wanted to check it out. Also I figured I could use a nickel of my extra money and get Katy Jean five peanut butter logs. While I thumbed through a few funny books, I thought maybe I'd pick up any rumors about a new magazine Billy Cohen had told us about, the particular magazine we weren't supposed to ever see. *Playboy.*

Squeezed between two buildings with an alley on one side, Bob's Tobacco House was a little narrow store that sold most all the comic books ever printed. And there were all sorts of men's detective magazines and hunting magazines and newspapers from all over the state and all over the South. They had bubble gum, candy, potato chips and hundreds of cigars and packs of cigarettes and pipes and pipe tobacco. And it had its own smell, like everything else had; the Bob's Tobacco House smell.

If we didn't stay too long he allowed us to read the funny books without buying any. Most stores would make you leave if you sat around and read. Henry and I were never allowed to buy more than one every couple of weeks. They cost a dime, except at Christmas, when a Walt Disney special cost a quarter because it had about twice as many pages.

I had the money to buy one today because of the extra money Daddy had given me, but if I bought it I might get in trouble for spending money just to be spending it. I wanted a new *Captain Marvel* but I didn't get it. Minnie said funny books weren't good for the mind after a certain age; and she had read to us, and encouraged us to read *King Arthur and Excalibur and Song of Roland*. They were great stories, but my personal reading selection was *Captain Marvel*.

In the alley separating Bob's from another building, a door opened into a pool room and domino parlor. We weren't allowed to go inside by my mother, or by the owner. The men smoked and drank beer and spit on the floor, in addition to gambling on the pool and domino games. But sometimes the door was left slightly open in the summer, and we would sneak down the alley and listen to some of the spillover talk, and peek inside. Also Billy had heard on good authority about a calendar on top of the Coke Cola machine with a picture of a woman naked from her belly button up to her eyes. You couldn't see the Coke machine from the doorway, but we thought if we kept watching, maybe one day the furniture would get rearranged and the Coke Cola machine might get moved in plain view from the doorway. Billy said he lived for the day that Coke machine had a better location.

Daddy said any guys in a poolroom before 5:00 PM didn't have any business there. My mother hadn't said, but I don't think she believed they belonged there before or *after* 5:00 PM. She probably wouldn't let us even go close to Bob's if she had heard about the one time Mr. Bob accidentally broke a Coca Cola bottle, slipped up, and said *crap* right in front of us. He apologized to us, but if Mother had found out about his language we would have been banned for life. Besides, she thought Bob's too close to a poolroom for her children to be visiting often, even if we were there for funny books.

"When y'all go back to school?" Dexter asked. Dexter was the colored shoeshine boy at Bob's. "Y'all jus' git in trouble plinkin' 'round downtown all day." He smiled when he said it. He was sitting at the stand waiting for a customer, eyeing the last couple of swallows in his Royal Crown Cola. "You look like you need a shine while you make up yo mind 'bout which funny book to buy. Only cost a dime. Not no mor'n a funny book."

I glanced at my tennis shoes. I kind of laughed. I had to shine my own leather shoes at home. The only time I remember having any shoes shined by someone else was when we drove up to somebody's wedding in Memphis one time. We stayed at the Peabody Hotel and before we left for the church, Daddy had paid for a shoeshine for Henry and me at the shoeshine stand in the hotel barber shop. Daddy said Tennessee had a long history of great shoeshine artists starting with The Chattanooga Shoeshine Boy. Daddy began some long story he probably had made up to entertain us.

The wedding was boring but the reception was okay what with free cake and punch. I remember my shoes were brown, because my mother said she was mortified I had brought the wrong pair for a blue suit. It was the last time, she had said, I could pack for myself until I married. And even then she said she might give my wife a list of instructions for me.

"We go back on September 14th, I think," I said to Dexter.

"That ain't so far off," Dexter said. He turned up his R.C. and gulped a slug.

"Not far enough," I said. "I wish we lived fifty or sixty years ago when you didn't have to go to school so much, and you could do things like build a raft and go down the river. Now everything is about things you don't care about, like learning where Brazil is and long division and stuff."

"You mean go down the Mississippi River on a raft?" Dexter said.

"Maybe. Maybe the Pearl. It goes all the way down to Louisiana."

"You mean y'all be like Huckleberry Finn?" He laughed.

"Better'n long division," I said. "I'd be Huck and you could be Jim. Jim, the colored guy."

Dexter laughed again. "Wooo-wee. I quit school when dey started wantin' me to do dat short division."

"You sound like Dizzy Dean," I said. "He quit after the third grade."

"And he jus' now, dis year, got hisself in the Hall of Fame," Dexter said. "But he didn't build no raft and go down no river, neither. Dat's cause he from Arkansas and Arkansas ain't got no good raftin' rivers, in my opinion."

"I'll bet he could still play for the Jackson Senators," I said.

"Naaa, he a broadcaster now. Didn't you see dat at the picture show last year, *The Pride of St. Louis?* Anyway, once you retire I think you gotta stay dat way."

"Oh yeah. That's right. He busted his toe and it caused him to hurt his arm. I'd forgotten." I blurted, "Dexter, do you know what *laying down a trick* means? Or *hoodoo*?"

He had turned up his R.C., gulping down the last swallow, but stopped and lowered his arm. His eyes widened a bit, then he nodded. "Do you?" he asked me right back.

I couldn't be sure if he was kidding me, sounding as serious as he did. Mary Hester acted as if it were strange but true. I had really wanted to ask Joe, but not in front of others at the warehouse. "No," I said. "I just heard about it is all. Is it like voodoo?"

"Oh no. Hoodoo is hoodoo. Voodoo is voodoo."

"Where-abouts you hear 'bout it?" I said.

"My daddy told me long time ago. I think colored folks take on 'bout it mostly. I don't think white folks b'lieve such doings." He bent over and put his bottle in the wooden case although he hadn't taken the last swallow.

"Well, what does *laying down your trick* mean?"

He glanced over my shoulder making sure no one else heard. He put his finger against my chest. "Dat's when you put a hex on somebody."

"A hex? What kind of a hex?" I said.

"Sumpin' to hurt 'em. Maybe even kill 'em."

"Is it forever? The hex I mean."

"Sometimes. You mostly take 'em off de same way you put 'em on. Bury 'em or burn 'em."

"Really?"

"Dat house out in y'all part of town had some *hoodooing* done to it. De one dat burned."

"How come it was hoodoo?" I said. "I thought it was lightning."

"Dat's what dey say. But cause they found a skull, folks think it wuz hoodoo. And if it's a skull and fire then it's hoodoo and not lightning. And somebody wuz laying down a trick."

I wondered what he meant with all his jabbering. He sounded like Mary Hester on the subject. And it scared me.

"But they found a whole skeleton, not jus' a skull," I said.

He peeked over my shoulder and shook his head. "No more now. Not now. Here come Mr. Bob."

Bob came down the aisle, weaving between the magazine racks slowly, because he was kind of old and fat. I could only guess his age, but I had heard he had opened the store before WWII started. Deafness in one ear had kept him out of the war. Billy had it on another good authority that years ago Bob and his brother had a whiskey still over in Alabama somewhere, and it blew up, his brother with it. Bob ended up with a busted eardrum and lost part of his left ear.

He had white hair on the sides and not much on top. A cigar with about two inches remaining hung from the corner of his mouth. Everybody called him *Mr. Bob*.

"Now don't keep Dexter from his customers, Young McCoy." He recognized me because Big Daddy and Daddy were in there every once in a while for cigarettes. And I think Daddy slipped into the pool room next door every once in a while on a Saturday afternoon and shot a game of pool with some of his old war guys.

"Don't got no customers, Mr. Bob," Dexter said. "Not many come in durin' dinnertime for a shoeshine."

"Why don't you run out then and get your dinner? Run over to The Big Apple Inn and get you a pig's ear sandwich. Here's a dollar. Bring me back a half-dozen tamales. And bring me some crackers."

The Big Apple Inn was a colored place down on Farish Street specializing in tamales, but for some reason had started cooking a pig's ear sandwich. Someone had told us the butchers around town threw the ears out as waste, so The Big Apple Inn said they'd take them. Somehow they must've figured out how to cook them because they sold a lot. I had never been in to sit down because only colored people were allowed, but I had heard the ears were pretty good. Anyway, Dexter loved them.

Dexter climbed on his bicycle in the alley and rode off. Bob blew lightly on the end of his cigar. "That boy ain't as dumb as he makes out. He shoulda stayed in school. He might've gone out here to Jackson State College one day." The college for colored people. No grownup ever passed up a chance to say something nice about school.

"Mr. Bob, you ever had a pig ear?" I asked. I wanted to get away from the topic of education. The next thing he would be saying would be how I should stay in school, although I had no choice about staying or not staying. Maybe he had heard me talking to Dexter about rafting down the river and thought we had taken on a notion to drop out of school and become pirates or something.

He cupped his hand and put it up to his good ear. "What?" But before I could repeat the question he answered. "Yeah, Dexter brings me one every once in a while. I'm more partial to the tamales." He reached over and put his cigar in the stand-up ashtray. "But the pig's ear is okay. Kind of like bacon in some kind of sauce."

"Well, I like bacon, but I ain't sure about a pig's ear. Maybe if it tasted like Spam. But I don't like sauces on stuff like bacon, except mustard on Spam. That's pretty good." I remembered something. "Say, Mr. Bob. Do you sell rabbit tobacco?"

He laughed so loud, everyone in the store turned. "Well, where did y'all hear about rabbit tobacco?"

"Well, somebody told me we ought to sell it. Said we could make a fortune."

"Well, y'all ain't gonna make no fortune sellin' rabbit tobacco, not when it grows wild and is free." He laughed again then changed the subject. "Well now, rabbit tobacco notwithstanding, you figured out which funny book you want?"

I had to tell him I couldn't buy one. I had just been reading until I met Ronny Erl at the picture show. I hated to say it, although he wouldn't get mad. I didn't want to take advantage of his good nature.

I also hadn't seen the new magazine Billy Cohen had mentioned, but I couldn't ask Bob about it. Asking about rabbit tobacco was one thing, but asking about magazines with pictures of naked girls another. Billy said when it came out, it would become known as the era of the great bosom explosion. Of course, Billy also had said we'd make a fortune selling rabbit tobacco.

"No, sir. I guess I don't want one today. At least I better not buy one. My daddy'll get mad prob'ly since I already bought one this week. I'm going to the picture show, anyway. It starts in 'bout twenty minutes."

"What're you boys gonna see?" He had taken off his glasses and had wiped them with a red bandanna. He held them over his head, squinting through the lens in the light.

"*Tarzan and the Amazons*," I said.

"Hmm." He paused, still occupied with his glasses. "What the hell is Tarzan doin' in South America?"

I left to go meet Ronny Erl. As I walked past Mr. Bob I glanced at the magazine rack and noticed the front of *Baseball Magazine* with its colored photos of Stan Musial, Duke Snider and Allie Reynolds along with a huge headline at the top about another probable Yankee/Dodger World Series. At the bottom margin I noticed a small headline in boldfaced print: *Have Negro Leagues Any Future?* I wondered what it meant. I didn't think there were any Negro Leagues left.

And hoodoo definitely remained a mystery.

When I got home I gave Katy Jean four peanut butter logs. I ate one on the bus.

Chapter 8

IT HAD BEEN OVER THREE WEEKS SINCE THE FIRE. THE SHERIFF and police hadn't determined any more about the skeleton. The belief still held they were dated to around the beginning of the century. According to the newspaper, my daddy said, title searches at the Chancery Clerk's office revealed no recordation of cemeteries in the land title, and even title to the area seemed uncertain, except some commercial interest in Memphis had been paying taxes. The case wasn't as much closed as there was no case to be closed. And in spite of what Hester and Dexter told me about hoodoo, the cause of the fire had to be lightning because the large chinaberry tree next to the shack was shattered, the newspaper reported.

I earned a dollar and a half for cutting the Riley's grass in the morning. Normally, for a yard that size, I'd get a dollar but since they lived about four streets over and I had to push the mower to get there, Mrs. Riley gave me fifty cents extra. They had three children, two of them in high school, but one, Cheryl, was a year behind me at Boyduling. She had a crush on me but I wasn't ready to settle down at my age; and besides, Billy kept trying to corrupt me with the Sears and Roebuck catalogue and talk of Hugh Hefner's upcoming exposé. But Cheryl *was* pretty, in my opinion.

When I had finished, Mrs. Riley thanked me and told me what a hard worker I was. It made me feel almost as good as the dollar and a half I had made. When I asked her about the fire and the skull, the only grownup topic I could think up, she told me, like most grownups did, she had not become aware of any more than what she had read in the newspapers but I shouldn't worry about it. I didn't bother to ask her opinion on hoodoo.

At home, Ronny Erl and Buck were waiting for me to ask if Henry and I wanted to go up to the Big House. We hadn't been there since the fire, so I stashed my earnings in my room and hopped on my bike.

We had never actually been inside the Big House, although we had been on the property, picking plums in the spring and exploring the Bobcat Creek swamp area down to the Pearl River, part of which crossed the property. It appeared strange, deserted. Houses weren't meant to be abandoned. You could see from Old Canton Road the front, back, and one side door were all closed and though we were sure no one lived in it we couldn't be sure, and it might be odd to walk in and find someone inside.

Next to the Big House, an old barn barely stood, a work shed close by behind the barn, and there had been three small houses standing, shotgun houses, before one burned. They were strung out along a dirt road almost a mile from the barn, down to the bottomland of the swamp. At normal stage the river passed over a mile farther into the bottomland, but sometimes if there were some heavy rains and flooding, the banks would overflow, the water would rise and close in on the dirt road and inch up to the shotgun houses.

There were several wild plum trees on the property. In the spring the trees would load up with plums and, as far as we were concerned, were free for the picking. They grew wild, and the taste shot through you with its sharp green bite. They were easy to reach as you could simply pick them from the low hanging branches. Sometimes we would fill a sack and take them home.

Sometimes on a weekend my mother wanted a family excursion to the countryside where we

would pile into the car and drive into the country where we were to labor filling sacks and sacks of wild plums, not eating a single one (disallowed by Mother), saving them all to make plum jelly or preserves.

This late in the summer, most of the vines and trees had dropped their fruit. They grew due to the fertile soil and rain, and mostly where the land had been left to nature and unattended. But the fastest growing weed ever, the ever-reaching kudzu, had come from Japan and grew fast and faster. Everything in nature left unattended grew wild, Daddy said. And kudzu was the wildest. It had wrapped around the Big House like a lover; and like plums, dandelions and weeds, it had wrapped the land.

There were remnants of an old barn, and a gray-boarded storage shed still stood, barely. The back of the land gradually sloped down to Bobcat Creek, which ran into the Pearl River and its swamp; the Pearl separating Hinds and Madison and Rankin counties. There were two remaining shotgun houses toward the creek. The one that had burned lay as a matted area of black grass and charred boards. It had been reduced to embers and collapsed timbers lying across the floor, the walls crumbled into stacks of ashes. A pot-bellied stove remained, exposed to the sky. There was no chimney. As I stared at the charred boards, I thought about the skeleton.

As we poked around, kicking burned boards and ashes, I had an uneasy feeling I was about to uncover a foot or an elbow. And I thought about Mary Hester and Dexter and their hoodoo talk. I had tried to convince myself there was nothing to hoodoo, but now so close to the scorched shot-gun house I teased myself with what Mary Hester and Dexter had said. Maybe we were in a *hexed* place.

The weeds and grass were dry and scorched by the sun; but it would be in October before the first frost would kill and turn most everything brown. The grass was above knee-high, so we stayed in the dirt driveway watching for snakes. The driveway led from the creek past the burned shack, past the storage shed up to the Big House, and ended at the old barn. The barn was held up with the remains of two old A-frames and some remaining planks boarded across the top and sides. We didn't go inside because we were afraid it would fall on us.

We couldn't recognize the property lines except at the front where the road ended, marking the city limits. An old barbed-wire fence marked the boundary along Old Canton Road.

There were scattered bits of junk lying around: old tire rims and pieces of rusty iron, things from some old farm machinery. An old abandoned tractor, as old as tractors were, with one rotted tire still attached set at an angle, lean-ing on the other rim. Billy was right. A lot of junk. An old windmill, nonoperational for years, its gears and pump fro-zen in rust, stood marking the skyline. It served blue jays and mockingbirds and starlings as a perch; to rest, to scan the land for bugs and worms. Occasionally, a hawk would bully its way onto the tail of a smaller bird in flight across the field and shoo away the weaker. The hawk having larger game in mind, like field rats or rabbits.

I wondered if any of this stuff had any value. If Joe had been up here working Gumbo, he probably already had seen any profits I could see. However, I was getting discouraged with the junk business. Joe had given me $3.95 for a handful of items from Minnie's. The rest he had hauled to the landfill. I had begun to think twenty- cents an hour or cutting grass might be my lot in life. And I wasn't sure Billy cared anymore since his rabbit tobacco business hadn't gotten a vote of confidence from Mr. Bob. We both might be destined for a life of labor.

A lizard skittered across Ronny Erl's shoe. "Watch out. Those things'll kill you."

"Aw go on, a lizard won't kill you," I said.

"Poisonous ones will."

"Well, there ain't no poisonous ones around here. Maybe in Mexico or South America."

The place was so overgrown, there could have been anything out there. But we stirred around poking into stuff as if we were archeologists. Those were the guys, Henry said, who traveled all over the world in search of little bits and pieces of stuff people left behind after they died. One time we had seen a special film on world travel and foreign places about the pyramids and sphinx in Egypt and old things. The pyramids were huge statues, built by hundreds and hundreds of workers. Also the sphinx. But the sphinx looked like something built by mistake; one part one thing, one part another. But anyway, archaeologists and people who rooted around for old stuff loved strange things like old pyramids. Henry said he didn't think an archaeologist would be coming up here anytime soon. An old beat-up windmill and a million tons of Kudzu probably weren't rated real high on some museum's discovery list.

"I guess nobody ever cuts the grass up here?" Ronny Erl said. "Wonder who actually owns this place?"

"I'll bet you anything that if we had a good smellin' hound dog we could find something up here if there's any-thing to find."

"Yeah. Maybe. But I think it has to be alive for him to track it," Buck said. "And there ain't no such thing as a smellin' hound. You mean a scent hound."

I picked up a dirt clod and threw it at the storage shed. "Well, whether or not it has to be alive, a dog could do better than us stompin' around in the weeds."

"Okay with me. But we ain't got one," Ronny Erl said.

"Maybe we could get Joe to bring Gumbo up here some-time when we're here," I said. "He said he comes up here around Bobcat Creek and the swamp every once in a while."

"Y'all wanna go inside?" Henry said. Although it was daylight, the Big House rested on the hill all dark and gloomy. I recalled the word *ominous* in one of Mommas' sto-ries. And what could be inside? Hoodoo maybe.

"Let's go," Ronny Erl said.

"Let's go in," Henry said. "Nobody's in there."

"What about ghosts," Buck said. "Gifford said a slave girl was supposed to haunt the place. And I've heard the same story a lot. I don't care what people say about 'no such thing as ghosts.' This place is made for ghosts."

I almost broke out in hoodoo talk, but I didn't.

"Aw, Daddy said that's jus' an old story colored people made up," Ronny Erl said. "A lot of 'em believed in ghosts back then and the stories jus' get passed along. And that was a Louisiana ghost about the slave girl. You remember? Red said so."

I thought about something else Red had said: "*But there're so many stories that go 'round, that you can't never tell what's true and what ain't.*" Daddy had also said there's a little truth in every story. Of course, he also said the problem had always been with the *little* part.

"Well, are we going in or not?" Buck challenged.

You could be sure the subject of *chicken* would come up. It usually did. I pointed my finger at my chest. "Well, I will if y'all will," I said.

"Chicken!" Buck said.

I knew it. "I'm not," I said. If you accepted the name *chicken* without a decent fight, you might as well start wearing a dress. "I jus' don't wanna get in trouble." I didn't care about getting in trouble as much as I had to deny the *chicken* label.

"Aw, you're afraid of something gettin' you," Ronny Erl said.

"I am not." I put my hands in my back pockets and shuffled my feet trying to think of a way to lie my way out. The house scared me even in the daylight. Finally I agreed. "Okay I'll go if we all go at one time."

"I'm gonna check some more out here," Buck said. "Y'all go on."

"Chicken."

"Drop dead."

The doorknob on the front door wobbled, broken. The door swayed, then creaked, opened. The house was still solid, although most of the windows were broken. Windows in deserted houses seemed to go first. Rabbit hunters passing and taking pot shots, slingshot marksmanship tested, rock chunkers, and a bunch of other window-killers, all viewed glass as a natural target.

Inside, crawling along the baseboard over and through the shards of glass, were the cobwebs, alluring for travel, but a trap for tiny critters to be eaten: beetles, redbugs, crickets, and some, unidentifiable. Then, as if by some magic design, the webs at once turned and climbed in some places to the ceiling and splayed like wings on a giant bird. Black widows were lurking.

Not much furniture to see. Except for a chair with a broken leg here and there, and a couple of old davenports, little decorated the downstairs. We found an old mattress, stained with something black, like dark molasses or maybe motor oil. No one wanted to touch it. Henry said it was probably old blood from an old murder. A couple of broken mirrors and more shards littered the floor, and cobwebs covered most of the other rooms. And, a single tidbit, an old can of sardines, unopened, swollen, about ready to pop open; maybe the road-stash of a passing hobo.

Upstairs an old roll top desk aged about five hundred years old, I thought, stood against the wall. It should have set on four legs except one had been broken off making it lean at a clumsy angle by the wall. Henry and Ronny Erl and I tried to force the top up, using as much muscle as we had. It seemed like the years of humidity and dust had wedged it like a tomb. Suddenly the top flew open, giving in to our efforts; a cluster of spiders and roaches raced out as if they were being chased by the brown rat leaping after them. I jumped as if it were a rattlesnake.

Before my heart stopped pounding, a window pane exploded and glass flew everywhere and we all dashed to the window.

Buck. From the outside he had thrown a rock through a partially broken pane.

Ronny Erl and I both spit from the second floor at him. Henry cursed him with a word I had never heard. Then he spit.

"I hope a moccasin gets you," Ronny Erl yelled.

Buck laughed. He had really scared us.

"Come up here," Ronny Erl yelled.

"What is it?"

"Just come up and see."

We gathered around the old roll top, piddling and grabbing at the series of stacked compartments, drawers and nooks and an old newspaper page. Mostly an ad page for things like ladies corsets and bottles of rye whiskey and hammers and knives; it had yellowed, and it smelled musty. Up at the top it had its name, *The Memphis Daily Appeal* and the date, August 10, 1908. We found all the drawers empty except for the one in the middle we couldn't open. We heard Buck climbing the stairs.

"It's locked," Henry said. "That's an old keyhole. Y'all see it, with the little metal hole around it." Everyone bent over trying to gaze into the hole, seeing nothing inside but blackness.

"Maybe we can break it open with a hammer or something," I said.

"Yeah," Ronny Erl said. "We could blow it open with an M-80 if we had one."

"I think we oughta get out of here," Henry said. "Somebody's gonna catch us up here."

There aren't any no trespassing signs," I said. "So what if somebody catches us?"

"Well, what if somebody sees us," Henry said. "We might get caught for breakin' in."

"Aw, I don't think anybody cares," Buck said. "You're just scared Henry 'cause this place is weird. Anyway, we didn't really break in, the doorknob was busted. Besides that, ghosts never come out except at night." He laughed. I glanced around the room.

The middle drawer was too sturdy to open without breaking the wood, and we couldn't pick the lock because none of us could pick a lock in spite of Ronny Erl's insisting he did. I wasn't sure if an M-80 would work even if we had one. We finally gave up and went back outside.

We looked under the windows and along the foundation. We took high steps through the grass, above our knees in most places, risking snakebite, and we'd kick dandelions to watch them explode like little bombs, their plumes scattering in the wind. And dragonflies buzzed and flew back and forth as we moved around. The field sloped in the direction of the creek and river down toward the swamp, although the main course of the river was over half a mile away. The driveway forked away from the path going to the creek and spiraled toward Old Canton, and now was nothing more than dusty tracts with a grass strip running down the center. It started down by the fence, where we had entered, by what used to be an old gate. The old entrance, barbed-wired-over and nailed shut with boards made it easier to crawl under the fence, so we had left our bikes there.

"Need a tractor to clear off this whole place, I bet," Ronny Erl said.

"Wonder if there are any gravestones," I said. "Red said there might be."

The tall grass made it difficult to see down the slope so you couldn't see much from a distance. You were forced to stumble over whatever you were trying to find. Almost noon, the temperature was rising and the bugs and gnats spun up and around our faces as we stepped through the grass, the sweat attracting them. We walked down the slope, hoping the heat would keep the snakes in their holes.

"Hey, let's just go back to the gate and get our bikes. We can ride down the road to the river," Ronny Erl said. "There probably ain't no cemetery out here anyway. Besides it's prob'ly a mile to the river."

"Let's keep on going," Henry said. "I wanna see if there's a cemetery."

"Let's get our bikes," Ronny Erl said again. "We'll never gonna find a cemetery. I'm tellin' y'all, there prob'ly isn't one anyway."

"Okay," Henry finally gave up. I could tell he didn't want to. He still wanted to find a cemetery. And I wanted to keep trying myself, but I was hot and the weeds were so high I wanted to ride instead of walk.

The roadway wound through the tall grass down toward the creek and the Pearl River. When we approached the water we saw several human tracks in the mud, though lots of tracks were no surprise since people came down to the river to fish or set out trot lines or squirrel hunt; and they didn't necessarily have to cross the property of the Big House. Some of them could be Joe's tracks when he brought Gumbo down here. You could go swimming in the river, but you had to be careful of the currents and eddies. And a few alligators lived and swam and waited. We skimmed rocks across the water or tried to hit turtles popping their heads up. Henry stepped in some weeds growing on the edge down into the water and scared out a water moccasin.

"Hey, snake, get him!" The snake slithered into the water. A barrage of rocks from the three of us followed. The snake ducked under the water, maybe hit, we weren't certain. Anyway, we returned to our skimming as we walked up and down the edge of the river.

"Watch out wherever you step," I said. "There are a million of 'em down here, I'll bet." Everybody laughed at my estimate. But there were a lot. Then I noticed Henry and Buck were standing over something, staring. "What'd y'all find?"

"It's an old satchel or briefcase, I think," Henry said.

"Pick it up and see if anything's in it," I said as I walked over.

"You pick it up. A snake might a' slithered inside it," Henry said. He pointed at Ronny Erl. "You pick it up."

"Not me! Hey Charlie, gimme that stick o'er there."

I pitched to him. He shoved the stick inside the flap and moved it enough to be sure there were no life forms in it. When we were certain sure death wouldn't jump out, Henry turned it over. He shook it until the contents dropped to the ground. A golden pin.

Chapter 9

THE DAYS, BEFORE SCHOOL, WERE GETTING SHORTER. LABOR Day was a holiday, and there were about two weeks before school started. Big Daddy said he never understood why people took a holiday for working. Labor was what you were supposed to do. And you did get paid. Unions and Communists thought up *holidays for working,* he said. But on a weekend holiday, our family usually did something together. My mother liked the idea of us doing things together as a family. Henry and I liked to do things together as a family if they were fun.

It had been over a month since the fire. The four of us agreed the pin belonged to all of us, certain of its great value. Henry and I kept the pin at our house, and Ronny Erl and Buck kept the satchel at their house.

We drove up to Canton on Labor Day weekend to visit some of Daddy's side of the family. Canton was about forty miles north of Jackson, and it took us about an hour to get there on Highway 51. Besides visiting, we were going to spend the day fishing in a tributary of the Big Black and Pearl Rivers. Daddy had an old war friend we called Mr. Georgie. I supposed his name to be George-*Something* or *Something-* George, but anyway we had called him Mr. Georgie since

I could remember. He and Daddy were in Burma together and realized, when they first met overseas, they both were from Mississippi and had relatives in the same area around Madison County. When he first came back, Mr. Georgie worked with McCoy Lumber and Supply, but I think he really wanted to live in Canton and be a full-time farmer and part-time fisherman. Or maybe the other way around.

Anyway, it was about an hour over there and Henry and I watched the passing fields of the countryside. But after sufficient boredom, about five minutes, we would start a game called "counting cows." It used to be fun when we were in kindergarten, but now we did it to pass the long hour. My mother would count a few for Katy Jean to put her in the game. Of course, whoever counted the most won, though we had nothing to win except the joy of beating the other. There was no way anyone could be sure how many cows there actually were, except for the guy's integrity who was counting on his side, so we were kind of on the honor system. This, of course, put Henry at a disadvantage. Between Richland and Canton, I reported a total of 1,626 cows. Henry said he had counted thirty-eight on the other side of the highway.

When my mother heard me announce my number, she turned and faced me without a smile, her eyes firing bullets. "Charlie, Are you sure you counted that many cows?" She really meant something else: *Stop lying or I'll slap you.* Then she would announce Katy Jean had counted 1,627 and was the winner. Katy Jean smiled, and Mother had just out-cheated me.

And every store or filling station we passed with huge signs advertising Coca Colas or Royal Crown Colas or

Barq's, whetted our thirst. So we constantly would plead to stop and let us get a drink. The answer mostly was *no*. In fact out of about a million times we asked, the *yes* answer came up maybe one or two times. And even then Daddy fussed, like we had broken some Bible rule. "If y'all keep spending money like this, I'm not gonna be able to send y'all to college." Or, my mother would say, "Those sugary drinks are gonna rot your teeth out and when you're old you'll have to gum your food." We pretended to agree, but we really didn't care about going to college then. I didn't care too much for the fifth grade. And as far as *no teeth — old*, it didn't mean anything.

But when the usual *no* answer came up, which it did today, it was followed by the, "You don't need one and we'll be in Canton in just a little bit." A "little bit" meant forever. An hour made for a long ride, even counting cows.

In Canton we were thought of as the "city boys." But Daddy said we were being teased and we weren't city boys like in Boston or New York. Big Daddy said we could be from Memphis or New Orleans and we still wouldn't be such a thing. He said for us not to count on finding a city-boy Southerner.

Canton had about six thousand people and if you didn't live on a farm you could spit about far enough to hit one. And, being a farming area, there were a lot of colored people.

At the house we saw our cousins and uncles and all that part of the family. We had to talk to everybody, while they mentioned about how much we had grown and asked how we liked school. I don't think they cared too much, but my mother said we learned to *socialize* by being sociable. Besides we didn't want to get in trouble for being impolite.

Being impolite would get you a switching about as quick as lying or stealing would.

Everybody called one of my cousins *Goose* about ever since he was born, I guess. Didn't have any idea where it came from. His real name was Richard. But it was a nickname he got stuck with and stayed with him. He shaved once a week and could buy cigarettes at any store where the clerk might not recognize him because he looked old enough to be in high school. His little brother, Pete, and I were the same age.

Goose would be fourteen soon. He didn't have a driver's license yet, so all he could drive was the tractor and the pickup around the farm. But he couldn't drive us around because his daddy said the bunch of us together in a vehicle might be a little too dangerous, the way boys had of getting excited and all. One time when Goose had a couple of friends in the pickup last summer, he hadn't been paying close enough attention, his daddy had said, and he drove through the watermelon patch. It was pretty messy from what I heard. I'm not sure because I never asked, but I'm sure Goose got in trouble. Destroying things like watermelons was worse than destroying something like cinder blocks. Cinder blocks were made in a plant. Watermelons were grown in the soil.

"I hear they're lookin' more into that fire in Jackson. The one where they found the skeleton," Uncle Walter said.

Uncle Walter was really a great uncle and was an Ole Miss Law graduate who had returned to Canton to practice law. He often liked to talk about things in the news having to do with trials and courts. He had been a small-town lawyer all of his life. A local judge for a couple of terms, most people still called him *Judge*. However, since he was into his seventies his practice of law pretty much covered talking about trials and crimes he had kept up with in the newspapers or old, famous cases. And a handful of lawyers in town who also were old, in-their-seventies, would get together with him down at the Bulldog and Rebel grocery store for a game of dominoes and discussions of old cases. Big Daddy said Uncle Walter was a very smart man. He had once revealed some history to Henry and me.

It happened that the B&R grocery had been opened in 1901 by two brothers. Robert Bobitt Sample, having inevitably become Rob-Bob, and Lester Leroy Sample. Rob-Bob had gone to Ole Miss and Lester Leroy to Mississippi A&M. The same year Ole Miss and State began playing their traditional rivalry on the last day of football season. The first year, State won 17–0 and the second year Ole Miss won 21–0. The third year a tie, 6–6. Mother said that would have been a good place to stop, but since she was probably the only one to think so, they continued until 1926.

Having been beaten the previous thirteen years, Ole Miss won 7–6 and fans were in such a joyous state they tried to tear down the goal posts at State's field. The on field fight that ensued became legendary and afterwards a decision was made for a prize to be awarded, which might prevent such mass mayhem. The prize became renown in Mississippi as the Golden Egg trophy. The fight that had broken out at the R&B grocery via radio contact with the game became legendary, as during the course of listening to the game, a highly contested domino tournament coincided along with the consumption of several bottles of bootleg beer by the contestants. With the notable players and beer-drinkers being almost evenly split between Bulldogs and Rebels, the riot that followed not only provided local doctors with business but local lawyers as well, at least a couple of whom were domino participants.

A fire broke out and fortunately through hurried efforts of volunteers, the R&B did not burn down. Rob-Bob had been punched so badly in the fight he wore an eye patch the rest of his life, forever claiming some low-life Bulldog alumnus gouged him in the eye. Uncle Walter said his eye wasn't hurt badly, but he wanted some settlement and some sympathy. Rob-Bob would never open his patch for any-one to see and had instructed that when he died, should he have an open casket, the patch should remain on, and there would be no *under-peeking*. He died in 1946, patch firmly in place and State won the Egg Bowl that year 20–0. But the next year, Johnny Vaught arrived at Ole Miss.

"Yes, sir," Daddy said. "I'm not sure what they have, or if they have anything. Not sure at all." The newspaper had run the story that in examining the skeleton it was noticed late in the examination the jaw was cracked and the neck vertebrae broken. Since there had been no disturbances such as a road grader or backhoe; and in fact only minor shoveling through the ashes by the firemen, they concluded the former body of the skeleton had been killed by a severe blow, around fifty years ago.

Henry and I and our cousins were all sitting out on the screen porch where we mostly listened. The topic ended after a few minutes. *Children should be seen and not heard* being the rule, so our listening seemed too much for the topic of old violent killings.

"Y'all goin' fishin'?" Uncle Walter asked, pipe smoke flowing through his lips. He rocked slowly in the porch swing, an occasional squeak from the old chain link. "Going with some friend of your daddy's?"

"Yes, sir. We supposed to go with Mr. Georgie. Well, he's gonna take us down the Lusa Tributary. Said we'd catch some big catfish."

Uncle Walter rocked back and forth in the old porch swing still puffing his pipe. "Well, I imagine y'all'll get some. I think old Georgie was born with gills. He understands more about fish than he does 'bout cotton and corn. Prob'ly the best fisherman in Madison County. Maybe best in Mississippi, white or colored."

Mother came out on the porch. Cousin Beck, Goose and Pete's mothers were standing with her. Mother started shaking her apron, a sign she had finished helping with the cleanup in the kitchen. She had heard us talking about our fishing excursion. "Well, y'all be careful. I don't want anybody getting drowned."

Cousin Beck reached over and smacked Pete right on top of the head with the fly swatter. "Stop that!" she hollered like she was at the ballpark. Pete had started picking his nose right in front of everybody. I couldn't believe it. Anybody with any sense knew that would get you smacked. But I still had to almost choke to keep from laughing. Henry couldn't keep his mouth shut, though.

"Pick a winner, Pete!" His laughter was interrupted when Mother smacked him on the top of his head with her hand.

"Just you shut your mouth. It's none of your business."

Henry always had a problem with one of our great lessons: *Mind your own business*. He should have learned, sticking your nose into somebody else's business was as bad as picking your nose in public. A rare moment though: two smackings within two minutes and I had cleared them both.

Uncle Walter kept rocking away in the swing, his amusement increasing the swing speed. He recalled the subject, trying to spare Henry and Pete anymore torment. "I think they'll stay out of the water. Old Georgie won't want 'em scaring away the fish."

"Well, if y'all do drown we aren't gonna spend a lot of money draggin' the river. You'll just be catfish food," Daddy said. "It cost money to go fishin' for drowned folks."

I had noticed over the years how grownups would try to lighten up the situation after somebody had been punished for something minor. It was called "easing the tension." I also found out later the Lusa is pretty shallow and not even over your head in most places. So I think Daddy believed drowning unlikely. I'm glad I didn't get smacked on the head. But the *picking* affair had passed.

The Lusa Tributary took its name from a Mississippi Indian tribe, the Choctaws. The name Lusa meaning *black*, although the Choctaws' primary area existed farther east than where the tributary flowed into the Pearl and Big Black Rivers. Lusa was like a small lake with a tunnel of cypress trees lining its banks, and unless the sun shone directly overhead it was mostly shaded. Uncle Walter likened it to a slough rather than a tributary. But it was fertile water, he had said.

We could feel the heat as we drifted under the large shroud of trees, and the branches spreading out from smaller willow trees along the bank that added shade. While Georgie did the paddling, working our way down to some secret spot, we watched turtles drop from snags into the water until we passed. We saw the occasional water moccasin winding and slithering across the surface, willing to get out of the way, although potentially aggressive. Except for gnats dancing around your eyes and a mosquito buzzing in your ear, we were happy. Of course, it was pretty hard for fishing not to be fun. Brother Milner, a deacon at our church, had said if fishing were illegal it would be the only law he'd break without being tempted. Even my mother laughed.

We paddled and drifted in two old, wooden, flat-bottom boats, with Georgie and Pete and Henry in one boat and Daddy paddling from the stern of the other with Goose and me.

The water wasn't brown from churned mud like many rivers, but dark, mostly settled, with little current to roil its sediments. I could see my face reflected like a mirror, and everywhere life on the surface: water spiders and all kinds of tiny water bugs. I had asked Henry one time how they could walk on water and he told me about something called surface tension, and I would learn all about it in sixth grade science. Every now and then a frog would dart from a floating log, the splash sudden in the stillness. Goose would spit to see if he could get a bluegill to rise and pop the offering; he did this about every five seconds until we finally drifted up to the starting spot. Mr. Georgie had found his place.

We fished until late in the afternoon, paddling up and down the short, shallow slough. I think I heard Daddy say Mr. Georgie was more than ten years older than he, although they were in the war together. Mr. Georgie's forearms were big, like Joe Washington's, like cement. I think you could strike matches on them. And on each a tattoo. One a hawk, the other the name "Rebel." He wore a brown Stetson with the brim pulled down low so you could barely see his eyes. Daddy told us Mr. Georgie had been awarded the Silver Star in Burma. It was the only reason my mother accepted

his arm-markings. She said tattooed people were *common*—
except for heroes.

Each boat had ice buckets full of catfish. Goose and I
guessed the smallest was two or three pounds. The smaller
ones were best for eating. We caught all of them on cane
polls using roaches and old gray worms for bait. Catfish
would eat anything. They were like underwater buzzards,
Big Daddy had once told me.

We started paddling back where we had left Georgie's
old 1942 Dodge pickup at a dirt trail leading to the river,
when we saw the distinctive figure of Joe Washington
standing on the bank. We waved. His dog Gumbo sniffed
and darted back and forth along the bank.

Georgie paddled up alongside. "Giv' us a pull up, Joe,"
he said as we bumped into the sloping bank. Joe reached
out and with his arm pulled our boat up so the bow set on
the land.

"What's going on with you, Joe?" Daddy said. "What's
Gumbo up to?"

"Ahh he jus' pokin' around. I been checkin' on some trot
lines. Gumbo jus' bein' out here where he b'longs. Runnin'
'round sniffin' up what he can."

"You think he's gonna be a good one, huh Joe?" Daddy
asked.

"Oh yassuh. He's gonna be fine. And he's gonna have
some good stock too. He bred wid a little bitch down at
Ridgeland. I got first selection of the pups. Need to find
someone who c'n raise a redbone, I guess. I can't feed
another jus' now."

No one said anything. We couldn't take the pup, but
didn't want to say so. Finally Daddy said, "You'll find a
home for him. He's good stock like you say."

"Well, if'n I don't, I'll might jus' take cash for him, if'n some owner kin come up wid the money."

"Who owns the bitch?" Daddy asked.

Joe shaded his eyes with the flat of his hand eyeing something above the cypress trees. "Y'all see de size of dat hawk," he said. He turned back to us. "Old Mistuh Franklin. He tryin' to raise dogs for a livin' dese days."

"Is he the same Franklin that's been around as long as I can recall?" Mr. Georgie said. Daddy's expression changed to a glare, eyeballing Mr. Georgie straight-on. But he said nothing.

Joe paused for a few seconds, removed his pocketknife and cut some fishing line. Finally he said, "Yassuh. Same one."

I exchanged glances with Henry and Goose. I could tell we weren't supposed to ask any questions. I changed the subject. "Joe, did you ever think of boxing instead of playing baseball?" He looked at me in a special way we shared. He seemed pleased I had changed the subject.

"Naw, Mr. Charlie, I never did. I'd prob'ly got myself kilt if'n I'd done that." He threw the paddle up away from the water then reached in his shirt pocket. He pulled out a small tin of snuff and scooped out a finger's worth and placed it under his lower lip. "I'd would've had to fight somebody like Jack Dempsey or somebody like that. Maybe even ol' Joe Louis."

"You might've had to fight Billy Conn," Daddy said. "He's as tough a guy for his size you'll ever see." He pulled a Chesterfield out and lighted it.

Joe smiled. Everybody had heard about the Joe Louis-Billy Conn fight. Conn was really a light-heavyweight, but fought Louis on better than even terms for twelve rounds until he was knocked out in the thirteenth round. "He wuz a tiger, Mistuh McCoy. He wuz dat."

"You think you could beat Jersey Joe Walcott?" I asked.

"Oh Lord no, child. Dat man near bout beat Rocky Marciano last year. And they say Marciano could really and *truly* knock down a mule with one punch."

Goose had counted the fish in the bucket and without looking up said, "Yeah, I was listening to the fight on the radio that night. Daddy said Rocky was just about to run outta rounds when he caught old Jersey Joe with his right hand. Daddy said Marciano wasn't much of a boxer, but if he hit you with his right, you'd better look out."

"Well, he's right," Joe said, talking about Goose's daddy. "Dat Rocky Marciano sho can punch—my goodness, he can. Now y'all understand why I wuz a baseball player." He flashed a huge smile. So did we. Gumbo wagged his tail like a new daddy.

We drove back to Jackson Monday night. Darkness hid the cows, so I kept thinking about the guy named Franklin. I wondered why his name had seemed to invite caution.

Chapter 10

Aman named Chambers Gallagher had been arrested in a motel just north of Jackson in Madison County. Suspected of having killed an antique dealer and stealing several items, he was also suspected of having killed a deputy sheriff in Biloxi earlier in the year. Tried and convicted in Hinds County, he awaited transport to Parchman for execution sometime after New Year's Day.

But most people seemed more interested in the county inquest for the skeleton than a killer.

The courthouse was the Hinds County courthouse, which is where criminal trials and inquests were held. People talked about the inquest throughout the day because it was something special. And what happened in court was in the newspaper every day for them to read about. Henry would usually tell me about it because he was getting interested in reading the entire newspaper, while I mostly turned through the comic section and the baseball standings. It seemed certain the Yankees would win their fifth straight pennant, which made a lot of people happy, but about as many unhappy.

It had been almost a month since the fire, and though little evidence had surfaced, the inquest lasted about a week, and they had called a jury. No one was sure why there had to be an inquest taking a week since there was barely a suspicion of a crime, and one that had happened four or five decades ago. It took up almost as much conversation as the pennant race.

Even my mother's bridge club ladies talked about the inquest, though why they cared remained a mystery to me. Daddy said since women didn't serve on juries, it was a natural thing to be curious about things they heard about but could not experience first-hand.

The bridge games were pretty much sissy events as far as I could tell, so talking about skeletons didn't seem to fit. However, if the game was as dull as it appeared, I guess they had to talk about something. A couple of the ladies smoked and the ashtrays would get filled with crushed cigarette butts with lipstick on the ends. The smoke wafted across the room and through the windows, propelled by the attic fan.

Even the refreshments at the bridge game were kind of pitiful. Mother would have some kind of punch or coffee and some of those little bitty sandwiches she called *finger* sandwiches. They weren't much to put in your mouth, and besides, I didn't like the idea of eating something that sounded like somebody's finger had been sticking in it. Plus there wasn't anything good in them like peanut butter or potted meat, only gooey white stuff with green things poked inside. And the crust was cut away like it was some kind of a fungus or something.

But when we passed through the room once or twice, you could hear parts of the conversation. And once I heard them talking about who might have been buried out there years ago. I guess they liked guessing since they couldn't be on juries. One of the ladies had remarked one day about who around town looked like an old killer. Later I told Daddy what she had said, and he said *looks* didn't have anything to do with it. He said if Jack the Ripper *looked* like a killer he wouldn't have killed as many as he had since people would've run when they saw him. When I ask him about Jack the Ripper, he told me to wait until I was older to ask.

The bridge games were held at our house every two or three weeks on Saturday night, and Henry and I had to mostly stay in our room, or sometimes Daddy would take us to the picture show, something fine with us. I don't think Daddy minded, except we usually chose something like *Frankenstein Meets the Werewolf* or *Tarzan's Secret Treasure.* He once took us to one he said we might like. He called it a show we could *all* enjoy, something called *The Maltese Falcon.* It turned out to be a little strange, and I didn't understand it as it turned out. Humphrey Bogart was in it, and it was some kind of mystery about a valuable black bird. He wanted to find the bird for a fat guy named Casper Gutman. And Gutman had a sidekick, a beady-eyed short guy named Joel Cairo. And the girl in it was always swooning and saying weird things girls say, like "Oh, Sam, I'm so tired of lying…" Then they would kiss and swoop in each other's arms and carry on with mush.

Anyway, I couldn't figure out what was going on, and when I punched Henry to ask he would tell me to shush so he could hear. And Daddy was too far to reach, and he probably would have told me the same thing. So I watched the picture show we *all could enjoy* and when it was over they ended up with the wrong bird, which just about gave the fat guy a heart attack and the police took Bogart's girlfriend to jail. I told Katy Jean it was a good thing she had stayed at home.

I had about as much fun as if I had stayed at home and watched the bridge game with all the "two hearts" and "one spade" and "double" talk and all. I thought I might smoke one day, but I don't think I'd ever want to play bridge.

The inquest finally ended, unlike the bridge games which never would.

Sunday morning before Sunday School started we sat in the rows of chairs in a common area. Before we went to our own class we sang hymns and had some kind of general discussion. But for a few minutes before Mr. Donahue, the administrator, came out, we were left to ourselves in the room to talk, and we could find out what everybody did during the week. One guy in our class named Theron Couch was a friend at school, who lived a few blocks away from our street. Theron grew up a Southern Baptist like my family so I saw Theron on Sundays, too. He thought of himself as a master of card tricks and high-dollar-wagering enterprises, like one of those gamblers and saloon characters in the picture shows. He often came to Sunday School with playing cards or some kind of magic trick, like the game with the three little shells where you try to hide a pea and get the others to guess which one it's under. A good guy, but it was kind of funny him bringing stuff like that to Sunday School. I was afraid he was going to hell.

"Now, Theron, do you think Sunday School is a place for such games?" Mr. Donahue said, coming up behind us.

"No, sir," he answered. He probably thought his game was about to get taken away. If it had been me, I'd been worried he'd tell my mother and daddy and I'd get a switching. Theron probably didn't mind a switching as much as he minded losing his games.

"Well, now, why don't you put it in your pocket and don't bring it again?" Mr. Donahue said. He didn't scream or anything like my mother would have. And thinking about it, I'll bet school teachers must've had a thousand things in their desk drawers for *games like that.* They just took them, period. Billy said we wouldn't be allowed to have them back until we entered college.

Finally the opening songs and prayer and announcements for the entire group were over and we climbed the stairs to our own boys class.

Mr. Kraft was our Sunday School teacher. About as old as Daddy, he was a deputy sheriff, and he always wore a blue suit and vest to church. He wore a suit during the week instead of a uniform like most of the deputies, but his weekday suit was usually brown. Daddy told us Mr. Kraft was next to the highest ranking deputy, and he usually didn't wear a uniform like most who were lower. We would see him during the week, and he had a pistol attached to his belt, mostly hidden by his coat, but I don't think he wore his pistol to Sunday School.

I overheard Mother say she sure hoped he didn't participate in the bootleg whiskey tax the legislature had passed, called the Black Market Tax. Whiskey wasn't legal in Mississippi but lots of it found its way in through bootleggers. Since it wasn't legal and people kept voting *dry,* the state couldn't get any tax money for it. Finally the legislature passed the Black Market Tax Bill, which said even though it was illegal, the bootleggers were going to pay a tax. And the county sheriffs would collect it.

While we waited for Mr. Kraft to come in, we almost erupted among ourselves with talk of the fair, which started next month. No one had a lot of money but everyone talked about all the things to do. Of course, if everyone did everything he wanted to do, it probably would cost a couple hundred dollars.

Theron claimed he would win every prize from every place where you could play a game. And someone always claimed that at the top of the Ferris wheel he would spit on somebody just to see if he could get away with it. And everybody talked about the new rides. I told everybody I had heard (though I didn't remember where) one new ride put you in some kind of a rocket and it spun you so fast your guts would be pulled through your ribs.

"Aw, who told you that?" someone challenged.

"I don't remember. But it's true. Anyway, that what they say."

"They who?"

"I've heard the same thing," Theron said. He probably hadn't, but it made him sound as important as me. "I have. Really." Adding *really* to a statement was almost like an oath.

"Aw, c'mon. It would be against the law if they had something like that," Johnny Dale said. Johnny's daddy was a lawyer and he acted like he had learned as much about the law as his daddy.

"Well," I kept on, "I heard about them having the same ride down in New Orleans at the Lake Pontchartrain carnival, and some man was killed and they made them tear it down."

Terry McNair changed the subject. "Y'all remember last year they had those two piranhas in a fish tank, and the guy who showed them to the customers put a piece of ground meat in the tank and they gobbled it in like maybe a second. Like a demonstration. Well, this year I'm gonna smuggle a wiener in with a nail stuck in it and see if them piranhas can chew up the nail."

"They'll arrest you for destroying private property," Johnny Dale said.

"Not if the fish eats the nail and nobody sees. They won't even know I did it."

"Aw, you're full of cr…"

Mr. Kraft entered. "Okay, boys, let's settle down."

Theron asked Mr. Kraft if he could tell us anything about the inquest. Mr. Kraft said it probably would go down as an unsolved crime, although there was one old case where a moonshiner turned bootlegger had had some political troubles in Canton back when Mississippi voted whiskey illegal. An occurrence around 1907 or '08. The bootlegger was pretty famous and one day simply dropped out of sight.

When all of us, almost in unison, tried to follow up, Mr. Kraft raised his hands, then his voice and said, "But Sunday School isn't the place to talk about it. I shouldn't have mentioned it."

We all moved to a semicircle facing Mr. Kraft at his little table. "Did all of y'all have a good week before school started?" he asked.

Of course.

"Well, who's learned the scripture for today's lesson?"

"The lot is cast into the lap, but the whole disposing thereof is of the Lord. Proverbs 16:33." Everyone stared at Theron.

"Praise the Lord," Mr. Kraft said.

 Someone couldn't hold it in. "Mr. Kraft, did you know the fair starts next month?"

"Praise the Lord," he repeated.

Chapter 11

SCHOOL STARTED MONDAY SO SATURDAY MORNING MY mother took me downtown to get new clothes. We usually shopped at J.C. Penny's on Capitol Street, downtown. Sears and Roebuck seldom saw *our* business for school clothes for some reason. My parents were often talking about the price of clothes in different stores and that probably had something to do with it—the price. But I thought it was because Penny's was in the middle of downtown and it gave my mother a chance to shop in some of the small stores with large windows, where you could see everything. And Capitol Street had a long row of stores. Naturally, I had to participate in the *shopping holiday.* Sears did get our Christmas business though.

"Now, y'all have a seat and I'll be right back," the shoe salesman said.

That meant he had to get his foot measuring device; a big, metal, thing built like some kind of Rube Goldberg contraption the salesman would use to encase your foot, like he was going to make a plaster cast. I always thought it would be easier to hold the shoe up to the side of your foot and see if it matched. However, I didn't get to offer advice much.

"Well, young man, are you ready for school?" He pulled up a stool and sat down with his contraption.

A standard question had to be followed with the polite answer: "Yessir. I guess so." Again, this meant no.

I had no sooner pulled off my tennis shoe than Mother almost busted my eardrum. "Charlie McCoy! I cannot believe you wore a sock with a hole in it." My big toe stuck out.

The salesman smiled. If I had taken my shoe off at home and she saw the sock with a hole in it, she would have said, "Throw those socks in my sewing basket and I'll fix them." But displaying your big toe in a public place for all the world to see was like belching out loud.

"I didn't know it had a hole in it when I put it on," I said.

"You didn't know? A hole as big as a quarter, and you didn't know?" She was really embarrassed, I could tell. And worse for me, it made her mad. Going shopping had enough problems without your mother being unhappy.

The salesman spoke up. I think he wanted to help divert the crisis, although I don't believe he was as shocked as my mother. An old man, about sixty maybe, he had probably seen a lot of toes coming out of socks. "Aw, he's just being a boy. And he's in a lot better shape than some who come in here. There're are more than a few who come in here barefooted."

"Oh, my," Mother said. "Well, my boys go barefooted in the summer sometimes, but they don't go out into stores that way."

"Yes, ma'am. I understand. But some of these little boys come in here with hookworms. They do, I'll swear. I don't make any comment. I usually jus' ask their mommas if they want a pair of socks, too."

"Well, I say," Mother said, "I get goose bumps thinking about those nasty little things."

He pulled my foot up on the contraption. I wiggled my toe through the hole which brought on a slap on my arm by my mother.

After he measured, he began the great search for sizes and colors and styles. I had little to do with the selection. Henry usually picked his own shoes because of his age, and also he had begun to care about what kind of shoes he wore. And he almost always picked loafers. But my mother made sure I *chose* something I could wear for school and something for playing in. And I also had to get a nice pair for Sunday.

In a few minutes the salesman came back carrying a bunch of shoe boxes and I agonized through the process of trying them on, using a little metal shoe horn, then I stood up and squeezed my foot up and down for the same old questions.

"How does it feel?" Mother would ask.

"Fine."

"They're not too tight, are they?" She would then poke my toes with her thumb as if that would reveal tight or loose. I had to be careful about giving her the wrong *look*.

"No, ma'am," I replied. The truth was, the salesman could have glued them to my feet and I would have said they were okay. I just wanted to finish as quickly as it took to get finished, and go home. This was one of the extra bothers of going back to school. My mother had to take us shopping. I didn't really care about clothes except blue jeans, and since she had my size memorized she could have come alone. Other than blue jeans, she could have grabbed up some socks and shirts, yellow or brown or blue, I didn't really care. As far as shoes, my Keds were okay for me. But everybody had to have a pair of school shoes and a pair of church shoes, and neither of them could be tennis shoes.

Going into junior high, Henry didn't have to come on this shopping trip but could go by himself. He had come downtown on the bus last week with Buck and shopped for his own clothes. He seemed to care what colors he wore.

"Why don't you walk around a bit and see how they feel?" the salesman said.

I walked around some and then, pretending to really care, lifted each of my feet and flexed my arches. "Yessir. I think they feel okay."

"Of course, you'll have to break them in a little. But that'll just take a day or two. Just take them off if you start gettin' a blister."

The shoe ordeal finally ended. Mother bought me a pair of loafers, too. And later Henry showed me how you could put a penny in them, one of the few things Lincoln pennies were good for; that and rolling up to get ten nickels. But the loafers did make me feel like I was racing into the double-digit age bracket.

We left the old shoe man with his contraption and moved into the counter areas where new clothes were stacked, hung, and laid out.

Shirts and underwear and stuff like that were easy, as it didn't require anything but checking the size. Although my mother would take a few seconds to examine everything costing money: three pairs of underwear in a plastic bag, all the same size. I wondered what could be so interesting? But she would hold them up and glare at them. Sometimes she would put one down and pick up another, an identical set. When it came to spending money, my mother and daddy really made it something special.

Of course underwear mainly came in white, but some of the sport shirts with the button-down collars were worth spending time going over. Blue jeans and Levis were simple too, but if she bought me what she called a "nice" pair of trousers, I had to go to the dressing room and then when I came out, the guy would make chalk marks all over the bottoms and stick a bunch of pins in them. I was glad I didn't need a new suit, one of the worst things about shopping ever invented. Lord, you could be in there half a day with some salesman measuring you like he was designing an airplane; your arms sticking out, and your legs spread out so he could run his hand up and down your leg and all kinds of measuring stuff. Getting a new suit was almost as bad as getting a smallpox shot.

After my school clothes had been taken care of we had to stroll-the-streets so Mother could stop and see what the window displays had in them, another lovely treat for me. She loved to window shop, but actual shopping, another story. Like buying underwear. She really might want something, but actually buying it didn't happen often. Sometimes we would go in a store after she saw something special in a window so she could get a closer view or maybe try it on. Once I started to ask if I could go down to Bob's Tobacco House and wait, but I feared her day would be ruined and make her even madder.

Finally, Mother tired of walking, or maybe she thought I was tired of it, so she said we could eat dinner at the Mayflower Café. Though I would rather be at home, getting a hamburger at the Mayflower sounded good to me. And with my birthday two days away, I think she wanted to do something special for me since I hated shopping. The hamburgers were big and cost a quarter so it was kind of nice to sit down under the ceiling fans with a glass of ice water and wait to be served. Mother ordered some kind of a grilled cheese thing that came with little, flat, pickles. I piled my underwear, collected in J.C. Penny bags, next to me in the booth.

"Why, hello, sugar."

I, of course, was *Sugar*. One of the ladies in my mother's Sunday school class had spotted us as soon as we walked in. Her name was Mrs. Littlefield. And she was pretty nice, but like most ladies she would kind of hover over children under about twelve or so. If Henry had been here she would have called him "Dear." Somehow around junior high you were labeled with a name change. Anyway she walked up to speak to my mother and patted me on my head.

"I guess y'all are shoppin' before school starts? Still like August out there I tell you—ooowee, hot."

"Oh my, yes," my Mother said. She nudged my foot under the table, meaning I should stand up for the lady. I started scooting out of the booth when Mrs. Littlefield stopped me.

"Oh you just keep your seat, sugar." She motioned with her hand at Mother to make her aware she had recognized my effort. Mrs. Littlefield rubbed my hair again then asked, "Are you ready for school?"

"Yes, ma'am. I guess so." This made about the one-thousandth time I had been asked. The mystery of this would remain with me forever. No one was *ready* for school. It was like being ready to have a root canal. But they asked just to be nice to your parents, I guess.

"Oh, Linda, honey, I heard there were some more problems out where y'all live with bobcats comin' up from the woods down by the river. I hope y'all are all okay."

I picked the menu back up and pretended to read it. We had ordered, but I wanted them to think I didn't notice what they said so they might say something in front of me they ordinarily wouldn't. However, I really didn't understand what she was talking about. There had been a single bobcat sighting in the neighborhood almost six months ago, and it had scared some little girl who lived about a mile away from us. She didn't get hurt or attacked or anything.

"Yes, but that's been some time back. I don't think there have been any recent sightings. Randy told me the carcass of one had been found sometime back off Old Canton Road. Apparently it had been hit by a car or truck."

"Yes, that's what I heard," Mrs. Littlefield said. "And I hope there haven't been anymore fires out that way."

Charlene, the waitress waiting on us, brought over our iced-tea. She was kind of pretty, although a bit chunky, and she had her hair piled up on top of her head like a hornets' nest, and it had a couple of pencils sticking in it. "There we are," she said. "Two iced teas." Then she asked Mother, "I'm so sorry, did y'all want a li'l slice of lemon, ma'am?" She was very nice. Chunky people always seemed to be a little extra nice.

"None for me, thank you," Mother said.

Charlene put her hand on my shoulder and asked, "What about you, sweetie?"

It always depended on the lady as to whether or not your name came out Honey or Sugar or Sweetie. Waitresses tended to call you *Sweetie,* friends of your parents used *Sugar,* and *Honey* was thrown around like a wild card by all of them. But she was just being nice so I said, "No, thank you." Besides if I had said something sassy, I would have really been in trouble. The best way to get in trouble with my mother or daddy was to be cute or rude, especially with grownups.

"Well, y'all's food is fixin' to come out so I'll see y'all tomorrow at church," Mrs. Littlefield said.

"Okay, Cheryl, we'll see y'all tomorrow."

"Bye, bye, sugar." A good-bye pat on the head. I smiled.

About a half hour passed before we finished and got up to leave. While we were at the cash register, I overheard some people talking about the inquest. I heard someone say he thought something had been covered up.

Chapter 12

THE START OF SCHOOL AT LEAST MEANT YOU DIDN'T HAVE TO hear the *are you ready for school* question anymore. It would be my next to last year before I began junior high. Henry had finished the sixth grade and was headed to junior high, where school took on great changes. This would be Henry's first year, but he had already started talking like he had been in junior high all of his life. I guess it was because he made friends with some of the guys who were going to be in the eighth grade and already had a year behind them. Some of them had paper routes at the same stop where Henry and Ronny Erl picked up their papers, and Henry and Buck talked to them about the same things, like smoking and cussing—advanced things. And the rumors were getting around to all of them about this Hugh Hefner guy and his *Playboy* magazine. But when I went through the Sears and Roebuck catalogue I was more interested in pocket knives and electric baseball games than in ladies' underwear.

I could tell Ronny Erl would have to get used to his new paper route or he would have to give it up. He kept falling asleep and the teacher had to keep nudging him on the shoulder. Ronny Erl and I were in the same grade, but because he was four months older than me he would turn eleven before the school year ended and would be old enough according to the *Clarion Ledger* to have a route. Henry and Buck had been delivering papers for two years and had gotten used to getting up early and sleeping for another hour before they got up for breakfast. Ronny Erl had been delivering for about a month. But if Miss Ashley reported him falling asleep in school, his daddy would make him give up the route and go back to sweeping out the hardware store.

One thing about going back to school after three months off was you saw some friends you hadn't seen for a while. If they lived pretty far from your own neighborhood, you didn't see them much during the summer.

Tim Whitman was a good friend, but he lived a couple of miles from me and he didn't play baseball much, so I didn't see him a lot except at school. Tim did a lot of interesting things like starting a weekly newspaper on notebook paper and drawing the pictures in by himself. He could draw a picture of somebody's head and it really looked like some-body's head. I thought maybe he would be like Walt Disney when he grew up. Most of us would draw a circle and put in little circles for eyes and dots and a circle for the nose and mouth. So it looked like a circle with stuff drawn in. Tim's were like something one of those *sketching* guys at the fair would draw, and people would actually pay for.

The janitor of Boyduling Elementary school, July, was in charge of emptying trash cans and unstopping toilets and most everything that needed fixing or undoing or redoing. A tall colored man, he wasn't as muscular as Joe. His name was stenciled on his khaki shirt pocket: *July Goodman.*

Miss Ashley taught us. A pretty lady, she had finished college the year before, I think. We couldn't be sure if she had a boyfriend from college, but she had about twenty boyfriends in the fifth grade.

"Charlie, would you go down and find July? He's probably in his room at the end of the hall on the other side. If
not, he might be in the principal's office. Ask him to come
up here and bring his mop."

"Yes, ma'am."

Tim had smuggled two chocolate-chip cookies back
from the cafeteria. While we were at our desks waiting for
Miss Ashley to return, Tim asked Mary Ellen Hoover if
she wanted to play *Show*. She said, "I guess. What's *Show*?"
I couldn't believe she had led such a sheltered life that she
couldn't figure out what was coming. Tim chewed one of
the cookies into a mouth full of gooey, chocolate cookie
paste and then opened his mouth. Anyway, it made her sick
and she threw up on her desk.

I walked down the hall to the janitor's room at the end
of one of the two wings of the school. It was my first time
to the other wing. I inhaled the aroma of soap and cleaning
fluid. The room contained a hot water heater in the corner,
brooms and mops and supplies, towels hanging from a long
wire across the room, and a wooden desk that held a framed
photograph of three colored men and a small boy. I guessed
they must have been some relatives of July. All of the men
were in overalls, and the boy had a baseball bat propped
on his shoulder. Another was of a well-built man like Joe,
with an old wagon harnessed by a pair of mules in the background. Anyway, July wasn't in his room.

When I walked into the principal's office Mrs. Thomas
was hunched over, her back arched, her face and finger in
Tim's face. We all feared Mrs. Thomas like a bunch of sparrows feared a blue jay. Ronny Erl said she must have been
about a hundred years old. She had white hair and lines in
her face, like the picture of a small-plowed field. She smiled

mean. And her fussing at Tim, meant July might need his mop right there. They say she got so fierce with a guy named Allen Albritton one time in the third grade that he peed in his pants sitting in the office.

Tim got a breather when she turned to ask me what I wanted. "Charlie McCoy, what are you doing? Has Miss Ashley given you permission to be up here?"

I felt a slight tremble come over me, my lip quivered, but I didn't want to pee in my pants in the fifth grade, so like John Wayne, I got a hold of myself. "Yes, ma'am. She sent me for July and his mop. She told me if I couldn't find him in his room to come here."

She stepped away from Tim for a minute and went into her inner office where July stood on a stool, fixing her electric fan set on top of a filing cabinet. I could hear Mrs. Thomas talking to him.

"July, please get your mop and go down to Miss Ashley's room." She turned back to Tim. "Looks like someone...," she planted an eye on Tim, "...has made a mess for you to cleanup."

"Yes, ma'am," July stepped down from his stool. July gave me a light smile. "Come on, young-un. Let's go see what we got to clean up."

When we were leaving her office, I glimpsed in the nurse's office and could see Mary Ellen lying on the couch with a wet cloth on her head. It looked like they were treating her for malaria or something, instead of puking.

I walked with July down to his room for the mop. I knew Miss Ashley wanted me to come back with him and not just tell him to come. Besides, not being in class even for an extra few minutes was special. When you were allowed to leave the classroom without the entire class, you felt like a trustee in a prison or something.

"Now, you boys need to behave better. Y'all get yo teachers all worked up and they can't teach you what you s'posed to be taught," July said. "Besides I 'spect if y'alls mommas and daddys find out about any mischief, y'all'll have more at home to worry 'bout."

July's character made him a special friend to everybody. I hadn't ever seen him except at school, but he must've lived in a colored section of town. "Well, I think Mary Ellen oughta have figured out by now not to ever play *show* with somebody," I said.

"Well, y'all don't need to be pickin' on girls anyway," he said. He chuckled a little bit, then broke his smile. "That's a failing, for boys to pick on girls."

"I'd get a switchin' if my daddy ever heard I *hit* a girl," I said. "But makin' them vomit's not the same. But I don't think I'd like my mother and daddy to find out."

"Oh, my. You young-uns. You young-uns."

"Say July, who are the people in the picture on your desk? The one where the little boy has the bat on his shoulder? The picture where everybody is kinda young?"

"Why, child, that's my cousin. Bout my third one I b'lieve." He didn't offer a name. "And Joe's daddy, Isaiah, and the lean one is me when I wuz 'bout fourteen years old." He rubbed the top of my head. "Now, come on. Let's get down to yo room and see to dat mess. And whad you mean, 'kinda young'? We still kinda young."

Chapter 13

FRIDAY, THE THIRD GAME OF THE WORLD SERIES. THE YAN-kees had beaten the Dodgers the first two and everyone thought they were headed for their fifth straight World Championship.

Because our recess came early in the afternoon, right after dinner time, Miss Ashley gave us the choice of listening to the World Series for thirty minutes or going outside to play, as we usually did. She had brought a Philco radio she plugged in next to her desk, and the entire class had to sit on the floor close to her desk so the radio didn't have to be turned so loud it could be heard in other rooms. As soon as she instructed us to move to the front we broke into a charge to the front, most of the boys getting the closest to the desk and radio, clobbering a few girls in the process.

Miss Ashley's displeasure focused. "Now, I think if some of you boys can't be gentlemen and allow the girls to move ahead of you, we can turn off the radio, skip recess altogether and do our *times tables*." The boys then held back until the girls got the places they wanted. Mary Ellen prissed to the front like Rosemary Clooney or somebody.

Ronny Erl leaned and whispered, "Mary Ellen wouldn't know a baseball from a horse turd. She just wants to be up front so she can show off." His whispering didn't go unnoticed.

"Now, Ronny Erl, would you rather spend the next thirty minutes listening to the ballgame or would you rather spend it with Mrs. Thomas in her office?" Miss Ashley had the instincts of a rat terrier. "I'm sure she would be delighted to have you visit."

"No, ma'am. I would rather listen to the ballgame."

"Then keep your mouth shut!"

"Yessum."

By the fifth inning, Carl Erskine had struck out Yankees like he was Bob Feller. He would set a record. Miss Ashley allowed us to listen for almost forty minutes, ten minutes longer than our regular recess period. I think she liked baseball like most of the boys did. She would tell us sometimes how her older brother and she would go fishing at Eagle Lake and bird hunting with him and her daddy. She was pretty but no sissy.

One time Grover asked her if she baited her own hook. She said of course she did. Grover asked her if she put on worms and crickets. She said, "Why, certainly."

"What about roaches?" Ronny Erl asked.

"No. I don't touch roaches; too many germs."

From the back we had heard, "Ooo, roooaches!" Apparently Mary Ellen didn't like roaches either. Tim and I smiled at each other. The thought of pitching a roach on Mary Ellen's desk wafted through our minds like a great fantasy.

After recess time ended, Miss Ashley asked me to take the radio down to July's room. Miss Ashley had told him he could borrow her radio to listen to the end of the game, as long as he had Mrs. Thomas' approval. I had become the official July errand person, I guess.

I inhaled the aroma of cleaning fluids as I entered July's room. He sat at his desk, a bottle of Coca Cola set on a piece of paper on the desk, a package of peanut butter nabs next to it.

"Now you tell Miss Ashley I do 'preciate the loan of her radio," July said.

"I will." I set the radio on the desk.

I wasn't supposed to stay and visit with July. We were instructed to get back to class as soon as we had done whatever chore we had been assigned. *Never dawdle.* If Mrs. Thomas caught you where you weren't supposed to be, you could really be in trouble. Sometimes she prowled the halls like a shark waiting for some little sea bass to come limping along.

"July, did you ever play baseball? I mean you and your cousin both seemed like you could have played." I pointed to the picture. I wondered about every Negro I saw now, whether or not he had played baseball. I didn't say *in the Negro leagues,* but that's where it would have been since they were both pretty old, at least compared to Jackie Robinson. He was pretty young and had only been in the white Major Leagues for a short time now. "I thought you might have played a long time ago, like Joe Washington, the ice man."

"Oh no, child. I never played baseball. Not as no professional. Just on the farm some with the boys." July told me Joe's daddy, Isaiah Washington, had been a powerful and moderately successful prizefighter a long time ago. "He took his family off to Chicago, long time back. 'Round 1908 or '09 as I recall. Had to earn a livin' and there weren't no land in Chicago to farm, so he took up prize fightin'. Even had a fight with the black heavyweight champion one time. Fellow named Frank Childs—called him de Black Hercules. Isaiah lost, but he put up a good fight fo ten rounds. He won a few fights tho. Made some money off it. Isaiah was a strong man fo sure."

"How come Joe didn't box when he grew up?" I asked.

"Isaiah advised against it. Told Joe he might make some money playin' baseball. They was some Negro Leagues startin' back then up North. But dat Isaiah—he could sho throw a punch."

The radio had warmed up and I could hear Mel Allen calling the game in the eighth inning. "But I've knowed Joe a long time, and he been knowin' my family for a *long, long, long* time. My boy plays shortstop over at Jim Hill." Jim Hill was the colored high school across town. "Joe wuz a good ballplayer, for sure. He wuz certainly. Now, you better get on back to yo' class before you git to being missed and git in a peck o' trouble."

I made it back to class in time for Miss Ashley to start our last lesson for the day: geography, which I hated more than any subject. We were always talking about foreign countries like Egypt and Belgium and Argentina and other places I didn't care about. We had to learn what their products were, like hay and barley and sugar beets, not to mention other boring things about how they got them to market and all.

But today we were talking about places in the United States. When I walked in I heard Boyd Hastings say, "I have a cousin who say the number one product in Kentucky is moonshine whiskey." He said it as seriously as if he were saying *pass the butter.* He wasn't kidding or trying to make the class laugh. He just said it so Miss Ashley could see he knew something.

Miss Ashley politely said. "Well, thank you for sharing that, Boyd, but I don't think we need to know that right now. And we're going to discuss some other things today. But thank you for trying. And try and remember that your cousin 'said' and didn't 'say.'"

Standing at the big pull-down map of the United States at the front chalkboard, holding a long pointer, Tim shifted impatiently from one foot to the other. He had been instructed to point to the five Great Lakes. Miss Ashley moved to the back of the class where she could observe the entire class and at the same time watch the front. "Okay, Charlie, take your seat. And thank you for taking the radio to July for me."

"Yes, ma'am, you're welcome." I slipped into my desk.

When she turned away, Tim pretended to swing at a pitch, and the pointer almost hit the vase of flowers on Miss Ashley's desk. She turned back in time to spot his swing. "Tim, do you want to stay after school and practice your swing for me? I can spare about thirty minutes after everyone else goes home."

"No, ma'am," he said. Minnie once told me this was a *rhetorical* question. It wasn't as if Tim really had a choice of answers; at least, not if he had any sense. In my entire school career I had never heard anyone answer a question like that with, "Oh, yes, I would love to stay after school." You would not only get an extra thirty minutes, but you would be sent home with a note telling your parents you had smarted-off. Then you would really be in trouble. The "No, ma'am," answer was the *only* answer.

"Okay, then point out the Great Lakes, and I want everyone to write them down in their geography notebook." Tim named them as Miss Ashley told an easy way to remember them. If you put all the first letters together, they would spell HOMES—Huron, Ontario, Michigan, Erie, and Superior.

Toward the end of our geography lesson and the study of bodies of water, someone asked about the Pearl River and we sidetracked to local geography. Miss Ashley used the opportunity to explain about rivers and the tributary systems and how they all ended up in the ocean. I guess since there were only a few minutes until the bell rang she let us explore the wild and adventurous tales passing among us. Someone brought up swamp monsters.

Supposedly, a creature called the Natchez Trace Swamp Monster lived in the swamps of the Pearl River. Boyd started talking about a seven foot, man-like monster who left tracks like the paw of an alligator. Before they had moved to Jackson, Boyd's family had lived in Tampa, then Mobile, and before that Texarkanna, so we believed a guy as well-traveled as he must have picked up a lot. No one considered how Boyd could learn so much about the Pearl River, never previously having lived in Mississippi, but his notions and stories sounded too good not to accept as truthful. Boyd had failed two grades, but we still recognized his travel experience. If Boyd failed the fifth grade, he would be the only *teenager* in the class next year.

Supposedly, the monster had been seen and tracked in Louisiana by hunters, trackers and even farmers, and his habitat came to be the Pearl River Swamp down where the river flowed from southwest Mississippi into Louisiana.

"Where did you hear 'bout this?" Mary Ellen asked in her snootiest tone.

"My cousin told me," Boyd said with a scowl.

"The same one who knows all 'bout Kentucky?" Mary Ellen oozed like a can of ant poison: shiny on the outside but full of sweet poison on the inside.

Miss Ashley quickly cut in. "Well, now, let's be courteous, children. Boyd, what kind of work does your cousin do?"

"He works for the carnival. The Royal American Shows. It brings the fairs to all the towns. He's gonna be here when the fair comes next month. He barks for the Tattooed Widow-Lady and sometimes guesses people's weights, if they ain't too fat. He says if they too fat, it's hard to get the *accuracy* you need. He don't wanna get fired for losing too many prizes. Now, the Tattooed Lady…"

"Yes, well, I see," Miss Ashley said. "But let's move on for now, and let's try not to say 'ain't.'"

"*My* cousin's a lawyer," Mary Ellen said. I thought Boyd was going to spit on her.

"Thank you, Mary Ellen," Miss Ashley said. "And turn back to the front, Boyd."

None of us, not counting Mary Ellen probably, could believe it. Here, right in front of us, one of our own, a guy who had someone with influence working at the State Fair. It could be a golden opportunity to get free rides and free entrances to the freak shows. Everybody started asking Boyd questions about this ride, and that one, and who would be the weirdest people in the shows, and if there were any new rides. It was like a small bomb had exploded.

Miss Ashley slammed her yardstick down on her desk with a sound like a rifle shot. "Now," she said in her firmest voice. "We do not all talk at once and act like a classroom of ragamuffins. We can stay after school, if that's the way y'all are going to act."

A long silence took hold of us. Her eyes moved from one side of the room to the other. When they focused in your direction, your eyes darted downward. The bell rang. Miss Ashley said, "I'll see y'all Monday morning."

At the rate Boyd was going, he wouldn't finish high school until he was thirty.

Chapter 14

THE WORLD SERIES HAD LONG BEEN OVER, AND FOOTBALL mostly took over our Friday nights and Saturdays. And the biggest event of the year came to town: the State Fair. The Mississippi State Fair arrived in Jackson at the end of October, usually right after the first frost. It was the first time of year you had to be sure and wear a jacket, because the summer heat had been chased by the autumn cooling, sometimes even shivering cold some nights.

When the World Series ended, summer ended. Most of the crops had been harvested; the *king*, cotton, and its season ended until spring. The days were shorter, and we talked about State and Ole Miss football, and Millsaps and Mississippi College. Some said the most underrated team in the South was Mississippi Southern.

Every year Henry and I got exactly five dollars for the whole week to spend on the fair, *free* from Daddy and Big Daddy. We were never sure who put in how much, but on the weekend before the fair started on Monday, one of them would hand us five dollars each and say, "Here's your fair money. Now don't spend it all on the first day." Henry had more success at this than I had.

As soon as school ended on the first day of the fair, Henry and I hopped on the bus and rode downtown and jumped off at the War Memorial Building, located on a bluff next to the old Capitol building. It offered us a vista of the fairgrounds.

You could see the entire length, beginning with the booths of cotton candy, candy apples, taffy and most any kind of creative foods imaginable. And the weight guessers and the sellers of little exciting items like I.D. bracelets you could have your name engraved on, or little hats with most anything stitched on them. Starting down the hill you could see the greatest spectacle to come to town the entire year. And you could smell it: the smell of sawdust and food and even manure. Even the people had a different smell.

There were a hundred ways to spend five dollars as soon as you entered. Beyond were the booths where prizes could be won by anything from throwing baseballs at wooden milk bottles to shooting .22 rifles at little metal ducks and rabbits. About half way down you could see a huge arch spanning the Midway with its various colored lights spelling out the name: *Royal American Shows*. Beyond this point were even more thrills. We were certain nothing in life's future could match what the RAS had to offer: the rides and the freak shows and the barkers calling you over with finely trained shouts. "Ladies and gentlemen, for one quarter, one fourth of a dollar, come inside and see the woman with six ears and a beard…the man with two heads…."

The call on my five dollars had no limits.

The livestock and crops on exhibition were next to the grandstand. The grandstand faced away from the fairgrounds in the direction of a baseball diamond, which is where our minor league team, the Jackson Senators, played. During fair week the field exhibited livestock and crops raised by young boys in various farm clubs. And sometimes there would be a fun event and contest like a greased-pig contest. The stables and metal barns at the back of the grandstand housed the prized farm products of Mississippi's soil. A reminder, my grandmother had said, Mississippi was mostly, and proudly, agrarian, and not Royal American Shows.

"How much does it cost?" I asked the man. He seemed nice and sounded like he really wanted me to win the giant panda bear. Though the weather had cooled, he wore a short-sleeve shirt revealing a tattoo of an eagle on one of his forearms. He wore a khaki apron with pockets on the front, like something carpenters used to hold nails. But he had coins in his, and he kept jingling them. He said he had been open since noon and, by this time, he had usually given away two or three big prizes. And, he persisted, it was so simple. He couldn't believe he hadn't given any away yet, but to tell the truth, he continued, he hadn't seen anyone yet with *my* skills.

"Son, all you gotta do is roll one of these little baseballs in the hole at the end of the board. There's nothing to it. And all it cost is one dime. Or two nickels. And you get three balls to try." The man smiled. "Now watch me," he said. He proceeded to roll three consecutive balls in the hole and he had me almost convinced I could win that big panda bear. I paused. "I tell you what, son, I'm gonna let you have three practice shots just to show you how easy it is. Then if you want to spend those two nickels on a chance, well, I guess I shoudn't say chance—I oughta say *certainty*. Then I'm gonna let you."

I then proceeded to roll three consecutive balls in the hole and life begin to have new meaning. My imagination swelled of the panda bear being mine.

The man raised his voice and shouted, "I tell you what, son. Because I can see you are a lad with character and competitive spirit, I'm going to throw in this gold watch, handmade in Albania. It's a Dretelix. One of the finest watches ever made.

"Man, a Dretelix," Henry said.

"Is that good?" I asked Henry.

Before Henry could confirm, the man spun me back toward him. "You put *one* ball in the hole and you get the panda bear and the watch, son. I can look at you and see you're a winner!"

Henry and I caught the bus back home. We had to be home for supper. The first day at the fair was what we called our scouting mission, meaning we were checking it over for anything new from last year. The big days were in the middle of the week when we would come with friends. I sat by the window behind the bus driver counting my money. I had $3.90 cents left. I had spent a dime on a candy apple and a dollar trying to get a total of thirty balls in the hole for a panda bear and a watch.

But the man acted pretty nice about my failure. He said because he had seldom seen such hard luck he wanted to give me a prize anyway. I stared down at it with my $3.90 cents in my hand—a plastic ring on my finger with a picture of the Lone Ranger.

Later, Daddy told me I had learned a valuable lesson. A lesson in *flattery*. He also told me he had never heard of a Dretelix. I asked him where Albania was.

Chapter 15

Daddy, you think Joe's dog Gumbo is a good trackin' dog? I heard that policeman, Mr. Burly, say up at the ice house today it was just an old nigger dog."

"Don't you have some homework?" he asked. Usually when your parents answered a question with an answer having nothing to do with your question, it meant they didn't want to talk about the subject at the moment. If they didn't want to talk to you at all, it would be: "We'll talk about that later; maybe when you're older."

The same thing happened when I asked about Hugh Hefner's magazine. Daddy told me we'd talk about it when I got older. Apparently twelve would be old enough but not ten, because Henry said Daddy had talked to him about the upcoming *Playboy* magazine, but had told Henry to not say anything to me yet. Henry usually told me secrets but I guess Daddy had been pretty firm with him about this, because Henry said I should be careful about what I got caught looking at in the Sears and Roebuck catalogue with Billy.

But when he asked if I had homework, it meant he didn't want to talk about the subject.

I stood next to his chair watching and waiting to see if he would pull his newspaper down. Finally, he slowly dropped half of it so we were face-to-face.

"Anyway, it's Friday. And Henry and me are going to the fair with Ronny Erl and Buck."

"Henry and I."

"Yes, sir. That's what I meant."

He picked up his pack of Chesterfield cigarettes, took one out and tapped the end of it on the lamp stand next to his chair, then lay his paper on his lap. "Well, I can't be sure what Burley thinks or why he thinks it. He didn't have to refer to it as nigger dog. Some of those guys down there are kind of rough on colored folks. I don't think it's necessary. But I'll tell you this. The fact is, that dog of Joe Washington's is prob'ly one of the best tracking dogs around, scent or sight. I'm familiar with some boys up around Richland and Madison who've been coon huntin' with him. Fact is, Big Daddy been huntin with him. It might've been before Gumbo come along, but Joe's always had good dogs. And I can tell you if he's being used as a breeding dog, somebody thinks he's good. That colored fellow, Franklin, apparently knows his hounds, no matter what else you say about him."

"What do they say about him?"

"Never mind."

I could tell he let something slip. It reminded me of when Mr. Georgie had commented on Franklin. It sounded like something Henry and I weren't going to be told anytime soon. Since Daddy had said "never mind," I changed the subject.

"They ever hunt anything besides coons?" I asked. I sat on the stool in front of him, my chin resting between my hands. I mostly wanted to listen, but every time he said something I thought of another question. "I thought Red Bones would track anything, like bloodhounds can," I said.

I had never heard about Big Daddy coon hunting with Joe. But he probably had when a lot younger.

"Well, they're especially good at tracking coons, for sure, but they might track anything. They are a lot like bloodhounds in that regard. Might track most anything; same as Blueticks, so they say."

"Big Daddy never told me he had been trackin' or huntin' with Joe."

"I guess he never thought much about it," Daddy said. "No secret or nothin'. But don't say nigger to Joe. Or Mary Hester either. You might hurt their feelin's. I realize a lot of people get in the habit of sayin' it and don't mean any harm, but don't get in the habit. It's an old word that means something far different than it used to."

"Yes, sir."

"Did they ever track bobcats down at the Pearl River Swamp? Or did they ever try and track the swamp monster maybe?"

He reached over and smushed out his cigarette in the ashtray and opened his paper again. I think my mention of the swamp monster had signaled our conversation had gotten silly as far as he was concerned. He lowered the paper. "Now where did you get that, about a swamp monster?"

I sat up straight. "Boyd Hastings at school. He knows a lot. Been all over. He as old as Henry."

He drew his chin in. "Twelve years old and he's in your grade? The fifth grade?"

"Yes, sir."

"Doesn't sound like he knows much to me."

"He's got a cousin who works at the fair. Guesses weights and stuff. And he's friends with the Tattooed Lady, too."

Katy Jean sat on the sofa and the Tattooed Lady comment drew a big smile. She started to laugh but it made her cough. Daddy put down his paper then held her hand until she stopped.

My mother came in. "Are you okay, Sweetie? You need some water?"

Katy Jean moved her head slightly.

"She okay," Daddy said. "Your brother's a little screwy, honey." He turned back to me, turned the paper to the comics. "Now, any swamp monster stuff is a lot of story and a lot of very little fact. As far as bobcats, Joe and Big Daddy never hunted anything but coons, as far as I heard. I don't recall them huntin' bobcats. Besides you hunt bobcats 'cause they're a nuisance, not for game. And you really need a lot of dogs—a pack. Bobcats are mean in a fight. Now go find something to do. I wanna finish my paper."

Our neighborhood extended to the edge of the Pearl River swamp and basin, and sometimes bobcats were seen in the area. One had prowled around in the neighborhood one night and frightened a little girl; the one Mrs. Littlefield had probably heard about. A neighbor had fired a couple of shots at it, but it got away. Those were the only wild animals to ever come up from the river into the neighborhood, though there were plenty of stories about panthers in the swamps.

He added, "Y'all better eat your supper before Ronny Erl and Buck get here, if y'all are goin' to the fair tonight."

Tonight, Friday, was the last night of the fair. Ronny Erl, Buck and Henry and I had decided to go. Actually, Saturday was the last night for white people, but on Saturday there were fewer rides going and fewer booths open, before they started back up on Monday for the colored folks' three-day week. And Friday was the busiest day anyway. On Sunday, a Blue Law day, the fair people rested, like the picture show owners did.

On Friday, people from all over the state would come to Jackson. The rides were shorter because of the crowds, but we came because it was the last big night. I had been two other nights, not counting Henry and mine's Monday afternoon trip. Down to my last fifty cents of my five dollars, I had to borrow a dollar from Ronny Erl. Actually, an advance on me helping him with his paper route for three consecutive Sunday mornings. It was harder to earn money during school than in the summer, so I had to do whatever I could, whenever I could, if I wanted any extra money.

After supper we caught the last bus to downtown that came out as far as our house. It was the same one Mary Hester caught when she finished work. Daddy had said he'd pick us up at ten o'clock at the Old Capitol Building and bring us home.

Since there were very few people on the bus so late, the designated seating sign between colored and whites was about in the middle of the bus. We sat in front of Mary Hester so we could talk to her.

She had two brown sacks with her, along with her small brown purse. "B'longin's," she called them. I couldn't be certain of the contents of the sacks, but I had seen her pull out a sweater, no matter August or January. And a pair of white socks. Always a pair of white socks.

"Are you goin' to the fair next week, Mary Hester?"

She lived over on the other side of Millsaps College with her uncle. Mother told me to never ask Mary Hester about him. When I had asked why, Mother told me when I was older she would tell me. It sounded like a Hugh Heffner answer.

Millsaps was the college Don Couples told us he might go to. Minnie had said she bet he didn't, because Millsaps was a Methodist college and if Don went to college around town, he's probably go to Mississippi College, since his daddy was a Baptist preacher. Of course, Minnie had been a Southern Baptist all her life, but also was one of the first graduates of Belhaven College in Jackson, which was a Presbyterian school.

Mary Hester's eyes looked at us through her horn-rimmed glasses. "I might go an' see some things. But I don't hav' no money. Cept I might git me some taffy and watch dem farm animals a bit. Somebody brought me one bag of taffy. But I got me saved up sixty-five cents, for maybe 'nother and maybe some of them boiled peanuts they sell and some of dat cotton candy, if'n I go."

"Aren't you gonna get on the tilt-a-whirl or the roller coaster?" Henry teased.

She let out a loud hoot; took her almost a full minute before she could answer, recovering from her laugh. "Not nobody ever gonna git me on none of dem rides."

"What 'bout the Ferris wheel?" Ronny Erl kept on.

She let out a holler. "Wooeee, my goodness. Jesus hav' to come git me right then at dat time, if'n somebody git me on dat thing. Dat thing be as high as cloud. I might even be high nuff to see Jesus." She grinned and laughed. "Lawd, y'all be crazy thinkin' somebody git me on dat Ferris wheel."

"Mary Hester, do you know Joe? The Joe Washington who works for Daddy and Big Daddy sometimes?" I asked.

She leaned back against the seat, both arms locked around her *b'longins'*. She inched one finger up to push her glasses up the bridge of her nose. "I 'spec he work for yo' daddy sometimes, like you say. But he stay out in the country, I b'lieve. He don't hav' no place in town, far as I c'n tell. I think he's from down 'bouts Madison. But I don't rightly really know him. He mostly in town when he haulin' ice or workin' somewhere."

"What 'bout July at our school?" Ronny Erl asked.

"July? He a white man or colored?"

"Why, he's a colored man," I said. "He's the janitor."

"Oh yeah, now I think 'bout it. But I don't talk to him too much. He got a older brother or cousin or sumpin'. Maybe twenty years older. He wuz brung up somewhere around Madison, too. I heared he sho worried 'bout his land git taken for the highway de guvment gonna build through dere. He worries all de time, dey say."

I resisted the temptation to ask her about hoodoo in front of everybody else on the bus. I hadn't told anybody about what she and Dexter had said, and about all colored people talking about what hoodoo is.

The bus lurched when a car pulled out across its path, running a red light. Everybody grabbed a seat handle except for Mary Hester, who had her arms full. One of her sacks came forward and almost spilled. A sizeable batch of snap beans almost spilled in the aisle.

"Oh me, I don't wanna lose dese snap beans," she said. "Yo momma give me a mess of 'em, and I mighta shouda taken on two sacks to put 'em in."

The driver had come to a complete stop and turned to the passengers. "Y'all okay back there?"

Everybody acknowledged they were okay, although there weren't more than a dozen people on the bus, counting us. "'Bout lost my snap beans," Mary Hester said.

The driver grumbled as though trying to apologize. "Well, y'all jus' hang on, I'll try to get everybody where they're goin' without killin' y'all." I think he mumbled a cuss word at the driver who had run the red light.

When we reached her stop, Mary Hester pulled the chord. "I'll see y'all Monday," she said as she stood up, hanging on for dear life with her b'longins'. She squeezed her snap beans. "Now don't y'all be foolin' 'round on dat Ferris wheel and fall off."

"See ya Monday, Mary Hester."

The sun had been down for almost two hours. The scene before us exploded into a sea of neon, twinkling lights, exhibitions, rides and the great arch of The Royal American Shows. We made our way to the rides, before the huge crowds took over, which meant the lines would be longer. Earlier in the week we had yet to discover the rocket *that would rip your guts out*, so we assumed it one of those rumors that almost never had anything to it. The rumors were always better than the fact.

"Let's hit the Ferris wheel. This time I really am going to spit on somebody's head," Buck said.

"Just make sure it's not mine," Ronny Erl said.

Buck said it, but I don't think anybody believed him. Just one of those *dare* things. But if he were caught they wouldn't only throw him out but would call a policeman and you'd really be in trouble.

We still hadn't seen Boyd Hastings' cousin.

Chapter 16

THE FAIR HAD ENDED. IT WOULD SOON BE NOVEMBER.

Boyd Hastings' cousin was gone at least for another year, free to roam the South barking for the Tattooed Lady or whatever he did. He would be back next October. "Of course if he was given something better at Ringling Brothers or another carnival, he might take it," Boyd said.

Often Henry and I spent the weekend at Big Daddy and Momma's house. I never met anybody who called their grandparents grandmother or grandfather except a boy named Dick Wessel I met in the first grade. Henry said it was because Dick Wessel came from New York. Everybody else had special nicknames for their grandparents.

Big Daddy and Momma lived on the other side of town but, unlike Minnie, they were only three or four blocks from downtown. Before the war Big Daddy owned a sawmill in Hermanville, Mississippi, before moving to Jackson and going into the wholesale lumber business.

When we were little boys, not old enough to read, Momma would read stories to us from a huge leather-bound book that included many of Aesop's fables as well as the story of Robin Hood and Chicken Little and Little Red Riding Hood. Stories were fed into me as if they were a food source. Henry and I grew up on stories from our grandparents. And Katy Jean loved to hear them read.

Momma still wanted to read to us, but I could tell she realized the time of us being *little boys* had passed. And Henry, being almost old enough to smoke and cuss, didn't have the interest like he did when we were little and crawled up in her lap. Mostly now, the book remained on the shelf. Once in a while I would ask her to read me a story, because I could tell it saddened her, watching us become older and grow away from her readings. Being too big now to sit in her lap, I sat next to her on the Davenport. I wasn't as much interested in the story as in watching and listening to her read. She read as if she were on the radio reading to children all over Mississippi. I thought she could have had her own program: *The Momma McCoy Radio Show.* But I never mentioned it.

The World Series had ended in six games by the end of the first week of October. Allie Reynolds had won the sixth and final game for the Yankees. Big Daddy especially liked Allie Reynolds, nicknamed the Big Chief because he was a Cherokee from Oklahoma. A big right-hander, he could really bring in a fastball, Big Daddy said. And Big Daddy knew sports as well as lumber.

Although Daddy finally said we'd get a television soon, Big Daddy still loved to listen to the ballgames on the radio, many of them at night, now. He didn't own a television. He said he didn't need to spend money on something that expensive. It shocked him some people were now buying second cars. He said he couldn't believe the way some people seemed to have money to throw away.

I loved to listen to the radio sitting next to him. Big Daddy would bang on the radio to get the static out. Henry said slapping the radio smoothed the static. Billy Cohen confirmed this theory. Billy said you couldn't hit it too hard though, or it would explode and blind you.

I liked listening to the heavyweight boxing championships as much as I did to baseball. Big Daddy knew boxing and baseball and he would explain strategies for both. It never occurred to me there was a strategy to boxing except to hit the other guy as hard as you could before he hit you, but Big Daddy said there was more to it than that. He said you *never ever* led with your right and if you dropped your left too much trying to fend off an uppercut, you'd get plastered with a right cross.

Last year after school started, Rocky Marciano and Jersey Joe Walcott fought for the heavyweight title. Jersey Joe was the champion and the oldest man to ever hold the title, and even at thirty-eight, Walcott was like a block of stone that could move. However, Marciano was not only popular but tough. Big Daddy called him a rotten boxer, but said he could dang sure fight.

In the thirteenth round, Rocky's dynamite right caught Jersey Joe on the jaw, and Jersey Joe became the oldest man to lose the title. Listening to the announcer, the way he called it and everything, was like I sat at ringside. A fascination, listening to the radio at night.

We had television later on at our house and, after a couple of years, Big Daddy finally did buy one, but I remembered the radio as a little more special. Later, Henry and I saw the news film of the championship fight at the picture show, *The Eyes and Ears of the World*, and that's when we had first noticed the resemblance of *our* Joe to Jersey Joe Walcott.

"Big Daddy, did you know Joe Washington played baseball?" We were sitting out on the back porch, waiting for

Momma to fix supper. He whittled with his little yellow pocket knife, yellow shavings dropping to the steps.

"You mean the Joe who works down at the warehouse once in a while? That Joe Washington? The same one who works for me sometimes?"

"Yes, sir. The same one. The one who delivers ice around."

"Yes, I did. He played in the Negro Leagues somewhere. If he'd been a white man he might've made it to the major Leagues."

"Like Jackie Robinson, you mean?" I said.

He discarded the piece of wood he had whittled to almost nothing, then blew away the shavings at his feet, reached over and broke a short limb off the wisteria bush. "Yes, maybe. Joe may have been better than Robinson. Different kinds of players though. Robinson's got a lot of speed. Joe's bigger and stronger. Best one of them colored boys they're using now is Willie Mays. That boy is some baseball player. The Lord really gave him some talent, even if he is colored."

"If he gave him so much talent, how come he made him a colored man?" I asked.

Big Daddy removed a new piece of whittling wood from his shirt pocket and scratched his ear with it. "Well, I guess God *made* him a baseball player, and God *made* him a colored man, but God wanted him to *make* his own character."

He had started whittling again. "What're you askin' 'bout Joe for?" He stopped for a second and eyed the whittled stick, up-and-down. "I mean he's too old to play ball now."

"Oh, I jus' wondered," I said. "I jus' saw a picture of him with July and some of his people at school. A picture from a long time ago. Joe was younger than me in the picture. And holding a baseball bat."

"A picture? You mean a photograph?"

"Yes, sir. A photograph. A picture a camera made."

"Who's July?" he asked. He didn't change positions. He kept his eye on his whittling. This being a feature I had noticed of grownups, especially older ones. They would be doing one thing while you were talking, but paying more attention to what you were saying than you thought by appearing to pay attention to what they were doing more than what you were saying. Big Daddy was very good at this. As a matter of fact, I think the older you were, the better you did it.

"He's the janitor at school. Anyway he and Joe know each other, but I'm not sure how much. He said they're cousins maybe."

"I see," he said. "Why didn't you ask him?"

"Well, I didn't want to be nosey," I said. "I asked July if he had played baseball with Joe. He said he hadn't. But I didn't ask him anything else."

"Well, that's something you don't wanna be—nosey. But I don't think it's nosey askin' 'bout friends. Depends on what you ask, of course." He had whittled the little stick down to almost toothpick size, stopped, and flipped it out in the yard. Then, again, he spread his legs and blew the shavings away, though this time he folded up his knife and took out his pipe. Next to the cotton seed plant, Big Daddy's pipe gave off about the best aroma in the world.

"Well, I was supposed to get back to class. Besides July was fixin' to take a break and listen to the World Series on Miss Ashley's radio."

A big cloud of smoke billowed up around the porch. "I see," he said. "Well, that might be worse than nosey, interrupting a fellow listening to the World Series."

"But how come they had Negro Leagues, Big Daddy?" I asked.

"Well, so the colored boys could play. They like to play ball, too. And some of 'em are good enough to make money at it."

"How come they didn't play with the regular players, like the Yankees and the Red Sox and Giants and all those guys?"

He scratched the back of his head with the pipe stem. "Well, I s'pose the teams up there jus' didn't want colored and whites playin' together. Colored and whites pretty much have been living in separate ways and places for a while now. Maybe the best thing considering the way the North—I guess I really oughta say the Yankees—*North* and Yankee aren't necessarily the same thing, After the War Between the States, most of this kind of thing happened. When the war ended, the South became a bit Northern-nized about Negroes. Except the North hated 'em and the South was mad at 'em."

"You mean a Northerner and a Yankee aren't the same thing?"

"Prob'ly are now. Didn't use to be."

"So now Jackie Robinson and some of those other guys like Luke Easter and Willie Mays are playin', huh? And Robinson is the first colored guy to play in the *real* big leagues since baseball started?"

"Well, most people aren't aware he really wasn't the first. The first was a guy by the name of Moses Fleetwood Walker. Played up in Toledo, I believe."

"Toledo? Where is that?" I thought maybe he meant Tupelo.

"It's up in Ohio. Don't they teach y'all geography anymore?"

"Yes, sir. Sometimes." I wanted to get away from geography. "Minnie said there was supposedly an old whiskey still buried out off Old Canton, somewhere around the property where that house burned from the lightning, where they found the skeleton. She said the whole place is probably cursed."

"Whiskey's been a touchy subject in Mississippi for quite a spell. Prob'ly always will be." Big Daddy turned his knowledge of history to prohibition.

Neither of my grandmothers had seen anything wrong with voting whiskey out since it presented the curse of temptation. Though my daddy only had a once-in-a-while fishing beer and was not a regular saloon patron, nevertheless he thought any government that would regulate one personal thing would probably get around sooner or later to regulating many more. My mother, who drank not, remained unsettled on the subject for the most part.

"What'd she mean when she said there was an old still buried out there?"

He banged his pipe on the side of the porch, emptying the black ashes. "Oh, there's an old story about a huge still out there somewhere. Supposedly it was in Bobcat Creek, but nobody ever found out. Then they said it was buried up out of the creek along the bank. supposedly one of the largest in Mississippi—maybe eighty gallon copper kettle."

"Is that big?"

"That's what they tell me. Pretty valuable to the owners, I imagine. If the story's true, that's why they wanted to hide it from the revenuers. Some have said there's several thousand dollars in hard money buried with it. Money that came up from New Orleans and the coast. "

"Like lost treasure," I said.

"Yeah, I s'ppose. But there're a million of those buried treasure stories jus' about anywhere you go." He put his pipe in his shirt pocket.

Henry opened the screen door and stuck his head out. "Momma said she's fixin' to put the iced-tea on the table. Y'all need to go wash your hands."

"Whether or not it's cursed is not for my judgment. But, maybe it is." Big Daddy banged his pipe on the edge of the porch. "Well, enough about Yankees and curses and whiskey. Too close to supper," he said.

"Yes, sir." I went into the bathroom and washed my hands.

Chapter 17

A T THANKSGIVING WE DROVE TO CANTON AGAIN IN our Oldsmobile. A cold day, though the sky was clear blue. It had rained two days before and the temperature had dropped to freezing Wednesday night. The summer and heat had passed and also with it the polio season, we hoped.

The friend of our family who had come down with it back in the summer had had many prayers answered. He had contracted the less serious virus of the three viruses. He would not be lame or confined to an iron lung, although Mother continued to pray for him.

Around Thanksgiving we began to see firecracker stands popping up. Small stands, wooden structures put up and taken down or easily abandoned, they were mostly occupied and run by people whom Boyd Hastings' family probably had kin with.

We would buy as many as we could afford, and even ask Daddy to buy us some too. For some reason he usually did it without admonishing us on the value of a dollar. "Firecracker" money was like "fair" money.

Mother would always tell us to be sure and tell Katy Jean when we were going to shoot roman candles so she could watch. And, she had said, "Under no circumstances are y'all to have *gunfights* with them. Somebody could get burned and then we'd have a doctor bill to pay." So when it came to roman candles we had to boringly shoot then in an arc across the yard. But Katy Jean seemed to enjoy them exploding and lighting the air. Like when she watched the seagulls on the coast.

"What all y'all got?" Goose said, opening our sack, when we got to Canton.

"Oh, we got a bunch of cherry bombs and M-80s," Henry said.

"The M-80s are mine," I said.

"Daddy said they're all together ours," Henry said. "So don't go trying to hog 'em all. He paid for them, you didn't."

"Well, it don't matter whose they are," Pete said. "Let's go blow something up."

Mother stuck her head out the door and yelled, "Charlie, put your coat on. It's too cold to be runnin' 'round out there without a jacket."

We liked to pack cherry bombs or M-80s in mud and drop them in a pond or stream and see how many minnows you could bring to the surface. We also jammed them in ant mounds and blew them up like the ants were Chinese Communists in a fort or something. We found out later the farmers didn't like this because it spread the ants. We had probably spread about six jillion Chinese Communist ants around the county.

We headed out in the field behind the house and were a pretty good ways out before we started blasting things all over the county. The branch, one of the places we fished during the summer, was a little cold for us to depth-charge many minnows. They were still and we couldn't find them easily. Nevertheless we blew up a few crawfish holes.

"Hey," Pete said. He pulled out four Lucky Strikes and a book of matches. "Y'all want one?"

Goose grimly stared at him. "Did you swipe those from Daddy's truck? You better be careful. He counts them, I bet."

Henry held out his hand. "Yeah, I'll take one. I never smoked a Lucky at home."

"At home?" Pete said

"Well, not actually *at* home. I jus' mean in Jackson. We aren't supposed to smoke anywhere. Daddy said if he ever caught us smokin' any damn cigarettes, we'd get a whippin'."

Pete and Goose asked me. "You smoke yet?"

"Naw," Henry answered for me. "He's too young to smoke. He doesn't even smoke crossvine."

He might as well have said, "He's still only nine-years-old." My own brother, the same one who had told me I was almost ten, *the great double-digit era*. I wanted to punch him. But my time would come, I figured. I didn't mention Grover and I had smoked about half of one of his daddy's Kools. It tasted so funny we flushed it down the toilet after a couple of puffs. And I had smoked crossvine. I just hadn't ever said so except to Grover.

Pete lit his Lucky. "Did he really say *damn* to you?" He coughed.

"Not the actual word. But he said *dang,* so we knew what he meant."

"There's a bunch of rabbit tobacco growing around," Goose said. "There used to be an old man who smoked it all the time. Said it was good for him; good tonic for cough and colds and it opens up his sinuses, too. He would put the old dry leaves in a corncob pipe. He said we better not smoke it though. Our momma and daddy prob'ly wouldn't like it, even if we had a cold."

Henry packed his Lucky on the back of his hand the way Daddy did. "Is he pretty healthy?"

"Naw, not really. He's dead," Goose said. "Choked on a green plum. They found him under a plum tree last spring all by himself. His eyes were wide open and he had a plum seed stuck in his throat."

"We have rabbit tobacco in Jackson," I said. "Well, close by in some fields outside the city limits. Mother is always tellin' us not to eat green plums."

"Didn't know it grew close to the city," Goose said. "Besides, I mean it's not like cotton or corn—something you plant—it grows in the fields and woods like dandelions and wild things. Y'all ever smoke it?"

"Naw," I said. "But a friend of mine thought we could sell it just like regular tobacco. Said we'd get rich, maybe."

"Really?" Goose sounded excited.

"Yeah, but Mr. Bob said there was too much of it free for us to expect to sell it."

"Who is Mr. Bob?"

"He owns Bob's Tobacco House in Jackson, downtown." I wish I hadn't brought it up since Goose and Pete knew so much about rabbit tobacco.

"Well, a guy who owns a tobacco house oughta be pretty sure," Goose said.

"This guy, our friend I mean, is Jewish and I figured he shouda known," I said.

"We got some Jews in Canton, but they sell mostly clothes. Make a lot of money selling them, Uncle Walter says," Pete said. He took a twig knocked off the lighted end of his Lucky. He appeared a little green. "I'll finish this later," he said.

Goose smiled. "Yeah—right after supper. Out on the porch, huh." We all laughed.

Henry lit his Lucky and coughed some, too. I laughed at him, and he said, "Let's see you do it, Mr. Rabbit Tobacco King." He had gotten mad because he hadn't wanted to cough like Pete had, on account of Pete being younger. "Let's see you really inhale it."

"Naaa," I said. "You said I'm too young."

"You're just chicken. 'Fraid you'll get caught."

"I jus' don't want a whippin'."

"You'll get a whippin' for smokin' crossvine jus' the same as smokin' cigarettes, if you get caught," Henry said between coughs.

"Yeah, but it wouldn't be as bad. You're smokin' stolen cigarettes. So you'd be a two-time loser. Smokin' and stealin'. Anyway I don't like crossvine. It burns your tongue."

"How do you know it burns if you never smoked it?"

"That's what Grover said," I lied.

Goose had lighted one of Pete's Lucky Strikes and had tried to blow smoke rings, but the wind kept bustin' them up.

"Let's go over to the cemetery," I said. "Check out the old Confederate stones."

We walked a little bit farther, smoking, coughing. Finally we reached the little cemetery on the hill. A lot of my family was buried there, going back to the 1800s, we had been told. But mostly we wanted to see the old markers of the Confederates. The markers had been worn down with time and the old sandstone markers had been scoured by the weather so they were not easy to read. But you could still see the letters, C.S.A. There were five of them all under a large magnolia tree in the back, up against the barb-wire fence separating the cemetery from the pasture. We wondered who they were, if maybe they were related to us. But nobody had ever told us.

They could have been killed anywhere and brought for burial back here to their home. Some men were buried where they died and some were buried where they lived. Big Daddy had said it was a special sorrow for our men who died at Gettysburg. They not only lost the battle, and with it our Cause, but they had to get buried *up there.*

"It was really good these guys were brought back to be buried in their own towns and counties," I said.

Goose tried some more smoke rings. "Lot of 'em are buried around places that weren't really cemeteries at the time. Some people buried them on their own farms," he said. "And sometimes you'll find a marker with *U.S.A* carved on it."

"You mean they buried Yankees?" I said. I hadn't really thought about Yankees *deserving* to get buried.

"Yeah," Pete said. "If they were dead and their people hadn't hauled them off. And they'd bury 'em even if they weren't Christians."

"How'd they find out whether or not they were Christians, if they were dead?" I said.

"Brother Milner said they'd hav' a smile on their face," Henry said.

I hadn't thought about Yankees smiling either. Not with all the burning and stealing they had done.

"Any dead Yankees around here?" Henry asked.

"Not right here. Not that we've found," Goose said. He sat down and rubbed his stomach. "But you'll find them other places. And I'm serious, you'll find old graves around old houses most anywhere. Prob'ly there are some around Jackson, and you just ain't located them."

I thought about the fire back in the summer. "You know, the skeleton they found after the fire last summer could have been an old Confederate grave. They never did find out who it was. Just said they found it when the firemen were siftin' through the burned floorboards."

"Maybe," Pete said. "Uncle Walter said he thought somebody died, maybe was killed, and whoever it was was buried under the house. I don't think that would happen to a soldier, Yankee or Confederate. He said the neck and jaw broken could mean a lot of things."

"Besides," Henry said, "the bones weren't so old. Maybe fifty years or something."

"You don't look so good, Goose," Henry said. "You inhalin' every drag?"

"We better get home," Goose said. "If we're late for dinner we'll be in as much trouble as for smokin'. Well, almost." He walked over by the barbed-wire fence and puked.

We were slower going back, what with Goose being a casualty, but we were back at the house before noon. Thanksgiving dinner usually took longer, what with all the food and everybody trying to help in the kitchen with all the different pies and turkey and stuff. They would all talk and cut celery and onions and mix things in bowls and things.

Sometimes the men would drift in to see how everything was coming along. They didn't actually say, "How's everything coming along." That sounded too much like "When is it going to be ready." They moved around the room eyeing the various pots and bowls then would say something like, "It sure smells good in here." What they meant was everybody was hungry, without actually saying it.

I had learned you had to be careful how you approached someone in the kitchen fixing the meal, especially if it was your mother. If you said something wrong, you would get a ferocious look or yanked by the ear and escorted out. So I had figured out the best statement was, "It sure smells good in here."

All of us guys stayed in the living room talking about Christmas coming up and what we would get. "What are y'all gettin' Christmas morning?" I asked. We didn't ask about the fictitious Santa Claus.

"I'm getting a double-barrel twelve-gauge Savage," Pete said. "But I can't go hunting alone. Not for a while yet, anyhow."

"I'm getting' a fly rod," Goose said. "I already have a shotgun."

"Y'all get to fly fish a lot?" Henry asked.

"Not yet. But Daddy is gonna teach me. He doesn't do a lot of it but he likes to snag bluegills when he goes with his friends. Bluegill's pop a fly right at the surface. It's just something different and fun, he says. He mostly jigs for crappie or bass fishes with Mr. Georgie."

"Dinner is ready," someone hollered from the kitchen. "Wash your hands."

Our place was in the kitchen at the breakfast table while the grownups sat at the dining room table. The grownups had their kind of talk and we had ours. Also they could talk about things we weren't necessarily supposed to hear.

However, sometimes we could hear them when they talked loud enough and didn't realize we heard.

We could hear Cousin Bill talking about hog prices and other such things, when right in the middle he would change the subject, as if one thing had something to do with the other.

"Did they ever find out anything about the remains they found in that fire back in July or August? Last I heard, prob'ly somebody who died or got killed around the turn of the century, right? Least that's what the newspaper said. You gotta wonder how his neck got broken. His jaw, too."

"That's right," I heard Daddy say. "But I think they've just about given up on it. The trail's too cold. They haven't changed their opinion on how old the bones are. I don't think they'll ever find out anything."

From our place in the kitchen we could hear most of what they said. I wasn't going to yell into the dining room how it possibly could be a moonshiner and the ground was cursed, according to Minnie, which would fit in with Mary Hester's hoodoo theory. I was still organizing my thoughts on the subject. I had even thought about asking Boyd Hastings' opinion. I really thought I could have added a lot to their conversation, but I kept my mouth shut.

"Would you like some more dressing, Bill?" I heard my aunt say. "But let's not talk about it now. It's Thanksgiving."

"I wonder if the guy who killed him is still alive?" Pete said.

He had just shoveled some dressing into his mouth, holding his fork like you held the handle on a bicycle. I kind of smiled to myself, because he probably had been told all the same table manners and stuff Henry and I had been told.

I also knew if his momma walked in and saw him eating like a *field hand*, as my mother would have said, he would get whacked on top of the head with a spatula.

"Nobody has said for sure he was killed," I said. "The inquest they had didn't really find out anything except he was dead and his jaw and neck were broken."

"But nobody is really sure," Henry said, to show he knew as much as I did.

"Do you have to be a grownup to go on trial?" Goose asked.

"Anybody can get tried for anything if it's illegal," Henry said. "Besides, who are they gonna put on trial after fifty years who's not old enough?"

From the dining room we heard an additional comment in spite of my aunt's plea. Cousin Bill asked if they had found any evidence on the property.

I thought about the pin. And I thought about the satchel at Ronny Erl's house.

Pete kept shoveling, bicycle style.

Chapter 18

W E OFTEN HAD FIRE DRILLS WHERE WE ROSE FROM OUR desks and moved as directed, "quietly," *always* "quietly," and in single file onto the playground; then after a sufficient period, and an all clear, we, again "quietly," promenaded back into the school and assumed our places before Miss Ashley offered herself at the front and told us what she thought of our performance. A frequent comment leveled toward the class seemed to be, "Well, y'all did quite well." Today a rejoinder followed: "Charlie McCoy may stay after school and write a hundred times, 'I will not throw rocks at the school bus during fire drill.'"

School wasn't fun in 1953. You not only had to behave and be extra polite, but you were forced under penalty of death to learn. How to speak, how to read, how to count so you learned "how much" or "how many" or "how to count change." School was like a job you didn't get paid for. So the best thing about school was getting out every day, preferably on time.

I walked home, later than the rest, since Tim and I had been victims of Miss Ashley's discipline. It was bad enough to have to stay after school on a Friday, but on the last one before the Christmas holidays, added extra injury.

I spotted Ronny Erl on his bike as I approached the house. He was lucky he still had the bike. His daddy almost took it away from him. Ronny had taken it down to Bobcat Creek during the Thanksgiving holidays and tried to jump the creek from a big overhang and crashed into the water and rocks and ripped open one of the tires and tore up most of the spokes. He also ripped a big hole in his blue jeans, which didn't make his momma any too happy. His daddy told him if he couldn't take any better care of something as expensive as a bicycle, he could do without it for a while.

To us, it seemed an ordinary thing to do—try to jump Bobcat Creek—the challenge and all, but parents took a different view of what they called *wanton destruction.* Just a waste of money, they said.

Last year when my mother had asked me what I wanted for Christmas, I told her I wanted a dollhouse. She gave me a concerned stare. "Why do you want a dollhouse?"

"Ronny Erl and me wanna blow it up with an M-80," I had said. Katy Jean laughed and I smiled to myself because she had.

Mother rubbed her brow and pointed to my room, saying, "Just go do your homework and think about something else for Santy to bring you. And it's 'Ronny Erl and I.'" Like Miss Ashley, my mother was adamant about *proper use of pronouns.*

I had crossed the street when a police car, siren blaring, raced past the school. Within seconds a sheriff's car and a Mississippi Highway patrolman sped past in the same direction. I ran across the street to see Ronny Erl. He had stopped on his bike to talk with Don Couples, who had gotten off the bus. "Hey, something's going on, Ronny Erl," I said.

"A train wreck maybe," Ronny Erl said. After pausing, "I'll bet a plane crashed."

Don shrugged. "Prob'ly be on the radio after a while." Being in the eighth grade, Don had had gotten off the bus from junior high. Fifth graders and eighth-graders didn't have much in common, but Don lived down the street. Don's daddy was the pastor at a new Baptist Church out on our side of town, five miles from downtown. A pretty nice guy, and one of the few eighth graders who wouldn't beat you up as a way to keep in shape. Also a pretty good ballplayer.

"I mean those guys were movin'. Musta been going a hundred," I said. "One a highway patrolman. What's he going so fast for, and inside the city limits, too?"

We had walked as far as Don's house when Gene Cooper came running down his driveway next door. As a second grader he had most likely been glued to Pinky Lee or Howdy Doody. Television being so new, most anything might be worth watching as far as we were concerned, even a kiddie show. Pinky Lee acted in a role as some goofy guy who did silly things to make little children laugh. Howdy Doody was a puppet, most of the time talking to some guy named Buffalo Bob. By the time you got to the fifth grade you watched it just to make fun of it. The little guys loved it though. *Before* we owned a TV, we were excited when we went to somebody's house who had one even to watch the weather, or a test pattern.

"Hey, did y'all see that police car? Who's he after? Where's he going? Y'all have to stay after school?" Gene could really talk. A nice guy, but too little to play football with us. He got a bloody nose one day and after that, his mother said he might be too little to play with us for a couple of years. But his mother let him watch. And we'd let him chase the ball when it went out of bounds.

"I think a spaceship landed," Ronny Erl said. I pretended I believed it. But I hated pulling dumb jokes on little guys. Gene did get excited.

"Aw c'mon there ain't any spaceship landing anywhere." Gene turned to Don, who didn't say anything. Don, being a preacher's son, wasn't used to lying so he had to smile and mostly keep quiet. He not only didn't lie, Henry said he had never cussed as far as he had ever heard.

"Yeah, there is. Didn't you see *The Day the Earth Stood Still?* That's a true story. One of the great picture shows of all time. A giant spaceship landed in Washington and had a real-life man and a big iron guy who got mad at some point and started disintegrating tanks and trucks and a few people."

"Ah, c'mon. It is not a true story," Gene protested.

"Yeah, it is. You wait and see. Some big giant guy is gonna be sauntering down Stonewall Drive in an iron suit anytime now, blowin' up everything in sight with his eyes. You better believe it's true."

Gene appealed to Don again. He lived next-door to Gene and Gene worshiped him, Don being an eighth grader. "Is he tellin' the truth?"

Don didn't want the joke go too far. Gene was only six. Don didn't mind us kidding with Gene as long as we didn't hurt his feelings. "Well, I can't be certain, for sure. I'll have to think about it."

Gene remembered his television program and back-tracked up the driveway to his house. He probably figured watching Howdy Doody had more to offer than listening to stories Ronny Erl and I were telling.

Don walked up his driveway. He had lost interest for now in the speeding police car.

"What'd you have to stay after school for? Cutting up during fire drill?" Ronny Erl remembered what we were talking about before the siren.

"Yeah, but Miss Ashley already had me and Tim Whitman staying late for something else."

"What'd y'all do?"

"During the Christmas play Miss Ashley had the girls run around like sugar plum dancers, so they had to take off their shoes. Well, Tim and I glued Mary Ellen's shoes to the floor with superglue."

"What'd she say?"

"She said we ought to be ashamed and—"

"No. What'd Mary Ellen say?"

"Nothing. She just started crying. That's how we got caught."

"You didn't have to stay after school *very long* for all that."

"Well, Miss Ashley said since it was the last day before the Christmas holidays, we could do some time today and the rest after the holidays."

"So you get to start the New Year by staying after school."

"Yeah. But that's two weeks away. Maybe she'll forget."

"I'll bet she don't."

"Yeah. Prob'ly not.

We had no school the next day since we were out for the holidays so we headed to the picture show. The Paramount had one on about WWII. Henry and Buck wanted to go to the Pix, closer to our neighborhood. It had *Invaders from Mars*. But Ronny Erl and I said we could see the War II picture show and also go in some of the stores downtown. We could see a lot of Christmas stuff. Besides we had all seen *Invaders from Mars* twice and it was hard to watch the show at the Pix because of people throwing empty popcorn boxes and making noise-makers out of candy boxes. Billy and some guy had gotten in a fight in the lobby a week ago and the manager banned them for a month. At the Paramount there were a lot of grown-ups, and you had to behave.

There were few people on the bus late Friday evening so we had our choice of seats. It had started raining just as the bus pulled up, and we had to keep our window closed so you couldn't spit, or try to grab the crepe myrtle bushes when the driver slowed down for a stop. The berries on the bushes were great for throwing at somebody at the picture show, but since we were going to the Paramount instead of the Pix we couldn't have thrown them anyway.

A few stops after us some lady stepped on carrying a huge bag of pecans. We recognized her as one of the waitresses at the Seale Lily ice cream store about a block from the Tote-Sum. There were plenty of seats, but for some reason she sat next to Ronny Erl. And she liked to talk. She was an older lady because her lipstick was awfully red compared to her skin and also she had a few liver spots. She would give you larger scoops than most of the people who worked there.

"Well, are you boys ready for Christmas?" she said.

We all said, "Yes, ma'am."

"Y'all all been good boys, I imagine."

Again we agreed. I asked her: "Boy, you got a lot of pecans. I'll bet it's a hundred pounds of 'em."

"Oh Lordy, not that many. But I tell y'all, my sister's friend giv' 'em to me for Christmas. And I got to get home and shell all of 'em. And I am just worn out from all my shoppin' and movin' around and workin' all day. I'm gonna make pecan pies for Christmas. After this storm gets through you can bet it's gonna get cold, so it'll be a good weekend to stay in."

"Yes, ma'am," I said.

"Where do you live?" Ronny Erl asked. I don't think he really cared, but she seemed like she wanted to talk. And I had already covered the pecan topic.

"Over close to Belhaven," she said.

"How far do you have to walk after you get off?" I asked.

"Oh, jus' two blocks. I got my galoshes and my umbrella though. So I won't get too wet. I'll bet dat convict who busted out gonna get drowned though," she said.

During the morning hours the convicted killer, Chambers Gallagher had hit a guard over the head with a pipe, somehow made his way out a side door and raced off. Every law enforcement agency in the county and state had been alerted. Roadblocks were established at major roads around the county, and policemen and deputies and Mississippi Highway Patrolmen buzzed back and forth across the county and state. The guard lay in critical condition, in a coma, they had said.

Mother had asked if it were safe for us to be out, but Daddy said a guy wouldn't last long on the run. No money, no clothes or transportation. He'll hole-up in some ditch or something until he gets hungry enough, he had said. He couldn't afford to show his face.

The lady must have been hungry being so close to supper time because she cracked two pecans in her hands and started eating. "Oh my, these are good ones." She dropped the shell, then cracked another. She moved some of the crumbs around in her hand like she was studying each little bit and piece. For some reason I wanted to help her, though I couldn't be sure in what way. She seemed poor. Her dress appeared plain and her hair like she had combed it with a toothbrush. I guess the wind messed it up, and she had tied a big bandanna around the top of it.

She smiled at me. "Oh my, my stop is coming up." She stood up trying to keep one arm wrapped around her pecans while she prepared to open her umbrella." Ronny Erl pulled the chord for her. "Thank you, young man," she said.

She stepped down through the front door, then turned. "Bye y'all." We watched through the window as the bus pulled away and a gust of wind yanked her umbrella when she opened it. She almost dropped her pecans.

The rain came down hard now, and when the bus hit big puddles along the curb it splashed water all the way across the sidewalk. I mashed my face against the window and could see front yards lit up almost like daylight when lightning flashed. Trees were bending in the high winds.

By the time we got off the bus downtown, the biggest part of the storm had passed and there remained a slight drizzle, though we could still see lightning flashes to the east across the Pearl River. The storm had been one of those fast moving ones. Daddy had said they caused the most trouble.

Before the picture show started we roamed around in some of the stores on Capitol Street and gazed at the Christmas stuff: games, toys, and all the fake Santa Clauses. Even though we had found out the truth about Santa Claus, we got a kick seeing him with all his Christmas cheer and stuff.

Course, it was a wonder how we ever fell for the story anyway, since there were about a million of them running around the different stores. But we still had to be careful so we didn't let guys like Gene Cooper find out the Santa fiction. I had almost slipped up in front of Gene one day when Don quickly *shushed* me.

The stores at Christmas time were special and we were out of school for two weeks, so going downtown where so many decorations were was kind of like being around Christmas before it came. Sears and Roebuck had the most stuff, but all the little stores up and down Capitol Street had a lot of things Sears didn't. Christmas had its own smells and sounds, like the sidewalks and cotton seed oil plant and the fair had theirs.

In every store it seemed Christmas music played in the background, and there were people standing around waiting in lines to get their presents wrapped. One week to go. We didn't especially care about the clothing stores, unless they had guns or knives or electric football or baseball sets, which they usually didn't.

Often a new picture show would come out at Christmas time. This year the new one, *Stalag 17,* was about these American soldiers who were in a German prison camp in WWII. One of them had been spying for the Germans, so the Americans kept getting caught when they tried to escape or sneak radio calls out. As it turned out, they caught the spy and threw him outside for the Germans to shoot. A pretty good show. All during it one of the American prisoners kept whistling *When Johnny Comes Marching Home.*

About half way through, when the Americans were beating up William Holden because they thought he had been doing the spying, the film stopped. If we had been at the Pix, everybody would have whistled and thrown drink cups at the screen and we would have all started stomping our feet. But not at the Paramount. The lights came on and a man, the manager I guess, strode into the middle of the stage to make an announcement.

"Ladies and gentlemen, I am sorry to interrupt the show, but I have been asked by the police to make an announcement. Will all members of the National Guard please report to the National Guard Armory. A tornado has hit downtown Vicksburg and there are some serious injuries and the governor has called out certain units of the National Guard. As soon as those men leave who need to, we will resume the show for y'all."

When the picture show ended, it was almost nine o'clock and the rain had completely stopped. The stars were out, the air colder. It probably had stopped by now in Vicksburg, too. We talked about the tornado and wondered how many people had been hurt or killed. It made me sad to think about somebody being in trouble at Christmas time.

Just after ten o'clock the bus pulled up. Since the rain had stopped, we could open the windows and you could feel the cold rush of wind against your hand. Daddy picked us up at the closest bus stop where we got off since the late buses didn't run all the way to our house. It had really turned cold by then.

My mother and Katy Jean were having a late evening snack of cornbread and milk sitting at the kitchen table. "They still haven't caught that killer."

"Now, Linda, don't start worrying. If he's out at three-thirty in the mornin' when they're delivering papers, he'll be half starved, wet and frozen. He's dang near necked, I understand."

My mother put her corn bread down, dabbed her lips with her napkin. "I don't think you should say *necked* in front of the children."

Like when Henry moons me, I thought. I focused on Henry. I tried to make him laugh.

"Oh my," Daddy said. "Well, I'm pretty sure the news said all he had on was prison pajamas. And pajamas aren't particularly comfortable sleeping under a bridge, or in the woods when it's cold. He won't last long. Let him die of exposure—good riddance."

"Anyway, I don't care what he's wearing, or not wearing, he's dangerous," she said. "I don't want the boys in danger. And the fact is, there is an escaped convict running around. And he might be close by. I just don't want to take it lightly. He could kidnap one of the boys."

"I don't want them in danger either. But, I'm tellin' you there's nothing to worry about. And he prob'ly isn't runnin' around. As cold as it's getting' he's prob'ly curled up in the fetal position. Even if he's close by he only *wants* one thing, to get away. Anyway, he's not a kidnapper. He's a killer."

She replaced her napkin in her lap, her eyes rolled. "Stop saying things like *fetal* and *naked.* And, would you listen to yourself? You just said he's a killer."

"Pass the milk bottle," Henry said. "Is there any dessert left from supper?" I knew he wanted to change the subject.

"Yes. There's some cake," Mother said. "Don't you want any cornbread?

"No, ma'am. Jus' cake."

"I was gonna go with Ronny Erl to deliver his papers," I said. "He can use the help more'n Henry, since he's probably in more danger. And I'll get fifty cents."

196 Paul H. Yarbrough

"Now, Charlie, I don't think there's any danger out there or I wouldn't let you go. Now y'all need to quit exaggerating these news stories. In the first place the police have roadblocks all over the place, in the second place if he isn't out of the state by now, he's probably hiding in some sewer pipe afraid to move."

"Even so, I'd still like to understand why he thinks Ronny Erl is in more danger than Henry," Mother said.

Daddy leaned forward placing his elbows on the table, a sin, and breathed a sigh. "Okay, Charlie, what's your story? What's so dangerous about Ronny Erl's route? Or why is it more dangerous?"

I told him about the Big House on the hill, and it stood barely yards from Ronny's last street on his route.

"Yeah," Henry said. "It'd be a great place to hide if you were on the run."

"Well, y'all ought to stay away from that old place anyway. It's abandoned and if there is another fire y'all might get blamed," Mother said.

"I'm sure the sheriff and police are aware of that house," Daddy said. "Anyway, there are thousands of places he could be. Anyway, he'll get so cold and hungry he'll turn himself in more'n likely."

"When have y'all been up there?" Mother asked.

"Oh, Linda, all the boys go up there from time to time. That skeleton business is mostly forgotten. They're never gonna find out who it was."

"Pass the cornbread, please," I said. I glanced at Henry.

Katy Jean pointed at the cake.

Chapter 19

Nobody on the planet earth likes to get up at 3:30 AM, except my brother. Henry would actually hum when he bounced out of bed. Buzzing like a fly. On the other hand, I could barely breathe. My mother could always come up with some Biblical Proverb for me when I demonstrated some character flaw such as a desire to sleep all the time. But I didn't care at 3:30 AM about my place in Proverbs. I wanted to stay in bed.

Twenty-three degrees. The sun would not rise until well after six, when the beginning of day would come as a pinkish glow in the east. Still dark at three-thirty, bitter with ice and frost, the alarm clock clattered like a fire bell. Our house was heated primarily by a gas heater centered underneath the house and exposed in the hallway as a floor furnace.

Henry and I piled our clothes in the hall by the furnace and began to dress for a cold morning outing: wool shirt, corduroy pants, a sweatshirt and a heavy winter coat; also gloves and wool caps. We were like knights preparing for a great battle.

The sleepiness had clung to my eyes like a cobweb, but when I stepped onto the front porch and the cold hit, I awakened.

The narrow asphalt neighborhood street, lighted with dim streetlights, provided a path paralleled on each side by darkened houses and bald trees stripped by winter. The air hit us in the face, the speed of our bikes making it even colder. My nose ran and I tried to cross my eyes to see if my nose had turned red. The cold pinched into my ears even with the earflaps from my cap covering them. It was almost a half a mile to the paper stop.

The papers were delivered in pickup trucks to different sections of town. The stop for Henry's and Ronny's papers was at the Broadmoor Food Store. Usually an older man drove while two younger men sat in the back and tossed the newspaper bundles. Each bundle was wrapped by a single piece of wire, and six or seven bundles were tossed, depending on how many routes there were at each stop. On Sundays and special advertising days the bundles were thicker since the papers had more sections in them, and, sometimes each route had more than one bundle.

"How're you boys doin' this mornin'? Not cold are you?" He laughed, standing in the bed of the truck ready to toss out the bundles. We shivered, wrapping our arms around ourselves. Just then, he spit a big blob of snuff in an arc, which splattered on the driveway in a brown splat.

The days when the papers were thicker than usual, Ronny Erl often asked me to help. I could use the money and the experience, in case I ever had a route of my own. Most guys could make around fifty dollars per month with their routes.

Today, Saturday, was the easiest day of the week. The papers had the fewest pages and therefore the lightest load, so normally I wouldn't have helped him. But for the killer-on-the-loose I would be at home, warmly tucked in bed. I thought of myself as something of a hired gun, like a shotgun rider on a stagecoach. Henry said I was stupid to come out and freeze my ass off, even for fifty cents. His cussing had continued to develop nicely as a seventh-grader.

Johnny Swaze had the job as district manager. He supervised the boys, making sure they kept their routes in order, they solicited for new customers and delivered on time. A grown man, though still a *somewhat immature man*, my mother had said. He wasn't much taller than me and weighed about two hundred and fifty pounds. He drove an old Dodge, the inside always cluttered with day-old newspapers, and on the backseat a couple of cartons of Viceroy cigarettes. When not eating or smoking, he had a toothpick in his mouth.

He had meetings about once a week at Seale Lily in the afternoons to see if the boys had any questions or any new orders to turn in, and to make sure everybody delivered their papers on time, and they hadn't been delivered wet when it rained. If a customer complained too many times, a guy could lose his route.

I often tagged along with Ronny Erl and Henry to the meetings. Mr. Swaze would buy the boys a nickel ice cream cone. He even bought me one. He bought himself a huge banana split, hunching over it like a lion gnawing a zebra's guts. A lot of times he liked to tell what I thought must have been dirty jokes to the older boys, but of course Ronny Erl and I listened in. They usually were the same kind of joke. About some traveling salesman and a farmer's daughter and how the salesman and the daughter ended up necked in the barn.

He got there at the same time as the paper truck. He sat in his car, the engine running and the heater on. He knocked on his windshield when he saw us, signaling us to come over. Most of the time he didn't arrive until after the folding process had started. Usually he would drive around to different stops checking in case the paperboys needed something, smoke a Viceroy, and leave after a minute or two. Since the escapee remained on the loose, Mr. Swaze probably had been told to keep a closer eye on the paper stops.

He cracked his window a bit. "Any of y'all want a donut? I got a dozen."

In the early morning hours you could buy bread products and milk products directly from the milk and bread drivers if you happened to see them making their deliveries. Fresh donuts were a favorite, because they were warm and fresh and everybody had a big appetite early in the morning.

"Yessir," we said, each voice visible in the cold air. We moved up to the window to catch a little bit of the escaping heat. We each took one donut. I figured at a dozen a box, if he gave one to each of the us, it would leave six for him.

"Hey, why don't we build a fire? There's an old garbage can in the driveway we can use," someone said. "Plenty of wood in the lot here."

The stores were next to a vacant lot with dead limbs lying around. And the old metal garbage cans in the driveway were empty since the trash had been picked up. So a roaring fire while we folded the papers would feel good.

"Naw, I don't think y'all oughta do that," Mr. Swaze said, stuffing a donut in his mouth. "I don't imagine the owners want fires close to the buildings. They jus' let us use the premises as a courtesy to the newspaper. And we don't want to make them mad. Besides I might get fired if I let you boys start unsupervised fires."

"Aww c'mon," Ronny Erl said. "Nobody's gonna care."

"Besides, it's cold as crap," someone else said.

"Naw. No fires. And you boys don't need to be using language like that," he said. This from the man who frequently told us jokes about a farmer's daughter and a traveling salesman.

Henry whispered, "I bet he'd say something else if his big fat ass was out here freezing. I'll bet he'd build a fire before you could spit."

I thought it pretty funny at the time: *Big fat ass.* There was a lot to learn in junior high, smoking and cussing and all. It would be very new to me. But with no fire to build we started opening the bundles of papers.

The headline on the paper read in large bold letters: **ESCAPED MURDERER AT LARGE**

"Say, Mr. Swaze, anything on the radio about the convict?"

Mr. Swaze rolled the window down. We could hear the radio. Hank Williams singing about his girlfriend's cheating heart and her crying and hollering, and Mr. Swaze keeping time to the music patting his knee.

"Have they said anything more on the radio about the guy who broke out of jail?" someone shouted over the radio.

"Don't think so," he said, his voice muffled by a donut mushing around in his mouth.

"Think he left the state?" Buck asked.

"Beats me," he said continuing to read the newspaper. He wiped some sugar off his mouth with his sleeve, then rolled the window back up. Even with the window up you could hear a giant Swaze belch.

We sat on the cold concrete sidewalk and folded the papers. Though freezing we had to take off our gloves. We had to roll the papers very tight for easy throwing, then with a rubber band they were doubled or tripled-wound and pulled down over the paper. Although a simple chore, it wasn't easy with gloves on. And if you stretched the rubber band too much it often snapped in mid-wind and popped your hands, which were almost dead numb from the cold; the pain was second to being stabbed with an ice pick.

"Okay fellows, I'm going up to the Pig Stand to see if those guys up there are okay. Prob'ly see y'all later." He drove off in the direction of the Pig Stand restaurant and drive-in, another stop where papers were delivered. The restaurant didn't open until 6:00 AM but he would be there when it opened. Mr. Swaze had two hours before he could actually get inside and eat.

He drove off with his donuts and Viceroys and a nice heater in his car while we sat freezing and folding.

"Is Mr. Swaze married?" I asked

"I don't think so. But I'm not sure," Ronny Erl said. "I never heard him mention his wife."

"I don't think he could have a wife," Henry said.

"Why not?"

"Nobody could feed him as fast as he eats."

We laughed.

When we had finished folding the papers we began pedaling through the dark, stopping every once in a while under a street light as if we could feel warmth there. For some reason, it didn't seem to be as cold under the light. Yard dogs would sometimes come out to bark. Buck said he once had a dog bite him, but since it didn't break the skin, he didn't worry about it.

We rode through the wet grass of each yard because you had to put the papers on the porch, and this made it harder than pedaling along the street. With the trees blocking the streetlights the yards had deep shadows casting peculiar shapes.

Old Canton Road seemed darker and colder than the rest. Ronny Erl's last customers were along it. We worked the side of the street where there were houses, the other side bounded by the barbed-wire fence. Along it were two streetlights. And, from where we were, the hill and the Big House were in total darkness.

"Listen."

"What?"

"Listen, just listen. Be quiet."

"Listen. Someone's comin'."

"Who is it?" I said. I wished now I had brought my pellet rifle.

" I can't see. And whisper. No tellin'."

"Let's hide."

"No. Wait a sec…" Out of the night a figure approached. At first a form, a silhouette, in the dim light. Then we could see Henry.

"Henry. Dang. You scared the snot out of us. What're you doing over here?" I said.

"I came to see what y'all are doin' over here. Are y'all finished? I finished twenty minutes ago. Buck's at home. He wanted to get back in bed."

"What time is it?" Ronny Erl said.

I pulled my glove back. "Five-thirty."

"I think he's up there," Henry said. "The guy who escaped."

"What?" Ronny Erl said. "You're crazy."

"I saw a flicker of light up there when I came down Old Canton. I'm tellin' y'all. Who else would be up there at this time of mornin', being so cold?"

Minnie had told me once the younger we are the more imagination *coaxes reality away* from us. When we stood on the frosty grass early on a December morning, across from the old house on the hill, I think I was beginning to understand. She had also said fear is the sinister cousin of imagination.

We lay down our bikes by the fence. When we finally crept up the hill through the grass, we stopped every few feet at the slightest night sound. Suddenly as if the sun was about to come up, we saw a slight hue of gold, a glimmer of light breaking the darkness at a point by the Big House. But it didn't seem as wide and arcing as the sun at sunrise. Some other light. We stopped.

"I think it's a fire?" Henry whispered.

"What's a fire going for if no one lives here?" Ronny Erl said. "Maybe it's a flashlight."

"I don't think it's a flashlight. It's not that kind of a light. It's flickerin'." Until now, I couldn't be sure my voice would work. "And anyway, why is there a fire?"

Although most of the grass around the place was dry and brown, its height still concealed whatever had caused the light. And high enough to obscure us as long as we crawled. I don't remember why we thought it was a great idea, but we crawled as close as we could for a better view. As we inched our way, like commandos, I thought my toes were going to freeze and fall off. My nose kept running, but I didn't dare suck it back up for fear I would be heard. So with frozen feet and loose snot, I continued with Henry and Ronny Erl toward the light.

Before the grass ended at the edge of the driveway, we could see a lantern, the small flame waving inside its glass enclosure, hung from the limb of a sapling. A man stood in a hole knee-deep, holding a shovel. He had stopped for a moment and wiped his face with a rag, though I couldn't figure how anybody could sweat. He appeared to be a colored man in the dim light. Wearing a black coat with double-breasted buttons like the navy guys sometimes wore, he also wore a dark Stetson. When he shoveled, little effort seemed spent. He had broad, slightly stooped shoulders, and probably thick muscles under his dark coat. A cigarette dangled from the corner of his mouth.

He dug next to the old work shed, but that's all we could tell from our position. We had checked the shed last summer and found nothing—nothing above ground.

We didn't speak, since we were too close. Anyway for all we knew, he had every right to be here. On the other hand, it seemed strange to be digging at five- thirty in the morning in freezing weather. But we had to get away before we froze or sunup revealed us. I elbowed Henry and flipped my thumb in the direction down the hill.

Suddenly, somebody's yard dog scared up a rabbit or possum down by the fence behind us and started barking. It got the man's attention, and he stopped and turned in our direction, lifting the lantern, holding it above his head, then advancing. He stepped down the slope toward us, stopping scarcely three or four yards from where we lay shivering in the grass. If he had come any closer he would have stepped on us.

I buried my face in the grass, but turned it slightly, just enough, and saw his face exposed to the light. Then I put my face back in the grass, snot squeezing up my face to my eyes. The dog stopped barking, the man paused and returned to the hole, putting the lantern back on the sapling. Remaining low, we backed down to the fence and to our bikes.

I thought about one thing on my ride home: Chambers Gallagher, *white man.* And this man was not white.

Chapter 20

WE DIDN'T TELL ANYONE EXCEPT BUCK. HOWEVER, OUR fear had faded by the time we reached the Pig Stand. I told them I saw the guy well enough to tell he was a colored man, so we dropped the notion of the escapee. We figured maybe some old hobo. Daddy had probably been right. Probably some old transients who poked around up there from time to time.

With no school, we didn't have to hurry home to sleep for an hour. We could go to the Pig Stand and get donuts. We got there as the inside lights were flipped on, and through the window you could see the manager and the waitresses getting the chairs and tables set up for customers.

Grover had been delivering as a substitute. He was riding up just as we got there.

Four of us piled into one oversized semicircular booth. Henry opened one of the leftover papers and began reading while the rest of us listened.

"Aw, we've already read that same stuff. Don't read it again," someone said. "What's it say about Ole Miss? They're still not going to a bowl game, are they?"

"Forget it. When State tied 'em it ended any chance to go anywhere. They probably would have gone to the Sugar Bowl again if they had won," Henry said.

Henry stopped when the waitress walked over with four glasses of water. Her name tag said *Marie*. She had a nice way about her, though she probably had experienced small boys and their tips. She set the glasses in front of us, one at a time. "Well, how are you hard-working gentlemen this morning? It is freezing out there." Ronny Erl inhaled snot from his runny nose.

"Very nice Ronny Erl," Henry said. Marie smiled.

"I couldn't help it," Ronny Erl said.

"Oh, just you wait, sugar. I'll bring you some Kleenex," she said.

"Oh, that's okay, thank you anyway," he said, trying to inhale again without a *blast*. He ran his arm across his nose. "I'm fine."

She pulled a green order pad from her apron and a pencil from the bun in her hair and spoke to me first. "And what are you going to have, young man?"

I tried to remember how much money I had. I reached in my pocket and pulled out a quarter and three pennies. "How much is hot chocolate?"

"It's a dime, honey."

"And donuts are a nickel?"

"That's right, sweetheart."

"And tax is a penny?"

"On fifteen cents or more."

"Okay, I'll have three donuts and a hot chocolate, please, ma'am."

Sometimes Grover tried to act like a man-of-the-world. "Can we have separate checks, please, ma'am?"

"You *may*."

Grover ordered two donuts. But instead of hot chocolate, he said, "And a cup of coffee, please, ma'am."

When you were under a certain age and you ordered coffee, you might just as well have ordered a double whiskey with a beer chaser. Coffee was considered a drink for adults, though some of us had been allowed to test the waters at a moderate level.

"Why, darlin,' does your momma allow you to drink coffee?"

We laughed a little bit at him: *a man of the world being asked about his momma's permission.* He tried to recover. "Yes, ma'am. Sometimes. If I use a lot of cream."

"Well, okay, this time. But if she ever asks me, I gonna tell her you said it was okay." She had Grover thinking she might ask his momma.

She had no sooner left to get our order when Mr. Swaze waddled in. Although there were plenty of empty tables and booths, he saw us. Now the four of us were in a booth with maximum space for three adults. And though we weren't adults, with all of our coats and caps and gloves jammed in between and behind us we had almost filled the space. But Mr. Swaze must have thought, *what's one more?* From across the room he bellowed, "Hello, fellows. Got room for me?" He struggled over like a hippo out of an African mud wallow.

Henry whispered, "The English Channel hasn't got enough room for him."

He collapsed in next to us. "Everybody got their papers out on time, I guess," he said. "Scoot over fellows." He lowered himself and wiggled his bottom against Grover while Grover tried to move the rest of us the same way. Finally we were all squished together: coats and caps and scarves and snot and fat guys.

He pulled out his handkerchief and blew his nose. It sounded like a train.

Marie came over, a grieved frown on her face, though remaining *gracious*, Mother would have called it. I'm sure all the waitresses at the Pig Stand were familiar with Mr. Swaze. "Well, good mornin', Johnny Swaze. Would you like some hot coffee? I'm sure you must be freezing—like my boys here."

"Well, good mornin' to you, you sweet thing. Marie, when are you gonna get rid of that husband of yours and take up with a fine handsome gentleman like myself." He roared at himself. "You could cook and wait on me instead of strangers all day and night."

Even at ten I suspected Marie would have rather cooked for General Sherman on his way through Atlanta than cook and wait on Mr. Swaze. "Well, if you're ready to feed three children, I'm ready to be yours." She put a glass of water and a cup of coffee in front of him then winked at us so he couldn't see it.

"Well, let me think about it a bit. But to tell you the truth, honey, I can't think on an empty stomach." He started reading the menu, then pulled out a Viceroy and tapped it on the table. "Whadaya say, how about six pancakes and four slices of bacon. And maybe a large orange juice. And keep the coffee coming." He fired up the Viceroy.

"Six pancakes, four bacon, large juice. Got it. I'll have that in just a few minutes, Johnny." I don't think anyone called him *Mr. Swaze* except the paperboys. She returned to the kitchen.

"Well, boys, I believe everybody is accounted for." He laughed at himself, then blew a couple of smoke rings across the table.

Marie brought Mr. Swaze his coffee. "Thank you, Doll Face." He winked at her at the same time he wiped his nostril with the bottom of his thumb. I noticed her eyes roll slightly. I don't think she minded us boys sucking snot as much as she minded a grown man picking his nose with his thumb.

She turned to Grover. "And, sir, would you like your coffee now, or do you want to wait for your donuts?" It was kind of nice the way she approached Grover with a "Sir." And though she *sounded* polite to Mr. Swaze, I'm sure he was lucky she didn't pour his coffee in his lap. She reminded me of my mother. She could be fierce, but a lady.

"Yes, ma'am. I'll wait for my donuts," Grover said.

A few minutes later she brought the entire order of donuts and hot chocolate, and Grover's coffee.

"Boy, those donuts smell fresh. Hmm, hmm," Mr. Swaze said. He made noises like a wild animal around food.

"Well, Johnny Swaze, your order will be here in just a minute," she said. She moved the donuts to the other side of Grover. "Just you leave these boys and their donuts alone." She could have been talking to a yard dog. Grover picked one up and stuffed it in his mouth, sugar spilling onto the front of his shirt.

Through the window, we saw a police car pulling into the parking lot. Two officers, wearing black leather jackets with fur collars, walked inside and sat down at the counter. They appeared solemn, their pistols strapped to their sides, their shiny badges and patrol caps. I wondered if they had been searching for the convict all night. They also made me remember the colored man. Maybe we should report our sighting of him. It seemed suspicious, him digging up there at that time of the morning, although he couldn't be the escaped convict if he were colored.

The manager and Marie were talking to the policemen before Marie brought Mr. Swaze's pancakes and bacon. "Well, now, Mr. Johnny Swaze, that oughta hold you for a while."

He used his fingers to stuff a piece of bacon in his mouth. "Those policemen over there have anything to say about the guy who broke out?"

"Not yet. Mr. Johnson, the manager, and I were just asking about that poor guard."

"Is he dead yet?"

"No. But I don't think we need to talk about it right now."

"Talking about that stuff while I'm eatin' don't bother me none."

"That's not what I meant," she said, a minor nod to us.

"Oh, oh, okay." He put half a pancake in his mouth he had sliced in half with his fork.

"Guess they'll have to try 'em again for another crime," Marie said.

Mr. Swaze didn't bother to swallow the pancake before he answered, a glob of food exposed in his open mouth. "Oh yeah. They'll charge 'em with bustin' out and assault on that guard. He's a real ass...excuse me... I mean a real jerk. He's from my part of the country, down on the coast. My momma and daddy knew about 'em. A wild one. Murder didn't seem to bother 'em." He scooped up three slices of bacon on his fork and shoved them into his mouth. "He deserves the electric chair. Cook 'em like this bacon." He roared again.

An hour later, and early light. Still below freezing, it wouldn't get much above that all day with the sky so clear. The weatherman had predicted cold temperatures all week, and some more freezing drizzle by Christmas Eve, a week away. However, as usual, no snow for Christmas had been forecast.

We had finished and watched Mr. Swaze finish his feast, and though it was Saturday we needed to get home so my mother knew no harm had befallen us.

"Well, you gentlemen come back and see me. And be careful on your bikes. And if I don't see you, have a Merry Christmas," Marie said.

"Yes, ma'am, you too. Thank you."

Mr. Swaze offered a parting sentiment. "See ya, Marie. And don't forget my offer." He laughed.

"I won't. Come back to see us." She held what my mother would call *a painted smile.*

I thought back to the man we had seen in the hole and wondered about him digging a hole so early in the morning. Maybe he was with those right-of-way people we had heard about. Maybe he had permission; maybe anything. Mother had told us most things had a simple explanation, if you didn't let your imagination run wild.

As we left, I saw a colored man getting out of a brown pickup truck across the street. He had pulled behind the Gulf Filling Station. The station was closed but had garbage cans lined up in the back waiting for pickup. He wore a Stetson hat and black navy car coat. He stepped, almost cautiously, to the garbage cans and put something in one of them then returned to his truck. When he turned toward us, I saw his face.

I called to Henry and Ronny Erl. "It's him."

"Who? Where?" Henry said.

"The guy at the house. The one in the hole," I said. "I'm sure."

I could tell he had caught me staring at him, and his eyes came back on me, and even from the distance, they were dark and hard.

We could hear the gears grinding for a moment as he forced the truck into low gear. He pulled away, smoke trailing from the tailpipe.

Why would a hobo have a truck?

Chapter 21

WE WANTED TO DRIVE DOWNTOWN TO SEE THE CHRIST-mas lights. We piled into our car, three of us jammed together on the back seat. Henry and I each had a back window and Katy Jean sat between us; Mother riding shotgun up front and Daddy driving. The temperature had dropped and it would continue to fall until the early morning hours when it would drop well below thirty degrees. Daddy had the heater on and we all were bundled in our winter coats. Daddy fired up a Lucky Strike. He had switched from Chesterfield because he said they made him cough too much. He cracked his window a bit as we drove, allowing some of the cool air to circulate. Each time we passed a brown pickup I squinted, trying to see the driver.

Strands of greenery wrapped with glittering lights crossed Capitol Street, each strand crossing from lamp pole to lamp pole, a wreath in the center, stretching the downtown length of Capitol Street from the train depot up to the Old Capitol building. Even Bob's Tobacco House had a wreath on the door.

If you stood on the balcony of the Old Capitol and viewed the entire length of the street with the Christmas lights crossing it, in the luster of lights you could imagine

Jefferson Davis giving his famous secession speech and gazing at the throng spread before him. The Old Capitol was just for offices now, no longer used as the center of state government. Often, passing, someone would comment on Jeff Davis and the past; always a lighted star topped the dome of the Old Capitol at Christmas.

The Christmas parade had taken place the week before and we had a special view from one of Daddy's customer's office on the second floor of a downtown building. Christmas parades were held in most towns, and they were mostly the same with everybody's fantasy about a White Christmas. Our parade in Jackson proceeded the entire distance of Capitol Street from the Illinois Central train station to the Old Capitol building. The entire procession sequenced Christmas-time displays: all visualizations of snow and cold and winter, whether the marching bands playing Christmas carols, or floats with Frosty the Snowman, or the grand finale: Santa Claus climbing from a red-painted cardboard chimney throwing candy to both sides of the street.

And, during the days following the parade, the downtown area with its shops and restaurants with decorations adorning them, with lights and green and red crepe paper, all had a brightness and cheerfulness portraying the season.

But the king of the stores at Christmas was Sears and Roebuck: music playing; columns wrapped in tinsel; and the greatest toy and game department.

Sears always sent its Christmas catalogue to arrive around Thanksgiving, putting everyone in the seasonal mood for buying. Daily, we flipped through the brightly colored book, constantly changing our minds as to what we would ask for, finally settling on what would fit Daddy's budget. Not that we cared about budgets, but he did, and so we had to pretend.

Prior to learning Santa Claus was not real, money had been no object as far as Henry and I were concerned, because Santa did everything for free. But Mother might say: "Perhaps Santa doesn't think you are old enough for a pony."

Or Daddy would say, "How the hell is Santa gonna get a pony in a sleigh?" One year, when he was five, Henry asked Santa for a hamster. Daddy told him there had been an especially hard winter at the North Pole and all the hamsters had died. Instead, Henry got a catcher's mitt.

We asked Daddy if we could go to Sears and walk around. He offered little resistance since he probably wanted to go himself, and it always made Katy Jean happy.

We were allowed to browse freely around the store. In the summer, they had installed an escalator, making it easier for people to go upstairs and down. We liked to ride on it but were told to not play around on it because, one, it could be dangerous and, two, we might knock somebody down.

Back in the summer a colored boy about my age rode up and down on it with a couple of his friends. They were barefooted, and one got his toes caught in the crack where the stairs close up. He almost lost his toe and blood was everywhere.

> Oh, come all ye faithful,
> Joyful and triumphant,
> Oh come ye oh come a ye,
> To Bethlehem.

You could hear the carols throughout the store, exciting you about the time of year and with the thought of getting something new. The music penetrated the chatter and baby-crying and multiple conversations throughout the store. For in spite of the hubbub, the people and the chaos and chatter among them, it was a *peaceful noise*.

I thought of the escapee and wondered what Christmas would be to him. But maybe he shouldn't have a Christmas, because of the guard he had hit over the head, still in a coma; and the guard's family wouldn't have a good Christmas. I felt sad for everybody in their families.

Henry said he wanted to go to the toy department, and my thoughts came back to where they normally were—about me. Though Henry was a seventh-grader, all important things were still in the toy department or the sports department, whether it was a bicycle, electric football game or a baseball glove. The two of us struck out for the basement.

We had seen pictures in the catalogue, but seeing what we wanted up close brought a special feeling, like they were alive. A hunting knife was top item for Henry, and there were an assortment to view in the sports department. For me, the newest electric football game, where miniature figures of players about an inch high moved up and down the metal field pushing one another, driven by electric vibrations. They had one on display that was allowed to run constantly, so naturally dozens of guys crowded around it. The sound screeched and crackled like radio static on a stormy night. I could tell it had the power to bring out some profanity from Daddy. I had to squeeze through the crowd to get a glimpse. Behind me, even through the crackling of the game, I heard my name.

"Hey, McCoy, what's y'all doing? Take a gander at this."

I turned and saw Billy Cohen. He had been ogling the store catalogue on the counter. I walked over to see what he thought so exciting.

"Pretty nice, huh?" he said. He held it up to the women's lingerie section, and there were all these women in their brassieres and panties and stuff.

"I guess," I said. I didn't want to dispute him. Although there was something aroused in me, it was a little embarrassing. Billy was flashing the pages at me. "Are the new football games in there?" I said.

"What grade are you in, McCoy?"

"The fifth," I said.

"Oh. Okay. Forget it." He closed the catalogue. "Where's Henry?"

"He's over in the sports department. He wants to see what knives they have. Are you here with your mother and daddy?"

"Yeah. I think they're upstairs talking to your parents. My father told me y'all were down here."

Henry approached us. "Hey Billy, what's up?

"My momma and daddy are down here shopping for Christmas presents," Billy said. "Daddy says we're running out of time. He said, 'only six shopping days left.' Take a gander at this." Billy opened up the lingerie section again. He had dog-eared it. The two of them started slobbering.

I wondered what the Cohens did at Christmas, since they were Jews. My mother once said, "the Jews are just one *testament* away from the Christians." Billy had an interest in most of the stuff Gentiles had an interest in: hunting knives and sports and stuff. I wanted to ask him if he ever got his tobacco business going, but I was pretty sure he hadn't. He might have asked me about my junk business which hadn't been so great either, clearing less than four dollars.

"What do y'all think about that guy who broke out of the jail? Think he's around here still?"

"I'll bet he is, but Daddy says probably not," Henry said. "And we gotta deliver papers in the mornin' while he's still on the loose. I could use a hunting knife *right now* instead of at Christmas."

"That what you're getting? A hunting knife?" Billy said. "There might be a reward if y'all caught him."

"Yeah, the main thing I wanted was a *twenty-two* but Daddy said, one more year. He said he might consider a .410 shotgun since it wasn't as powerful. But anybody can shoot squirrels with a .410. I want a rifle."

"If you had a good hunting knife you could rip the guts outta that guy if he attacked you. I kinda agree with you, about needin' it now," Billy said.

We stepped back so a lady could get to the counter and use the catalogue. Billy acted as if he had been moved out of his personal library.

"Well, anyway my daddy hired a night watchman while he's on the loose. If he want to bust in some place, a jewelry store would be as good a place as any."

"You know where a good place to hide would be? The Big House on Old Canton," Billy said.

"Yeah. Maybe."

I couldn't imagine why a half-starving, freezing guy trying to get away from the police would want to rob a jewelry store. I didn't think a guy would go into a store half naked and try to buy a suit and shoes with a diamond ring. But I didn't say so.

"My daddy says he thinks he's hiding in some hole somewhere," I said. "No money and not much for clothes. Maybe
not even shoes."

"Maybe so. But my daddy's not taking any chances. If
he needs money, he could steal watches and rings and sell
them to somebody. "

I didn't say anything else. It sounded like something he
had made up.

An announcement suddenly boomed over the storewide
intercom: *May I have your attention please. The store will be
closing in fifteen minutes. Have a Merry Christmas and please
drive carefully.*

"They oughta add, *And keep an eye out for murderers on
your way home,*" Billy said.

"Say, what time is it?" Henry said.

I checked my Timex I had gotten for my birthday. "7:45."

"I'll bet Mother and Daddy are trying to find us. We'll see
you later, Billy."

"Yeah, I'll see y'all."

We could hear the sounds of "The First Noel" as we left.
When we walked to our car, Henry and I stayed far enough
behind Mother and Daddy didn't hear us talking about the
escapee, and how the three of us had talked about the Big
House being a good place for him to hide. We kept it to ourselves about the colored man we saw digging a hole.

It had turned colder and the breeze coming through the
cracked window had a bit more of the December bite, and
the drift of the fumes from another Lucky seemed to fit with
the cold wind and the season.

Everybody liked Mother's idea of driving around looking at Christmas lights in the neighborhoods. Some streets

had a lot more than others, but almost all had some display. One street on the other side of town, Pecan Boulevard, laid straight as an arrow from one end to the other, and right down the middle, stretched a line of pecan trees. They were strung with series and combinations of lights and stars all throughout the trees and shrubs, along with fixtures of things like Santa Claus and reindeer cutouts and cotton stuff on the ground, supposedly snow, and all had lights shining on them like billboards. Many of the yards had manger scenes and angels concentrating on the sky. It reminded me of a new electric football set.

One of the more popular yards had a miniature of a small town with houses, a downtown area with little office buildings, and a church with a tall steeple at the end. They even had little tiny figures arranged like they were Christmas shopping or greeting people. Henry and I liked it, but thought it would be a great place to lob a few cherry bombs.

Finally, Daddy decided we had burned up enough gasoline and said we needed to get on home.

On the way home, Daddy stopped at the Tote-Sum store for milk and bread and talked to a policeman inside. Daddy told us there had been nothing especially revealing. The policeman had told the night manager to be wary of anyone knocking after hours. This little piece of information gave Henry and me hope there still might be some excitement.

The policeman had told Daddy there were all kinds of sightings and rumors; only one confirmed. Two white shirts had been stolen from a clothesline in one neighborhood. But no one had been spotted. And even if the shirts were taken by Gallagher, it would take more than a couple of white dress shirts to keep him warm and dry.

I thought again of the guard they had assaulted. Now, at Christmas, his family wasn't at Sears or Western Auto or Kress' enjoying the sounds and sights and smells and everything else about Christmas. They were at the hospital, hoping he lived.

The killer must be hiding somewhere. I tried to think how it must feel to be, cold and hungry, and hunted; no warm house with food, or with people who cared about you. I felt sorry for him; not because he was a criminal, but because he had become one. He would never again have a Merry Christmas—if he ever had.

"Well, I sure hope they catch him soon," my mother said. Mother often tried to relax us with positive thoughts. But this didn't mean she wasn't still worried.

When we turned into our driveway, we heard the news bulletin on the car radio: *Escaped convict apprehended. Details at the top of the hour.*

Katy Jean squeezed my hand and gave a gentle sigh.

Chapter 22

W E HAD NOT BEEN TO THE BIG HOUSE SINCE WE SAW THE man in the hole. The weather had been too wet and cold to bother. Our search where the colored man in the Stetson had dumped something behind the Gulf station had produced nothing but a handful of newspapers. There were four or five sections from the paper all dated sometime in 1953, but we just glanced through them before we stashed them at Ronny Erl's. Henry and I still had the pin, though we still hadn't figured out what kind of a pin.

One day at the Pig Stand, we asked Marie if she ever saw the man across the street in the brown pickup. She said she didn't pay any attention to people pulling up in the lot, let alone those across the street. Henry said anybody feeding Mr. Swaze would be too busy to watch for anything.

It rained all week and stayed cold. It didn't freeze, but felt like it with the rain and dampness. I was glad I didn't have a paper route. The week crept, and the closer to Christmas, the more time seemed to slow. Grover said it had something to do with Einstein's theory of time going faster or slower, depending on what you were doing. He said Einstein knew all about atomic bombs and time and stuff like that.

Henry said car salesmen could make you believe most anything, and since Grover frequented the Ford dealership he had learned how to spout off. Billy made sure we knew Einstein was Jewish. Anyway, it sure seemed like time slowed down around Christmas.

When I complained about how time dragged for Christmas in front of my mother, she said we should remember how slow it must be for the jail guard and his family. Still in a coma, unless he pulled out of it she said his family would have sad memories all future Christmases. She was right and I had almost forgotten about him. I did say a prayer for him although my selfish thoughts always returned to the loot I would get Christmas morning.

Christmas Eve we had a big supper at Minnie's. After, we sat around while Minnie played some Christmas carols on the piano, and we drank eggnog. Being Baptist, it contained nothing but egg and nog as far as I could taste. Henry said Catholics and Methodists put some pretty powerful stuff in theirs, and some of them got really plastered on Christmas Eve.

We found out Christmas morning the guard died. He never came out of his coma. He never spoke to his family again. Everybody said it was a shame about him and his family, especially dying right on Christmas day and everything. But Daddy said life was like that sometimes.

The day after Christmas Henry and I caught the bus downtown to see another picture show: *Shane.* Billy had called and said he'd meet us at Bob's Tobacco House before it started. He wanted to show us what he got for Christmas. Henry said it probably was a subscription to *Playboy.*

Mother overheard him. "Well, I don't expect Mr. Cohen has allowed anything so perverted. I don't care if you're Jew or Gentile, anybody who likes that filth is a heathen! And if Bob's Tobacco House has that nasty magazine y'all can just buy funny books somewhere else. Anyway, Mr. Bob's Tobacco House is too close to a poolroom in the first place."

We caught the bus. It had been cold for over a week but the rain had stopped.

Billy stood by the magazine rack thumbing through a detective magazine, *Strange Detective Stories*. As soon as we walked in, Billy said, "Don't waste your time; they still haven't moved the Coke machine." He nodded in the direction of the alley, then proceeded to flash a new wristwatch with a snazzy, gold elastic band.

Everybody had a watch by the second or third grade even if you couldn't tell time, but the first one or two were Mickey Mouse or Roy Rogers. Their pictures were on the face of the watch, one of their arms being the short hand and the other the long hand. But by the fifth or sixth grade, it would be a the new Timex watch with no personality. If you still had a Mickey or Roy by the fifth grade you were deemed a sissy—a name with its own problems.

Being the owner of a jewelry store, Billy's daddy had given him a real glamorous one, the price we could only guess. He beamed when he held it up. "I'm gonna go to the picture show with y'all, okay?"

"Okay."

"What time does it start?" He held his watch up in front of his eyes.

"Two o'clock."

He checked his watch. "What time is it over?"

"About four-thirty."

Again he held it up. "Okay. As long as I get home for supper on time." Another time check.

"You find out what's on?" I asked.

"*Shane*. Supposed to be one of the greatest westerns ever. Better than John Wayne in *Red River*. Let's go," Billy said. "Should take us about ten minutes to go over there. I'll time us."

Shane was great. But about half way through, Jack Palance, the evil hired gun, told a farmer from Alabama that he was Southern trash and so were Robert E. Lee and Stonewall Jackson. This brought a round of boos from the audience. But Larry Taylor, a sixth grader got thrown out because he threw a popcorn box at the screen. If he had been at the Pix it probably would have been okay, but at the Paramount the audience had a lot of adults and you couldn't do things like that. I wish Larry had stayed because at the end, Alan Ladd who played Shane called Jack Palance a "dirty low-down Yankee liar," then proceeded to blow his brains out. The audience, adults and all, cheered.

After the picture show, Billy went up the street to his daddy's store to see if he could catch a ride home. Henry and I were going to catch the bus. I had hoped to split up from Billy because I wanted to go back to Bob's before we caught the bus. I had decided to bring somebody else into my little secret I had with the colored people.

It was almost five o'clock and Dexter had started closing his shoe shine stand, standing alone popping his rag. His last customer had stepped away, tossing him a quarter. I waited until no one else could hear. He stood next to the stand, humming.

"Hey, Dexter, tell Henry what you were telling me about hoodoo."

"What? You mean voodoo?" Henry said, puzzled.

Dexter cast a glance down the aisle. He flopped his rag over his shoulder and propped one foot on the stand like the stance of a prophet.

"Well, I wuz jus' tellin' 'bout the hoodoo that's gone on out yonder where that lightning fire wuz last summer. Yo little brother here don't b'lieve me. But ever'body know 'bout it."

"Are you sayin' hoodoo or voodoo?" Henry asked again.

"Hoodoo. Hoodoo's from Africa. Voodoo's from Haiti. Hoodoo is straight from the Congo. And it works."

"On who?'

"On whoever you hoodooin'."

"What?"

"Yeah. You can hoodoo somebody or some-thing. It depends on your goal. Depend on the nature of your trick."

For the next few minutes Henry and I were hypnotized by Dexter's story on hoodoo. He reminded me of the guy at the fair who talked me into rolling balls for a dime. Dexter could get you to believing anything. He said many blacks had been sold by Massachusetts and Connecticut slave traders to the French colony, Haiti. And that's where voodoo got started.

Dexter had somehow found the *truth:* pure hoodoo came from Africa and voodoo from Haiti, mostly French. Those people in New Orleans were the only ones who really and truly performed voodoo. In Mississippi they used hoodoo through herbs, roots, fire and/or burial, combinations with personal objects or even human remains. Voodoo, he said, was likened to a kind of religion, like snake-handling religions.

"How do you know somebody put a spell that caused the lightning?" Henry asked. "How come it wasn't jus' regular old lightning that comes with thunder?"

"Jus' cause."

"Cause why?"

"Same *cause* that man who broke outta jail wuz part of somebody's hoodoo."

"Damn, Dexter. You're losing your mind," Henry said. "He didn't have nothing to do with anything except getting away." I glanced down the aisle to see if anybody heard Henry say *damn*.

"No I ain't. He wuz a bootlegger from the coast, and he broke out cause of that old still that's buried out there. He and his people wanted it," Dexter said.

"What still?" Henry asked. He turned his head back and forth between Dexter and me.

It occurred to me I had never told Henry what Big Daddy and Minnie had told me about the moon shiners' still and it being buried. "I'll tell you later," I said. "Anyway, Dexter how come you think he broke out 'cause of that?"

"Well, you c'n bet anybody from the coast who's a criminal is got some bootleggin' doings. You c'n jus 'bout be sure. And he wuz from down on the coast. And where you find fires and skeletons you c'n be sure of hoodoo."

"You're crazy, Dexter," Henry said.

Mr. Bob walked up. "Okay, Dexter, close it up for the day. You goin' over to The Big Apple Inn for supper?"

"Not tonight, Mr. Bob. Gotta big doin's goin' on."

"Dang. I wanted some tamales."

♦ ♦ ♦

Because he was in the seventh grade and I in the fifth, Henry not only assumed he knew more than me, he said so. "That's a lot of baloney," he said on the bus ride home. "Dexter's jus' talkin' 'bout stuff colored people talk about. It's some old superstition from way back when slaves made things up. We've been studying this stuff in Mississippi history. Dexter's jus' gotten wrapped up in old stories—jus' stories."

I didn't tell him Mary Hester had told me the same things about hoodoo. He might say something to her and it would hurt her feelings. You could tell Dexter he was crazy and he wouldn't care, but Mary Hester would be hurt.

"You know what?" Henry said. "We oughta ask Mr. Cohen about the pin we found. Ask him what it is. Ask him if it's valuable."

"What made you think of that?"

"Jus' did."

"Yeah, maybe you're right. He oughta know about gold pins and stuff. And what they're worth," I said. "What if he asks us where we got it?"

"We'll just tell him we found it in the woods. We don't have to say we found it by the river close to the fire. I don't think it matters anyway. We could have found it anywhere."

"Should we tell Ronny Erl and Buck?"

"Yeah, after we ask Mr. Cohen. If it's valuable they'll get to share. We're all partners."

"When do we ask?"

"Tomorrow. But you ask Daddy when we get home. He'll tell you I'm right about that hoodoo stuff. You and Dexter are nuts."

Go to hell, I thought. And I wasn't even old enough to cuss.

Chapter 23

MAYBE HE WAS JUST THROWING AWAY OLD NEWSPAPERS. But I knew he was the same guy in the hole. We rummaged through the old newspapers he had discarded, the one thing in common being the future of the new interstate highway.

The old Highway 51, which ran through Jackson, overlapped Mississippi from New Orleans to Memphis and beyond, to Chicago, maybe. After the Mason Dixon Line, we didn't care where it went. A federal highway, it had two lanes most of the way. Big Daddy said they were *national* highways; *federal* died after 1865. But after World War II, with a new burst of business, the new president, General Eisenhower, developed the concept for a vast system of four-lane highways, called interstate highways.

Initially Highway 51 was to be widened through Jackson to four lanes north through Madison County and Canton, and north along the Mississippi Delta. Widening highways and new right of ways meant clearing and buying new lands, grading and digging.

But maybe, after all, the man was just throwing away some old papers.

Thursday, the day before New Year's Eve, and we wanted to see Mr. Cohen. We had asked Billy if he thought his daddy would mind us coming by during business hours. Naturally, we had to tell Billy why we were coming, but as it turned out he didn't ask for a cut. His mad love for his golden watch, which he said was worth a lot more than some discarded pin, kept most of his attention. And his rabbit tobacco business having been a failure, he would still be supported by his daddy, anyway, so he didn't care about our little pin.

When we arrived at Cohen's Jewelry on Capitol Street, Mr. Cohen stood behind the front glass counter. It was filled with watches, rings, bracelets and all sorts of other gold and silver items. He had an eye piece stuck in his eye, peering at some kind of expensive stone. A big man with muscular arms, his examining the tiny stone reminded me of Joe peeling the apple at the warehouse. His gray hair didn't make him seem old, just wise.

Mr. Cohen came out from behind the counter. "Well, fellows, let's see what you have there."

Henry carefully unfolded our jewel from a white handkerchief as if he were about to expose something from King Solomon's treasure. Mr. Cohen picked it up and held it over his head against the light. He said nothing at first. But the slight shaking of his head and his wrinkled brow told me we didn't have a fortune in some rare old gold key. He pulled his eyepiece down and put it in his pocket.

"I believe you boys have brass key. It's old. No doubt about that. But it is brass."

Henry and I looked at one another. "A key?" I said.

"Brass?" Henry whispered.

"That's right. Y'all see the little tit on the end? And the little circle at the head. That's what it is."

"Sure would be a tiny door for it to unlock," Henry said.

"Yeah," I seconded.

Mr. Cohen smiled at the comment but didn't laugh. "No, no. It's probably for some small box, or maybe a desk. Lot of old desk drawers had keys like this. Some old roll top desks have several drawers and some have individual locks. Not so much anymore. Mostly the keys for the newer desks are the same pattern of any other key. Where'd y'all get it?"

"Oh, jus' out on the road somewhere." Henry was careful about saying exactly where.

"We thought it was a golden pin. Maybe worth a lot of money," I said.

"Well, it's not gold and I doubt anybody would pay you a nickel for it. Now, maybe it'll unlock a map leading you to great treasure. But by itself it's just a souvenir. Sorry, boys. Well, I've got to get back to work. But anytime y'all have a question come on by and I'll try and help. Tell your momma and daddy I said hello."

"Yes, sir. Thank you."

Since Henry had acted the way he had, I decided to ask Daddy about hoodoo. He told me I could put the hoodoo business in the same category as the swamp monster. Without mentioning any names he said there were some colored folks who believed it and probably always would; and they certainly wouldn't believe a white man telling them otherwise.

This had been a bad week. First I had been told the pin was insignificant, and now hoodoo was hogwash.

After going 9–1, including one of the biggest wins in Mississippi football history, beating number five Alabama 25–19

earlier in the year, on New Year's Day, Mississippi Southern won the Sun Bowl. 1954 began.

I had been sent to the principal's office. Sitting straight-backed in a wooden chair, I waited to be grilled by Mrs. Thomas. Tim waited in the other room, our separation dictated so we couldn't get together on our stories, we assumed.

Temptation had grabbed us by the throat and we had scotch- taped a spider to the top of Mary Ellen's desk before she came back from the cafeteria. We thought she'd just jump with a classic Mary Ellen, "Ooohh." Instead, she screamed like an Inner Sanctum victim and started crying. They probably heard her in China.

We were sent to the office with Miss Ashley's admonishment, "I don't think I've ever been so disappointed in y'all."

I had sensed her disappointment even if she hadn't blurted it out, and I suffered a little bit too, myself. But one of the guys in Sunday School told me later the devil really tempts you beyond your own strength, sometimes. He said only Jesus could have resisted taping that spider to Mary Ellen's desk.

While we were waiting, Mrs. Thomas's door was partially open, and I could hear her talking to July. "Yes, July, I realize Franklin has had his share of problems, but you have to help him the best you can."

July was banging on something, probably the heater. When hot it was the fan he was fixing, when cold, the heater. "Yessum. He's a bit better dese days since he done dem months in Whitfield. I think dem doctors fixed his mind somewhat. But he jus' worries all the time 'bout things he can't do nothin' 'bout."

"I understand," Mrs. Thomas said. "You've told me how he worries about the city spreading out and taking over all the land around."

Bang, bang. "Yessum. He worries 'bout dat highway comin' through and takin' over all huntin' and plantin'. He ain't got many places left to take his dogs, he says. And jus' worries hisself 'bout it."

"You mean where they're widening Highway 51? That's gonna be part of that interstate highway they're talking about."

Bang, bang, bang. "Yessum, but it do take away de land from folks wherever it go."

Mrs. Thomas must have realized he had left the door ajar, because I saw her step over and close it. Within a couple of minutes the door opened again, and July came out carrying his toolbox. He paused and smiled at me, then shook his head and walked down the hall.

Tim and I were invited into Mrs. Thomas' office.

I raced home, getting there about the same time as Henry. Junior high ended almost an hour after Boyduling, but since I had to stay after school for an hour Henry arrived at home when I did.

"Mr. Charlie been bad at school," Mary Hester said. "What you been up to?" She didn't wait for an answer. "I'll bet you don't tell yo momma and daddy you come in here an hour late." She stood, shaking a throw rug on the front porch while holding the screen door with her butt so I could slip past her. "I'll bet Mr. Tim or Mr. Ronny Erl been mischiffing wid you wid whatever you wuz doin'." She spit a brown glob of snuff into the flowerbed.

"What'd y'all do?" Henry asked.

"Nothing," I lied. "Uh, just getting' some extra credit so I stayed late." Mary Hester broke out in a giggling spasm. "Anyway, come on back to our room. I've got to tell you something."

Mary Hester kept shaking the rug, peering at me over the top of her glasses. Katy Jean didn't have her usual smile but grimaced at me with the same disappointment Miss Ashley had shown. She had heard the word "mischiffing."

"You remember that guy we saw digging? Back before Christmas?" I said.

"Yeah, what about him?"

"I figured out who he is. And it wasn't no convict."

Miss Ashley wanted us all to exchange Valentines; which meant you had to send one to some girl to be polite. No guy in his right mind would send a Valentine to a guy. But if you didn't give one to a girl, you couldn't have any Valentine candy at the Valentine party. It wasn't like a Christmas party, but better than no party at all.

Miss Ashley called Tim and me aside and suggested we each give one to Mary Ellen as a penitence for the horrible things we had done. Ronny Erl told me he would exchange with me his Valentine's draw, Nelga Arnesen, whose family had moved from Sweden to the United States last year. A nice girl, although very big and she could beat most of the guys at arm wrestling. But it didn't matter. I could tell Miss Ashley's suggestion was really an order.

Boyd had caught a coral snake and kept it in a box at home. He said he would sell it to me for quarter, if I wanted to really throw something good at Mary Ellen. I told him no thanks. I didn't want to disappoint Miss Ashley anymore; besides Mrs. Thomas had told me the spider incident would go on my permanent record.

I planned to peek in July's room when I returned from the cafeteria. It was about the only chance you had to be in the hall without a teacher watching you. If you ran an errand like taking a message to the office or going to get July and his mop or to get him to replace a light bulb you were briefly free, but I remained low on Miss Ashley's list when it came to doing any special chores. Her disappointment in Tim and me had kept me on the bench.

I wanted to see the group picture, the one which included his cousin, so I took the risk and sneaked into his room. I didn't see him, so I had a second chance to view the picture of him, Isaiah, and his cousin Franklin. Franklin had been the man digging the hole.

Chapter 24

How do y'all know it'll fit that desk up there? That's not the only roll top desk in Jackson, you know," Buck said.

"So what?" Henry said. "Might as well try. Like Mr. Cohen said, it might lead to some treasure."

Still, nobody believed me when I told them the man in the hole was July's cousin Franklin. I wanted to see if the key fit as much as they did, but it made me a little nervous thinking about him. What if he were inside the Big House now? And what if he had a pick axe instead of a shovel? He had been in Whitfield, the place they kept crazy people and lunatics. And just because they let them out didn't mean they weren't still crazy.

"Sometimes," Mary Hester had said, "if they couldn't get them un-crazy, they just sent them home 'cause they didn't want to feed then no more."

"You can't tell," Buck said. "How old is that picture? The one in July's room?"

"July said it was taken about fifty years ago."

"Well," Henry said, "then this guy Franklin is over seventy."

I think Ronny Erl wanted to be on my side since we were in the same grade and almost the same age, but even he had a hard time believing me. "How can you see a picture of a guy who's about twenty and recognize him from the picture when he's over seventy?" he asked.

I couldn't explain it. But something in the man's face and eyes in the picture, and something in the face and eyes of the man I saw early that morning were the same.

"Well, who is Franklin, anyway?" Ronny Erl continued. "He's just some old colored guy who stopped sharecroppin' and started raising dogs. Even if it is him, it doesn't mean anything necessarily."

Henry and Buck and Ronny Erl and me were climbing over the barbed wire fence, the house and the field deserted as always.

"Ouch." I stuck my finger on a barb and then sucked my finger while I held the wire for Ronny Erl.

"I heard Mrs. Thomas and July talking about him like he was still a little funny; like he still wasn't *all there*. But I think July kinda worries about him 'cause he's family."

"Funny?" Buck asked.

"Funny like." I spun my finger in a series of circles at the top of my head. We worked our way through the weeds, our shoes sinking in the soft ground which had taken a lot of rain since Christmas. "But he knew Joe's daddy, Isaiah Washington. Joe and his daddy look almost alike. Like Jersey Joe Walcott. Joe's daddy was a fighter. Did y'all know?"

"Where'd you find out?" Henry asked.

"July told me one time."

"You never told me," Ronny Erl said.

"What's that got to do with Franklin," Buck said.

"Nothing, I guess. I jus' wondered what he would be doin' up here diggin' at five o'clock in the morning."

"Well, you jus' said he was crazy," Buck said.

"He's July's cousin, anyhow," I said. "That's all I was sayin'."

We stood in front, weeds still grew through the porch boards, with additional ones crowded in. We entered with less reluctance. Having been inside before had given us a bit more courage, somewhat like jumping off the high diving board for the first time. Daytime or nighttime, it seemed strange. Its silence, its battered and desolate image, stood before us; stood above us. The Big House seemed bigger today. Its boarded structure seemed like something written in an old storybook.

We climbed the dusty stairs, seeking the old roll top. The room hadn't changed. The broken furniture, the stained mattress, even the old can of sardines was in the same spot we had left it last summer. When we hovered around the desk we paused, hoping another rat wasn't lurking. We had closed the roll top after we had tried to pick the lock back in August. It had gotten stuck again, some recent dust or mildew wedged in the edge. I took out my new pocket knife and handed it to Buck to scoop out the impediment. Reopening it freed a dozen roaches.

Henry stuck the key in the locked drawer. With little effort it opened.

There were seven or eight old pages of letters, a couple with dates in 1891. We didn't care if we were thieves, we took them; our treasure. Ronny Erl had brought the old satchel and we stuffed the letters inside with the discarded newspapers. We all agreed to go over them thoroughly at either our house or Ronny Erl's house.

At Ronny Erl's driveway I realized I had left my pocketknife at the Big House. Buck had handed it back to me, but I put it down when I helped push back the roll top.

"Who's gonna go back with me?" I really didn't expect any volunteers, being almost two miles, and everybody tired. Besides, they wanted to go through the letters.

"You better go back and get it. That's the knife you got for Christmas," Henry said.

"I hate to go back by myself," I whined. "It's scary when you're by yourself."

"You better go on before it gets dark. Anyway if you go on right now you won't be late for supper. Besides, we've been up there twice. There's nothing to get you except brown rats." Everybody laughed but me.

"Well, y'all don't tear up those letters before I get to see 'em," I said.

"We ain't gonna tear 'em up," Buck said. "Might sell 'em to some museum or something."

I mounted my bike and headed again for the Big House. Daylight wouldn't last long. The sun lingered at the top of the trees. I carefully climbed over the barbed wire fence again, my finger still sore from the earlier puncture. I crossed the field at a jog and made my way to the front door, the sunlight dropping under the porch overhang.

Every step up the stairs seemed like a mile. Alone, there were no voices to drown out the creaking stairs or the shifting timbers. The dimming daylight, blocked by evergreens growing above the windows, reduced the light inside to shadowy grayness. When I climbed to the top of the stairs I could see into the room, my pocketknife still opened on the desk. I walked over and picked it up, paused and stared at the desk top. I tried to imagine someone writing letters back in another century. I tried to visualize a mailman coming to this house on horseback.

When I closed the blade it was as if I had switched on a radio—voices—voices from downstairs. My heartbeat rattled me. I tried to find a place to hide and saw a closet. I didn't care if it had a hundred brown rats in it. I feared them less than the unknown downstairs. I sat down in an old broken chair to take off my shoes so whoever had entered wouldn't hear me. But before they were off, I recognized one of the voices, a deep hoarse one.

I tiptoed over to the door, slightly open, and stood behind it. Through the crack I could see down the stairway into the front foyer.

"You got to stop dis snoopin' 'round and spreadin' all dis hoodoo business, Mr. Franklin. Dis land is gone. We ain't never gonna get it. An' all de hoodoo in de world ain't gonna do nuthin'."

Peering through the narrow slit I could see them. Joe Washington and Mr. Franklin. And as sure as the Stetson hat he wore now, he was the same man, fifty years older, than the man in the photograph.

"It's yo land. And it's my land too. Jus' 'cause dem shiners and bootleggers stole it back when you wuz jus' a boy and I wuz jus' a young un, don't mean it ain't our'n now. We got a right to it. An' de money dey buried out here."

"Mr. Franklin, de highway people comin' through pretty soon now. And dis land b'long to some folks in Memphis, I understand. It don't make no difference if'n it right or wrong or nuthin'. An' they catch you doin' yo hoodoo stuff, they'll put you back in the hospital. July done told you de same thing. An' dey ain't no money to be found here."

"We can *spell* de land, Joes. I'm tellin' you, we need to burn a cat and bury it. I already got some big holes started.

We need a big cat. A bobcat. And dat hound you got c'n sniff out bobcats, good as mine. I know you been workin' him 'round here. Burnin' a cat is the best trick to lay down. An' bobcats is the biggest and wildest. They'll spell it. They'll hex it."

"Mr. Franklin, I jus' work old Gumbo 'cause it's easy place to git to when I work in town. I ain't tryin' to get no cats to kill and burn. An' you can't be hoodoin' things you take outta dat house. You jus' scatterin' stuff around; dem vases, and old lamps and satchels and stuff. Yo hexes don't mean nutthin'. And yo spells don't neither."

Through the crack I saw Franklin step up to Joe's face when he spoke. Close enough to whisper, but I could hear every word.

"Dat lightning fire wuz a *sign.* It wuz the right time to uncover de bones of dat shiner yo daddy murdered. Murdered him on account he wuz tryin' to steal de land to bury his still. Murdered him right in front of you and me, when you weren't no more seben-years old, and buried him under the dirt floor of dat old house. An' old lamps I hoodooed take away de light, and satchels gets 'em packed up, and vases—"

"Mr. Franklin, now you know Daddy didn't murder dat man. Dat man wuz gonna hit him wid a axe handle and Daddy punched him dead. Broke his neck. Wadn't murder though. Daddy didn't mean to hit him dat hard. Dat white-trash shiner thought he could get away wid jus' runnin' us off on account he wuz white and we wuz colored."

"Y'all went off hiding in Chicago, and dat's how we lost de land. Nobody ever b'lieve me when I told 'em I had claims 'round here," Mr. Franklin said.

"Well, Daddy jus' took us away. Said dere wuz mostly fair-minded white folks 'round here, but dere wuz enough white trash to 'cause trouble. He didn't have no witnesses 'cept me and you. And he said dere weren't no turnin' back. It wuz jus' over."

"And de white folks took de land."

"No, no, Mr. Franklin. Wuzn't white folks dat took it. It wuz white trash dat took it," Joe said.

"Like dat escaped white man. He be comin' up here to git dat old still," Franklin said. "He wuz a bootlegger and he wanted it. All dem whiskey men on de coast after things like dat. An' he be up here an' found him some dat money buried. Dey know it buried all over different spots and hidin' places on my land. Dey got ol' maps dey stole from de coloreds. An' dey know where it got buried and hid. But he gonna die now cause I done a hoodoo on him."

"Mr. Franklin, he jus' a no-good killer wid nuttin' to do with dis place. He jus' happened to be in-de-world at de same time as us. He jus' sorry trash. And he jus' wanted to git away. Jus' shows dat dere's some sorry white folks jus' like dere's some sorry colored folks. And we don't even know if dat still got buried, and even if it did it long been trashed underground. And anyway, it don't matter. Dat killer gonna get what he should git. He back in jail now. And I sell ice and collect junk and you hunt dogs. An' dat's de way it gonna be."

I saw Joe reach out and put his hand on Franklin's shoulder and turn him toward the door. "Now you come along and go on home. And you stop yo hoodooin'. Start livin' what yo life got left."

Franklin lowered his head, stared at his feet for a moment, and shuffled toward the door. Joe followed. I waited until I could be sure they were both gone, then charged down the stairs. I was barely in time for supper.

"What took you so long?" Henry asked.

"I couldn't find it. I didn't remember where I put it."

"It was right there on the desk unless a ghost stole it," he said.

"I forgot."

"How could you forget? That was the only place we did anything."

"I jus' forgot." I twisted my face as if I wanted to shout, so he'd stop asking about it.

"Well, you're the one that's gonna end up in Whitfield," he said.

Katy Jean sat motionless. She smiled when I was happy. She grimaced when I was sad. Now she appeared frightened.

"Supper's ready," Mother called.

Chapter 25

I WONDERED HOW I COULD KEEP WHAT I HAD HEARD TO myself, although probably nobody would believe me anyway. Henry would call me crazy; Daddy would say: *Now don't tell me a story.* My reply would be: *I'm really telling the truth.*

But then he would call the police or sheriff and I feared getting Joe in trouble. Joe hadn't killed anyone, but his daddy had. And his daddy was dead. I couldn't be sure about Franklin, who I thought was nutty as a pecan pie.

I started to ask Theron in Sunday School the next morning, he being so wise in the ways of the world: *How should I reveal I had overheard two guys talking about a killing almost fifty years ago?* But I didn't. Any guys my age couldn't keep their mouths shut, and I worried about what might happen to Joe. Besides Theron was busy concealing a pair of loaded dice he had bought at the Magic Shop across the street from Bob's Tobacco House.

Mr. Kraft might be a good choice, for telling a grownup besides Daddy. Mr. Kraft had said back in the fall the skeletal remains would probably be part of an old unsolved crime, if anything should be discovered indicating one. It sounded like maybe nobody really cared since it had happened such a long time ago. I could be a hero with the sheriff's department. I had the solution to the unsolved crime but didn't want to tell anybody.

The only one besides Franklin and Joe and me who had heard the conversation, I figured had to be Jesus. And I was already on probation with Him for the Mary Ellen spider incident. Right now, Jesus was probably saying either, "Go tell your daddy," or "Keep your mouth shut." The biggest difference between Daddy and Jesus, Jesus wouldn't give me a switching for doing the wrong thing.

As usual we ended church services with the *Doxology*. But my heart wasn't in it.

All Henry, Ronny Erl, and Buck wanted to do was read the old letters over and over, so I didn't say anything to them. We gathered around Ronny Erl's bed and laid out the pieces of the letters. Several pages of separate letters and parts of each of the pages had been smeared beyond legibility, exposed to water apparently. Only parts could be read. They were dried and brittle and the edges flaked off. Ronny Erl and Buck had scotch-taped all around the edges and up and down the middle. The writing was legible.

One read:

June 22, 1891

... give unto Samuel Washington and his son Isaiah ...and sixty acres in the county or counties of...

Another:

Samuel Washington, a free man of color whose farm was confiscated by confiscatory taxes forced by occupational Yankees and Scalawags beyond his ability to pay... was able to claim in my name with gold coin...

Another:

February 18, 1905

Samuel Washington, a free man of color, and his two servants having served loyally as cooks and wagon drivers in The C.S.A., I will bequeath when I sign my final testament …erage south of Canton Mis…

The other pages were as limited, vague, choppy, references, most having been smeared.

"That must be Joe Washington's daddy and granddaddy," Ronny Erl said. "Charlie, y'all remember when the three of us were workin' down at your daddy's warehouse last summer? Joe said his granddaddy was a free black man."

"I remember," Henry said. "You remember that Charlie?"

"Yeah, I think so." I thought about Franklin and Joe and the conversation I had heard.

We spent the next hour guessing about what may have been left out and what we had read in front of us. I didn't contribute much. I mostly nodded my head.

The next night at supper we talked about Joe and the letters. The four of us had decided to tell Daddy and Mr. McGinnis about the letters, in case they had some value. They took them to the sheriff, who later stopped by the warehouse to see Joe and ask him some questions.

They asked him what he remembered about Isaiah and Samuel Washington. Joe told them he remembered working in the fields as a boy, and his daddy had left all of a sudden and go up north to Chicago. He said his daddy wanted to be a prize fighter. His daddy was Isaiah and his granddaddy was Samuel, but his granddaddy died the same year they left for Chicago; about 1909, he told the sheriff. Joe told them as best he could recall he was ten years old.

A county lawyer ran through the Hinds and Madison County records in the Chancery clerk's office, finding in some old dusty records the title into a Joel R. Cranston at least as far back as 1860. There also had been filed a record of death of the same Cranston, dying in 1919—intestate.

And a record of Samuel T. Washington, listed as *a free man of color* owning over three hundred acres in four tracts in both counties, some of it contiguous to Joel Cranston's. However, in 1869 it had been sold for taxes to some interests in Boston. Samuel T. Washington, a free man of color became a free man of color without property. Daddy said the sheriff surmised from the partial letter the statement *was able to claim in my name with gold coin* may have indicated Cranston somehow paid his taxes through the Reconstruction period and lived there until he died. Apparently record title showed heirs from Biloxi claiming descent and distribution from Cranston's estate and this property had been sold by the Biloxi *heirs* to some company in Tennessee.

Daddy said Joe insisted all he could say was he and his daddy left in the middle of the night for Chicago. Joe said he worked his way back South playing baseball in Nashville and when he retired he came back to Mississippi. Daddy flipped his eyes at me. I had been staring, my mouth open. "Is there something you want to say, Charlie?'

"Oh, no, sir." Katy Jean had a penetrating stare. I turned my eyes from her.

"And that was it?" Mother said. "They just left in the middle of the night?"

"That's what he said. Anyway they made copies of the letters. Gave back the originals. I put them over there on the coffee table for you and Henry. I guess y'all get to keep them. I'd be surprised if they're worth anything. But they're y'all's." Daddy had kept his focus on me. "Are you sure you don't wanna say something?"

"Yes, sir. I'm sure."

"Well, then eat your supper.

The next to last day of February. Cold, dark clouds with moisture and wind blew through during the night, and when I awakened I saw the four inch blanket of snow covering everything. From top-to-bottom and end-to-end.

Henry said when he went to deliver his papers it was coming down hard. He tried to wake me, but I mumbled and snorted and refused to come out from under the covers. So at 6:30 AM I had my first view, and the news on the radio said school had been cancelled.

The clouds were dark and flakes were still coming down as they would until almost noon, giving rise to a rumor school would be cancelled tomorrow, too. My mother's biggest concern seemed to be for people who might not have brought their plants inside or got their shrubs covered. I didn't really care, but for some reason I had a thought about old Mrs. Nettleton and her flowers. Grover couldn't do nearly as much damage to them as a snow storm could. Katy Jean sat at the living room window and seemed to absorb the beautiful sight. Her bright face stared at the whiteness. I wish she could have played in it with us.

Mother stayed home from the office so Daddy had to stop at Mary Hester's and tell her she didn't need to come in today. He had to go by her house since the only phone she had access to was a pay phone at the grocery store at the end of her block. Mother suggested Daddy pay her for the day anyway since it wasn't her fault she couldn't come in. And Mother told Daddy we could afford it right now. Daddy grumbled, not because of the money, but because the snow made such a mess and driving to the office took twice as long, let alone going out of his way.

By noon we had built three snowmen, had a dozen snowball fights, and with a few cars daring to get out on the roads, the white landscape had been reduced by a third to mush and slush. Mother had become so frustrated with us tracking in and out she finally threw us out, saying we could freeze to death but we weren't to track anymore snow inside. "In or out," she said.

I decided to see if I could ride my bike to the Tote-Sum. The snow had mostly been cleared from the road by the cars driving over it, and since Ronny Erl hadn't come down to our house, either he was up the street at his house or he was at McGinnis Hardware store.

Henry and Don Couples were helping Gene Cooper build a snow fort. Gene didn't have any boys his age within a block or two, and when Mother saw Don helping Gene she suggested Henry help, too. "Little boys like it when older boys show an interest in them." She was probably right, but not even Pinky Lee or Howdy Doody could have kept Gene inside with snow available, whether or not he had anyone to play with.

A single car had parked at the hardware store besides Red's and Mr. McGinnis'. They wouldn't get much business today, but they were open anyway. Same thing across the street at the Tote-Sum. The Seale Lily had not even opened.

"Ronny Erl and Buck are both at home, Charlie," Mr. McGinnis said. "I told Buck since school was out for the day, he could come up here and earn some money or play in the snow. So guess where he is?"

"Yes, sir. Everybody's been playin' at our house. I just came up here to see if I could make it on my bike."

"Well, you be careful out there. Those roads are slick, and although there aren't many folks out, they don't have as good a control as they ordinarily do."

"Yes, sir."

Red came up to me and put his hand on my shoulder. "I tell you what, Mr. Charlie. Let's go over to the Tote-Sum and I'll buy you a Co-Cola."

"Yes, sir. Thank you."

Gifford peered from behind the counter, his green jacket zipped up, his hands in his pockets. Only one of the front roll-up doors had been opened, and since it faced south the wind didn't hit him too hard. He had an electric heater going on the floor behind the counter. Lewis walked out of the cooler and remarked how much warmer the cooler was than outside.

"They oughta make you boys go to school since they make me come to work," Gifford said.

A customer drove up and skidded to a stop against the curb. Red and I stepped back. No one had ever driven into the store, but today could be the first time.

"Mr. Red, did your daddy ever meet Joe Washington?" I asked. "I mean, did he really? Like did he ever see him in Chicago? How about Joe's daddy, Isaiah?"

"Aw yeah. He knowed Joe pretty good. Just cause he saw his daddy fight one night. He found out Isaiah came from Mississippi, and Daddy knew the men who were backing him. Some white men from Canada. Daddy stopped by his dressing room one night and talked to him. Daddy wanted to buy into Isaiah's contract. But the men told Daddy they didn't want to sell none of him."

"Was your daddy a scout for the White Sox then?"

"Here go, Gifford." Red flipped Gifford a nickel for a bag of Tom's Peanuts. "Yeah. He did some bird-doggin' for the Cubs too. Funny thing. Cubs and Sox fans hated each other even back then."

"Like State and Ole Miss, huh?" I said.

"Naw. Up there they hate each other. Down here, State and Ole Miss jus' mean to each other." He laughed at his own comment. "Anyway, Daddy never did get into the fight bidness. And if old Isaiah had started younger and had a fair chance, I b'lieve he could of even whupped Jack Johnson. Isaiah was as strong as a mule, and tough as wet rawhide. Had a heck of a punch, too.

"But Daddy watched Joe around the colored schoolyards up there playin' baseball; and around 1916 or so, there was a black that slipped into the Pacific Coast League and Daddy thought maybe if coloreds started playin' in the major leagues again, Joe might develop into a pretty good prospect."

Freezing, standing there, I kept sipping on my Co-Cola. I wanted to hear more. I sucked snot up my nose.

"But old Judge Landis, a Yankee from Chicago, put his foot down and said no blacks were gonna play as long as he was commissioner. He said people in the South wouldn't stand for it. Funny thing. All the major league teams were in the North except St. Louis, but the South *wouldn't stand for it.* Funny thing, too—I never saw Joe playin' in them Chicago school yard games with any white players."

"So what happened?"

"Well, Joe played some semi-pro ball while he worked for a livin' in the stockyards 'til 'bout 1924 or '25. His daddy had died by then. And I think Joe wanted to get back closer to home. Anyway he got on with a team in the Negro Leagues. Played for Nashville for a while. By the time Robinson got in, Joe was in his forties and too old. And another real funny thing. It was a Southerner, Mr. Happy Chandler, who took down that color line. He said he didn't see how you could send colored men to war and not let 'em play baseball."

I stopped sipping and slugged down the rest of my Co-Cola. I suppressed a belch and finally asked the question I really wanted answered. "Why'd they leave Mississippi? Every time I've talked to Joe, he seemed like he just wanted to be a farmer. And I can tell he likes to hunt, the way he is always workin' Gumbo."

He reached over and put his empty bottle in the wooden drink box. He pulled out his pipe and packed it. He struck a match and pulled on the flame until the smoke started flowing. "Well, Mr. Charlie, I'm not sure, exactly. And what I think I know, I prob'ly ought'n tell you."

I didn't say anything. him being a grownup and me being a boy. I couldn't argue with him, and I couldn't tell him what I'd heard.

It had stopped snowing and the sun started breaking through the thinning clouds. We probably would have to go to school tomorrow.

Chapter 26

THE MONTH OF MAY APPROACHED. SCHOOL WOULD BE OUT in a month. Oh Lord, how the event began to rise like the sun in the morning. Freedom.

Chambers Gallagher had been convicted again in March for the killing of the guard. The trial had lasted two weeks and he was sentenced to life. However, his initial sentence of death had to be carried out. Then he could serve the life sentence for killing the guard. The execution which had been originally set back in December had been reset for June 19. The newspaper reminded us of the date: the first anniversary of the Rosenberg execution.

It also printed some information for anyone interested, notes of personal possession. One item jarred our attention. The night Gallagher was arrested he had in his possession a dozen silver dollars, all 1907 mint. The rumor spread immediately from one end of Stonewall Drive to the other. There had been, indeed, bootlegger money buried at the Big House, and Gallagher must have been there at some time.

The police squelched such gossip, issuing another press release that more than likely the silver dollars were stolen from the antique dealer he had robbed and murdered. Gallagher had simply picked them up from some previous hiding place. Daddy said the police passed this information to prevent a stampede to the area by imaginative youngsters like us.

The old letters we had found turned into nothing valuable, like the pin. Henry and Buck, who were studying Mississippi history in school, asked their teacher, Miss Kyle about the letters. She told them partial correspondence, such as we had, was not uncommon in deserted farmhouses. In any event, they had been so damaged by water, except for the few lines of script, there was nothing for a museum to care about or an historian to use for research. Ronny Erl stuck them in his dresser drawer.

I had not said anything to anyone about Franklin and Joe's conversation. I knew nothing could be done to Joe because he hadn't done anything. And his daddy had long since died. I didn't know if Franklin had tried any more hoodooing, but the area close to the Big House and across the land where it stood had been partially cleared with dozers for the right of way. I think Joe probably kept an eye on Franklin.

I had not even told Henry about the afternoon when I had returned to get my knife. Once, I thought about telling Katy Jean. I wanted to tell someone. I didn't though. But she would have kept my secret. I knew that. I hadn't seen Joe since that day, and I had tried to avoid him because I feared I might blurt out what I had overheard.

I rode my bike up to the Tote-Sum after school just as Gifford's brother, Larry, drove up in front of the ice house in his dusty and dented Ford pickup. A crowd of people gathered quickly. Anybody who had ever hunted gathered to see Larry's pride and joy—his redbone coonhound, Lucky. Lucky was going on nine months old. Larry grabbed her around the head and gave her a big kiss.

I had seen the same pleasure from Daddy when Henry or I did something in front of other people that pleased him. Of course, he didn't haul off and kiss us. You would have thought Gifford's wife had given birth to that dog herself. Three or four men were standing by the bed of the truck commenting on Lucky, and each giving her a pat on the head when she nuzzled toward them.

"She is pretty," Larry said. "This little bitch is gonna tree a lotta coons." He beamed. "I'm gonna breed her, too."

"Whereabouts you gonna work her?" someone asked.

"I'm gonna take her over to home. I'm pretty familiar with them woods. But I been training and workin her out there off Old Canton, where old Joe takes Gumbo sometimes. I think old Gumbo is proud of his little girl, Lucky." Joe had sold his single pick from Franklin's litter to Larry Gifford.

I thought about our collie, Streety. He was old and tired. Not a hunter, a companion. It was his job. His life's work was Katy Jean—*doppelganger*—that's what Minnie called him one time. When I asked, she told me the same thing all grownups in my family would tell me: "Get the dictionary." Daddy would never let us have a hunting dog as a yard dog. A hunting dog hunted—it didn't lie around waiting to die. It didn't matter, anyway. Streety didn't have time to hunt.

I remember Miss Ashley reading to us about George Washington and his plantation in Virginia. She said George would walk all around his plantation and look at his animals. He would greet them as he would greet friends, she said. She said he even had each of his hunting hounds specially named and as part of a test she made us memorize them: *Tipler, Truelove, Sweetlips, Singer, Music, Trial* and *Taster.* My mother thought it a wonderful idea Miss Ashley had had. My Daddy said he wasn't sure how useful it would be learning all of George Washington's hound dogs. Big Daddy said it sounded more useful than memorizing the names of the Great Lakes.

Miss Ashley said farmers, *agrarians,* were of such fiber, and they cared for every living thing God had put in their care.

Once, when Ronny Erl and I were riding home on our bikes, an old colored man passed us carrying his mule in a trailer with a wooden floor. The mule's leg crashed through a weak board in the floorboard and shattered as it hit the asphalt road. The mule's horrible braying and screaming could've been heard in New Orleans.

Anyway, two or three cars stopped, and one of the men took out a rifle. He offered to shoot the mule for the colored man. Burly's police car pulled up and Burly, cussing and fuming, stopped the man. "Nobody's gonna shoot a gun inside the city jus' to kill some damn nigger's mule," he roared.

The old colored man took his axe and smashed his mule in the head, putting him out of his misery. He was still crying when the wrecker hauled the trailer and mule away. I didn't want to cry in front of Ronny Erl, so I held back until in bed later that night. I actually prayed God would take the mule to Heaven. I never told Katy Jean about it.

And it seemed the same with Lucky. She was more than a dog; a member of the family to Larry Gifford; somebody to be cared for. I guess it had something to do with what Big Daddy meant when he told me one time most everybody in Mississippi had farm roots. Of course, I couldn't think of many people who didn't like dogs, except my mother said they make some people sneeze. I watched as each man around the truck bed stuck his arm out to give Lucky a rub or a pat. And each time Lucky responded with a tail slapping the air with love.

Joe walked over from the ice cooler where he had been checking the ice supply. He had come in the back door and had noticed all the enthusiasm for the dogs.

"Hello, Joe," Larry Gifford said.

"Hello, Mistuh Gifford. I b'lieve dat pup I sold you is a big hit 'round here. Y'all gonna spoil him."

"Yeah, I'm prob'ly the baddest at spoilin' him. But she's learnin fast, so I got no complaints." He pulled out a cigarette and lit up.

"Say, Mistuh Gifford, It kinda late to be deliverin', but since it's Friday I thought I'd see if you need any ice before the weekend. I jus' now checked the cooler an' y'all seem a bit low."

Gifford stuck his head in the cooler for a second. "Yeah, Joe. Maybe giv' me another 450 pounds. That oughta last us 'til Monday."

Joe pulled at a load of ice with his tongs while I held the cooler door for him. The big door slammed. "I ain't seen you lately, Mr. Charlie. You must been busy wid school. You gonna work fo yo daddy dis summer? Bet he could keep you busy at de warehouse."

"I might. Some, anyway." My eyes were focused on the floor. I wondered if he thought I had been avoiding him.

I never thought Joe old before now. Fifty-something, he had always looked like Jersey Joe Walcott. Now he looked like *Old Black Joe* in the song about the old worn-out Negro man. Now I realized, although he could have been a great ballplayer like Willie Mays, he was merely a guy who hauled ice and did odd jobs and collected and sold junk.

He didn't even have any land anymore. Yankees had stolen his baseball career, and moonshiners and bootleggers had stolen his land. Most anybody could figure out the baseball part, but I was one of the few who knew about the land. I hated to see Joe in a pitiful way.

"Well, I'm gonna be haulin ice 'round. 'Cause I believe we gonna have a hot summer. A hot summer in Mississippi be as sure as a coon runs from a hound dog."

"You gonna be workin' Gumbo? Maybe chase some bobcats?" I said.

"Might be workin' him some. Git him ready for next fall." He paused a minute. I wasn't sure if he were taking a breath after lifting the ice, or if he were thinking a bit longer about my second question. "I don't think he need to be sniffin' out no more bobcats."

"Cause they're dangerous?" I still remembered what Franklin had said about the hoodoo.

Joe laid his ice tongs on top of a stack of milk boxes, and pulled his leather serape over his head. "Well, Mr. Charlie, dat's part of it. An' bobcats can be dangerous for a lot of reasons."

"Are they dangerous because of hoodooing? And buryin' in holes?" I blurted.

"Why child, wad you thinkin'? Wad you been hearin'?"

I was afraid I'd scared him. A little white boy knowing about a colored man and his problems, a boy who knew about somebody getting killed, even if it had been almost fifty years before.

"I heard you and Franklin talking way back in February, that day up at the Big House." He had a blank stare. "I wasn't sneakin' around or nothin', I was upstairs trying to find my pocketknife when y'all came in. I was scared because I was all by myself and I didn't know who y'all were at first."

He set the tongs down on the ice. In the cooler, I could see his breath when he finally spoke. "Well, I guess if you heard, you heard. And, I guess you ain't told yo momma or daddy since ain't nobody said nuthin' to me."

His eyes had asked a question. I wondered if he was afraid I'd tell the police. Somebody like Burly. "I haven't told anybody. I wasn't going to. I mean, your daddy's dead and everything. And I heard you say he killed a moonshiner when he hit him. But he didn't mean to. I mean, didn't mean to kill him." I stopped for a second. "Is Franklin crazy?"

Joe picked up an ice pick and started chipping a block. "It's gettin' cold in here," he said.

The inside handle clicked and Lewis pulled open the heavy cooler door. "Gangway ever'body. I need a case of Co-Colas."

Joe picked up his tongs and stepped aside. "Well, Mr. Charlie, we better git outta dis workin' man's way. Come on, let's git on out."

I followed him to his truck and asked him a second time, "Is he? Franklin? Is he crazy?"

He climbed up in the cab. His eyes averted downward to me. Finally an answer. "Mr. Franklin jus' an ol' man now. He prob'ly ain't no more crazier 'n me or you. He got some good points and some bad ones. He kinda like Mr. Burly—he got some irritation in his soul dat jus' want let go."

"Irritation? What you mean?"

"Sumin' dat botherin' you. Sumin' won't let go. Mr. Burly be fretful 'bout colored people. And Mr. Franklin got vexed

'bout white trash folks dat stole land from us colored folks."
Joe pulled out a red bandanna and wiped his brow. His
huge arm rested on the open window. "But wad happened,
happened a long time ago and dere ain't no goin' back.
Mr. Franklin got dis idea dat he can find some bootleggin'
money out dere and buy back dat land. And he think he
can hoodoo and hex any highway, or anybody makin' highways comin' through dat land. He jus' won't giv' up. So he
mos'ly makin' his-self crazy, I s'pose. He ain't gonna find no
money. And like I say, der ain't no goin' back. Jus' like dere
ain't no goin' back for my daddy and wad he done—right
or wrong."

I wished I was old enough to say something smart—as
smart as someone who knew that Tarzan didn't belong in
the Amazon; as smart as Miss Ashley who could correct
Boyd for poor English; as smart as Big Daddy who could
talk about a lot of different things at one time and have
them make sense. Finally I blurted, "I'll never tell on your
daddy. I never will."

I saw sweat. As the sun beat down I saw those same little
rainbows I had seen on him last summer at the vacant lot.
He turned the engine over and revved it, then after grinding
the gears, he pulled out of the parking lot.

Chapter 27

A WEEK TO GO BEFORE SCHOOL ENDED. SATURDAY WE drove down to the fairgrounds to watch the baseball game. It was early in the season. The Jackson Senators were a minor league team in the Cotton States League. Most of the teams were from Mississippi, Arkansas, and Louisiana.

Today we were playing the Meridian Millers. Meridian had a pretty good team but the Senators were doing okay today. Eleven to three in the sixth inning. There were several hundred people at the game but the stands weren't filled, so there were a lot of empty seats.

There were guys who would mosey through the stands selling peanuts and cold drinks. You would constantly hear their calls, "Peanuts, hot dogs, cold drinks, cold beer!" The sounds of baseball Daddy would say.

There were a couple of people two or three rows in front of us who had ordered five or six beers each already, a man and a woman. I don't know if they were married or not, but they seemed happy drinking their beer. And they seemed happier now in the sixth inning than they had in the first inning. My mother had contorted her face for them, and though they hadn't been cussing or anything, they had been loud. The woman dropped a belch once sounding like a stuck hog. I started laughing and Mother turned on me. Daddy shook his head.

The Senators played downtown at the fairgrounds. Actually, the field had been laid out off the midway in a big open area where the field and diamond had been constructed. The grandstand rose up three tiers of steps on the third base side, where most of the fans sat to watch the game.

By the time the fair came to town in October baseball season had ended and the grandstand served as a viewing area where such events as greased-pig contests were held, as well as show horses and other things. Almost every year a drawing of some kind took place, and one year we all were excited because everybody in our family had a number on their ticket and Katy Jean won the fifth and final prize.

The first prize was a John Deere tractor and the other prizes something less valuable, down to Katy Jean's fifth place prize, which was a twenty-five pound sack of fertilizer. She accepted it, and smiled. She told Mother she was happy because it was the "stuff that grows things." Katy Jean was like that: she could always find happiness.

On the first base side there were the bleachers, which were put up for the baseball season and taken down afterwards. My mother said they had to put all the "ruffians and ne'er-do-wells" somewhere, but she preferred Henry and I not sit there. Naturally, one day when we went by ourselves we sat there. The Senators had a playing manager by the name of Duke Doolittle. He also caught for the Senators. So when they were in the field Mr. Doolittle came about as close to the bleachers as you could get. When the Senators did something bad, the men in the bleachers would blame it on the manager. One time after a bad play a man yelled out, waving his beer bottle in the air, "That's the way to go Mister Duke Doo-Doo!"

Today I had come to the game with Mother and Daddy while Henry and Katy Jean didn't come. Katy Jean stayed at Minnie's house, watching her shell butterbeans. My mother really loved baseball as much as Daddy did, and all sports really, especially if the teams were from Jackson or Mississippi.

Henry didn't come today because he had promised Don Holder he would help Don and his daddy with some work their new church needed. I think Henry would rather have come to the game but Mother told him it was *thoughtful* of him to make the sacrifice. A real sacrifice required at least a little pain. My mother and daddy mostly gave good advice, but I think Henry still would have rather been at the game instead of painting door frames at a church. Billy said Jesus would have been a great shortstop if they'd had baseball back then, because Jesus was Jewish.

Louie Shoffel, our left fielder and one of our favorite players, had hit two home runs over the Falstaff Beer sign on the center field fence. One time when Louie took off down the base path trying to beat out an infield hit, his baseball cap flew off and we could see his bald head. Afterwards he seemed more like a grownup to me than a ball player. But he was still a favorite.

The whole outfield fence had signs advertising things like Golden Crust Bread and Kyle Brothers Auto Shop, and all kinds of other things. Mr. Cohen had an advertisement for Cohen's Jewelers. One sign had a picture of a pretty lady smiling which showed what a good smile you could have if you used Ipana Tooth Paste. But somebody had gone out to the fence when nobody was around and painted one of her front teeth black so it looked like she had a missing front tooth. The first time you saw it, you laughed, but afterwards you got used to it.

When my mother saw things like that she would say something like, "I better not ever hear of you and Henry doing that to somebody else's property."

I had asked Daddy why he and Big Daddy didn't put a sign saying McCoy Lumber Company, Dependable Lumber, like they had printed on their stationery and pencils. He told me they were too expensive. And signs had to pay for themselves. I wasn't sure what he meant, but I always thought it would have been nice to have my family name up on the fence of the Jackson Senators.

We sat down toward the end of the grandstand close to the colored section, and when somebody hit a foul ball down the left field line I turned and saw Joe sitting among the twenty or thirty colored people. He waved, and I waved back.

Every once in a while I would watch the guys way across the first base line in the bleachers to see if I could tell if they were yelling at the umpires and the players. And I'm sure they were screaming at Mr. Doolittle plenty. I tried to focus my ears to tell if they were calling him *Doo-Doo* again, but they were too far.

Ronny Erl and his daddy came over to where we were sitting. Ronny Erl bit into a peanut in order to crack it. Mr. McGinnis gave him a light smack on top of his baseball cap.

"Don't do that with your teeth. Crack one peanut against the other in your hand. That's what hands are for: *work*. Teeth are for eating. You'll ruin your teeth and I don't wanna have a big dental bill." Mr. McGinnis was like most parents, always talking about bills they didn't want to have. He started talking to Daddy about some business stuff.

I held out my hand for Ronny Earl to give me a peanut. He dropped two in my hand so I'd have two to crack. "I didn't know y'all were comin' to the game," I said.

"Yeah, I was up at the hardware store when daddy decided to come. He asked Red if he could take care of things for the rest of the afternoon. Say, where's Henry?"

"Ah, he's helpin' Don Couples do some church stuff with his daddy."

"Where's Buck?'

"At home or at the store, I guess. He jus' didn't wanna come. He may be helpin' Red."

The crowd erupted and stood, as the crack of the bat had alerted everyone a ball had been tagged. Sure enough our first baseman, Banks McDougal, had cracked one over the right field fence. With a man on, we led 13–3. The man-half of the pair in front of us exploded: "Boy, he slapped the shit out of it." An immediate eruption spewed vomit all over the seat below us. I thought Mother was going to have a seizure. Daddy shook his head and glanced at Mr. McGinnis.

I think either of them would have said something about using vulgar language around women and children except the man had become so sick his lady-friend, or wife or whatever, started leading him out, talking to him as they left. "We need to get you something to eat, sugar."

I decided to go over and talk to Joe. Ronny Erl said he had to got to the bathroom down under the grandstand. "I'm 'bout to pee in my pants."

"I'm going over to see Joe," I said. "Come over there when you get back."

Joe sat next to the rail separating the sections. There was a much older colored man with white hair sitting in front of him, clutching a bottle of Falstaff in his hand, peanut shells in his lap, his head tilted back, his eyes closed, sound asleep. Daddy told me one time baseball was a relaxing game to watch. This guy appeared relaxed.

"The Senators are doing pretty good today, huh?" I said to Joe. "Louie is really havin' a pretty good day."

"Yeah, he doin' okay Mr. Charlie. But hittin' dem home runs ain't enuff always. He need to get his average up. He jus be hittin' 'bout .255. He need to be hittin' more'n dat."

I took a swig of my Orange Nehi. "I think as long as he hits home runs he's a good player."

"You here with yo momma and daddy?" he asked.

"Yep. They're o'er there…" I pointed back to the white section, "trying to get another place to sit."

He strained his eyes to where I had pointed. "Whats-a-matter? A post blockin' their view?"

"Naw," I said. "Some guy jus' vomited in front of them and they weren't so happy 'bout stayin' where they were. But I don't think we're gonna stay much longer with the Senators so far ahead. We prob'ly will leave before the ninth inning."

"I see Mr. McGinnis over dere. I guess he's got some help to run de hardware store today if he's takin' off for the ballgame."

"Yep. Red and Buck are down there, I think," I said.

Joe rubbed his chin then set his cap on the back of his head. "Well, where's yo friend Ronny Erl?"

"He went to the bathroom. Be back in a minute."

He pulled out his pipe, packed it, and lit it. "Back on de farm when I wuz a boy we didn't have no Saturday's off.

Sometimes we didn't have no Sunday's off. Course I wuz only a bit of a boy when we left the farm. But dere weren't much time off."

"Who owned the farm?" I asked. "Was it yours?"

"Well, I'm not rightly sure who owned it. I jus' know we worked and hunted on it." It wuz as if we had never talked before. He didn't care about what I'd heard because he trusted me to never tell. He changed the subject. "Well, you boys still in the junk bisness? Or y'all moved on to bigger things?"

"We went outta business," I said.

He laughed. "Well, maybe it jus' not yo callin' in life." He took a couple of puffs. "What 'bout dat little Jewish friend of y'all. He talked 'bout makin' it big in rabbit tobacco. What's his name…?"

"Billy Cohen," I said. "That's his sign out there on the right field fence."

"Aw yeah. His daddy owns dat big jewelry store downtown."

When he said that, I thought about the pin, and it made me think of the letters we had found at the Big House; letters with the name Washington mentioned. And the name Isaiah mentioned. And, after we found them, the conversation I had overheard between Franklin and him. Things I wanted to talk about, but I couldn't bring myself to.

"Do you come here much? To watch the Senators, I mean?" I asked.

"Oh, I come ever' now and then. Can't spend as much money as it cost here; fifty cents jus' to git in. Den a hotdog and a Co-Cola. By de time I leave I spent over eighty cents."

The old guy in front of him started drifting to one side as if he was about to fall over. Joe reached out put his hand on his arm and prodded him back upright, then took the Falstaff out of his hand and put it down on the seat next to him. Half asleep, the man swatted a fly off his nose.

"When you played in Nashville did you get free hotdogs?"

"Oh my goodness, no. We wuz jus' paid a little bit to play. Anythin' we got we had to pay for, except to get in the park," he said. "We got in free for dat."

"You think you'll ever get out of the junk and ice-haulin' business and go back to farmin'? Maybe get you some land?"

The man in front of Joe had started softly snoring. "Naw, too late in life for dat. De only time I get out on any land is when I take old Gumbo. Be nice to have my own land, but I guess I'll be drivin' dat ice truck 'til I die. Maybe pick up a little junk ever once in a while."

The Senators shortstop made a diving catch for an out, and the fans jumped to their feet and cheered. I almost spilled my Nehi jumping to see.

"Watch out, young-un, you 'bout to lose yo soda." Joe pointed to the White Section. "Yo daddy's wavin' at you. And I see Mr. Ronny Erl over dere. I b'lieve y'all are 'bout to go."

I turned. "Okay, I'll see y'all later, Joe."

"Well, I sho hope so, young-un. I sho hope so."

Before the season was over, Louis got traded.

Chapter 28

A T FIVE O'CLOCK WE DROVE UP TO MINNIE'S. WE parked in the shade out front which covered most of the street, the sun almost down. The two huge pecan trees were like giant umbrellas spreading over the yard, shading almost every inch and extending into the street. The pecan trees had begun swelling in March and the buds were showing what would be a large crop in the fall. By then the branches would bow downward, each pecan reminding me of a tiny green egg with its husk. There would be hundreds and hundreds of pecans to gather after they fell.

This late in the afternoon I knew Minnie would ask us to stay for supper, and since Henry would be eating with the Holders, Mother wouldn't have to worry about him getting a good meal. She forever concerned herself we get a *good* meal, she put it. To my knowledge, Henry and I never had had a *bad* meal as far as we were concerned—except at school, maybe. And of course squash.

When we climbed the steps to the house we could hear the sounds of the piano playing. Minnie could play it just by sitting down and punching the keys. The piano, a baby grand, had the name Steinway painted on it, and had been in her house forever.

We could walk in without notice since we could see both she and Katy Jean through the window, but I loved the doorbell. It was loud like a fire bell and fun to ring.

Minnie taught music to lots of people around town, and she had even written some songs. She could play almost anything and often played songs we loved like "Old Smoky" and "Sewanee River." My personal favorite was "Barbara Allen," which Minnie would sing as she played.

She would play anything anybody asked but one she played often was Daddy's favorite, "Casey Jones." He had first heard it as a little boy and when Henry and I would ride with him in the car he would often sing it. Minnie would start on the piano, then point to Daddy; a signal for him to sing.

I guess he loved it so much because it expressed a Mississippi hero: Casey Jones, a railroad engineer. He had been killed when his engine met another engine head on, but he had warned his fireman, a colored man named Sim, to jump in time. When Minnie played it Katy Jean smiled, and I thought Minnie played "Casey Jones" a lot for Katy Jean.

One time Minnie had told us the story of Beethoven and how he demonstrated no matter what handicaps life throws a man's way, there is a way to overcome if you love what you do. Beethoven, though deaf, wrote some of the greatest music ever written, she had told us. She played "Moonlight Sonata" often, and we loved it almost as much as "Dixie."

Her house had aged over decades, but I think everybody's grandparents' house has an old history. Old people had old stuff. But my mother's childhood home offered a special place to Henry and Katy Jean and me. There were old photographs lining the hallway, and more on small lamp tables in the living room and many on the piano. Photos of individuals; some of uncles or cousins; photos of groups of family members, most dead and gone to heaven, we believed. And a bookshelf with everything from works of Samuel Johnson, to Jefferson Davis' *Rise and Fall of the Confederate Government;* and *The Story of My Life,* Helen Keller's autobiography; and *King Arthur and the Knights of the Round Table.* And a must reading she had told us, when we were old enough to understand: *A Defense of Virginia, and the South* by R. L. Dabney, who'd been Stonewall Jackson's chaplain and chief of staff.

"Well, who won the game?" was the first thing Minnie asked.

"The Senators!" I yelled it before anyone else could.

"Well, that's wonderful. I'm glad y'all had a good time."

"Of course, we can't be sure," I added. "We left before the game ended because the Senators were so far ahead."

She turned on the piano bench and pointed at me. "The game's not over 'til the last man's out. That's what your daddy always says."

"I'm pretty sure we won anyway," I insisted. "And Louie Shoffel hit two home runs and Banks McDowell hit one. Louie is great."

She turned around on the bench, facing the keys. "Well, they're going to trade Louie if he doesn't get his average up." She knew baseball, too. Having started following the Black Sox scandal in 1919 she had told us, she took an interest in the resurgence of baseball and began reading the sports section every day. I thought it interesting how Grandpa Charlie had died in the same year she started following baseball.

My mother changed the subject. "Did you get all your butterbeans shelled? I realize y'all had a lot. If you haven't finished, we'll help."

I really didn't like the way she had said *"we'll."* It sounded a lot like it might include me. I would as soon watch that guy at the ball park puke again as shell butterbeans. Fortunately I was saved.

"Oh, no thanks, honey. I've finished all of them. Now I'm going to get up in a minute and fix y'all some supper."

"Oh no, Julia," Daddy said. "You don't need to be feedin' us." Julia was Minnie's real first name. I seldom thought about it. Of course, it was one of those polite things to say. I knew all along we were going to eat there.

"Now I have plenty. And there's still some leftover chicken and some meatloaf that's going to waste. So y'all just don't worry about it. You said Henry is eating with friends, didn't you?"

"Oh, yes," my mother replied. "He's been helping Pastor Holder at his new church out toward our house. Henry and Charlie are friends with Don, the pastor's son. They just live a couple of houses down from us. I think they've been doing some painting at the church. So the Holders are havin' Henry over this evenin' for supper."

"What'd Joe have to say?" Daddy asked me. "I saw you ov'er there talking' with him. Was he enjoyin' the ballgame?"

"Yes, sir, I guess so. Seemed like he did." I sat down next to Minnie and Katy Jean on the piano stool. "Joe played in the Negro Leagues a long time ago. Did y'all know that?"

"I don't think I ever knew it," Mother said. "But I don't keep up with things the way y'all do."

"Do you mean Joe Washington?" Minnie asked. "That colored boy who hauls ice around?"

"Yes, ma'am," I said.

"Yes, I knew it." Daddy finally squeezed his answer in. "Played back in the twenties, I believe. Not sure who he played for. There were several of those Negro teams and leagues. Most were up North."

"Was he tellin y'all something about the ballgame?" Mother asked. She always showed interest in what somebody might have said to us at the ballpark, with the *Duke Doo-Doos* afoot.

"Yes, ma'am. Some things. But mostly we talked about Gumbo and stuff like that." I reached out and plunked a couple of keys on the piano. I hit the black ones then the white ones to see what sounds they would make.

"Charlie, don't bang on the piano," Minnie said. "If you want to learn to play, we can set up time for you to take lessons. Saturday's are a good day for me. But a piano is not a toy."

I moved over to the couch. "No, ma'am. I guess not." I turned the subject back to baseball. "Joe was talking about the players and all that. Just wondered if y'all knew he had played when he was young."

"Well, he's pretty knowledgeable, I imagine," Daddy said.

"Think he could play in the Major Leagues with Robinson and Doby and those other colored men?" I asked. "I believe he's strong enough. Big Daddy said he prob'ly could. Red said so, too. And his daddy was a scout for the White Sox back when Joe was younger."

"Well, I don't know," Daddy said. "He's older than I am now, and you've got to be young to play. It's a young man's game. I imagine his playing days are long behind him. But he mighta been able to, back when he was younger."

"How come they didn't have black players in the Major leagues before now?" I asked.

"Well, up North, where all the Major League teams are, they don't want them playing together. Same thing down here. We think it would be better if they played with their own people."

"Red said his daddy thought they might let coloreds play in the Major Leagues back then, for a while. But nothing ever come of it."

"*Came.*" From my mother.

"Came of it," I corrected myself.

"I believe someone told me his father, Isaiah, left for Chicago to become a prize fighter," Minnie said. "I always wondered why they left the land they owned. At least that's what I understand, they owned it. They weren't sharecropping. They had some good land. Why go off up to Chicago and get into that kind of business? I can't imagine who was giving them guidance back then. Of course, there was the story about the big whiskey still buried and hidden up there. I never did learn where that story started."

My secret about Joe and Isaiah and the moonshiner. I turned around on the piano bench to avoid anyone seeing my face. Among Minnie's many talents was the art of needlepoint. Behind the piano on the wall I had turned to face a framed quotation:

To keep your secret is wisdom; but to expect others to keep it is folly.

Samuel Johnson

My mother held up her hand and said, "Now, Mother you and Randy don't need to talk about these things anymore. These children are not quite ready for talk about these things." Daddy and Minnie agreed, making it unanimous. Katy Jean smiled at me. I wondered what Mother meant by "these things."

Minnie pushed the piano bench back and started for the kitchen. "Come on in the kitchen with me, honey," she said to my mother. "We'll start fixin' something." Minnie turned to Daddy and Katy Jean and me. "'Bout six we'll eat, if that's okay with y'all."

I bound myself, to never give up what I knew.

Chapter 29

SUMMER MEANT BASEBALL AND FISHING AND SWIMMING. And those things had their own smell. Again, a special smell, a smell of summer. Everything I came to be familiar with seemed to have its own smell. I was my own coon dog.

The previous spring the conclusion to a famous trial had taken place, and even the least of us heard about it though mostly grownups talked about it. I mostly read the papers for the comics and box scores, but the front page had huge photos of the Rosenbergs.

This spring, the conclusion of another trial had taken place and set off alarms both North and South. First in Kansas, by the Supreme Court ruling in the Brown versus Topeka Kansas Board of Education. It's effects would be greater than the Rosenberg's.

On Saturday my mother and daddy wanted us to go over to the Farmer's Market, a place where a bunch of the farmers brought all kinds of crops to sell in Jackson. They would have all sorts of things from watermelons to tomatoes to sugar cane and beets and carrots to just about anything you could think of; and butterbeans and snap beans, too. I hated them the most, because I had to help shell them. A boring job and also they weren't very good to eat raw.

Unlike pecans where you could shell one, eat one, so your work didn't go unrewarded.

My mother would say, "Now Henry and Charlie, I'm gonna let y'all help me shell some beans." It sounded like we were being rewarded, like letting us go to the picture show with her or something.

In a huge parking lot a large metal roof covered a long raised platform. There, trucks could unload boxes of crops and display them for customers. My mother ambled along, poking at the useless things like squash and beets while Daddy, with Henry and me, strolled by the wooden bins thumping watermelons. Daddy seemed to understand the art when he thumped them, while I had no idea and just did it because it might make people think I, as a ten-year-old, had some expertise about something. It had something to do with how ripe they were, but that's all I could figure.

Watermelons were not only good to eat, they provided a nice competitive game. In addition to being one of the great jelly sandwich stompers, Grover also had the record for longest watermelon seed-spitting distance, though Henry had always maintained it was wind-aided.

"How 'bout this one," I said. "It's huge. A monster. Can we get it?"

"I don't know," Daddy said. "We'll see how much it costs. And we need to ask your momma. She may want another one. Or she may not even want one today. And we're not buyin' something jus' to be buying it."

"Here's a ripe one," Henry said. I don't think Henry could tell any better than I could but he thumped it and spoke as if it were a certainty.

"Maybe," Daddy said, thumping it himself. Henry frowned at the *maybe*.

Everybody loved watermelons, especially if they had been iced down until they were very cold. They were also good even when they weren't cold. One of our neighbors who had a vegetable garden also had a watermelon patch. Last year he had let us boys have a free one as soon as they ripened. He told us watermelon plants were brought over by slaves from Africa maybe three hundred years ago.

All the stuff at the Farmer's Market came from farms all over Mississippi, brought in to sell. But a lot of people, white and colored, grew different fruits and vegetables in their own back yards right in town. And some lived a little bit outside the city limits and raised crops for their own families and even had livestock, too. The Farmer's Market was kind of a huge outdoor store anybody could come to.

Across the expansive asphalt parking lot we could hear shouts and cries coming from beyond a storage building, as if there were some sort of game being played behind it. We couldn't see what caused the commotion.

"Daddy, can Henry and I run over there and see what's going on?" I asked.

"Naw, y'all jus' stay here. We're jus' gonna stay for a few minutes. I don't wanna have to go scrambling 'round trying to locate y'all when we're ready to go."

We shopped, and thumped and sniffed and smelled for about fifteen minutes when Billy Cohen came up. The shouts from beyond had subsided.

"Hello, Billy," Daddy said. "Your daddy here?"

"No, sir. I came over on my bike."

I noticed he had come from the area of the cries and shouts. "What was all the shouting about?" I asked.

"Ol' Boyd Hastings got in a fight with some colored guy," he said.

"What about?" Daddy said. Mother frowned. She didn't like to hear about fights.

"The colored guy said The Royal American Shows cheat colored folk at the fair. Pretty good fight though. The colored guy lost a couple of teeth, and Boyd got a pretty good busted nose. Bled like crazy. Prob'ly broke."

"Let's go on home, Randy," Mother said. "I don't want to hear any more."

The final day of school came. A great day. Getting out of school might have been the greatest holiday ever made, except for Christmas. The sixth graders were allowed to leave early and go on a picnic. In the morning they had kind of a graduating ceremony. They marched into the auditorium singing *God of Our Fathers* while the whole school plus parents and teachers sat in attendance. Mrs. Thomas made some comments about what a grand group they had been and they were now going into junior high, a new adventure for them. We all stood when we sang *Dixie,* and afterwards the sixth grade class left for the rest of the day for their picnic. The rest of us returned to clean out our desks and wait for the final bell.

I had done my time after school for all my infractions. By the spring Miss Ashley had a backlog of all my things for which I, or some of my friends and I, had been forced to stay after school for, or having to write a hundred times or more: *I will not put chewing gum in the pencil sharpener* or *I will not flip Jello with my spoon across the table in the cafeteria.* We never did have a real fire, though Boyd considered starting one in one of the garbage cans. But he was afraid it might backfire and burn the school down and he would have to go to summer school. And he was already two years behind.

As it turned out it didn't matter. Boyd Hastings was the only guy I ever knew who was expelled from grammar school. One day Mary Ellen popped off about *her cousin the lawyer* once too often. Boyd turned around and shouted, "Well, nobody really cares about your damn shyster son-of-a-bitchin' cousin."

I hadn't imagined Miss Ashley could get so mad. She dragged Boyd by the ear down to Mrs. Thomas' office and it was the last I ever saw of him at Boyduling. It erupted as something of a scandal for days afterwards among teachers and parents, that some *youngster* would use that kind of language. Minnie's reaction: "Now, who are Boyd's people?"

I had the whole summer ahead. But first, I could clean out my desk of old notebook papers and old art pictures and folders containing junk you were supposed to keep track of during the year. And now you could destroy it like some great feast of destruction.

Miss Ashley told us how much she had enjoyed teaching us and would always remember each one of us. She said she would be back next year teaching the fifth grade, and we were to remember when we became sixth graders we would be something special, so we needed to remember and not do the silly things some of us had done from time-to-time as fifth-graders. I'm sure I noticed her eyes focused on Tim and me during her goodbye speech. But I think she still liked us anyway and had recovered from her disappointment.

Some of the class brought little gifts, ones probably their parents had bought, and put them on Miss Ashley's desk. Mary Ellen put down one wrapped-up about the size of a torpedo, and smiled as she backed away. Tim leaned over and whispered that he dared me to superglue it to the desk after we came back from the cafeteria.

"Now it's time for dinner so let's make our last trip to the cafeteria a good one," Miss Ashley said. "No talking in line and no rough-housing." Again a focus on Tim and me. "I don't want to keep anybody after school on the last day."

And with our instructions we made our way to *the food trough from hell,* an expression Henry and all the older guys had labeled the cafeteria. I think Benny Stephens made up the name. Benny had started cussing very early in his school career. Maybe even in the fourth grade because I remember he was the first guy I ever heard say *shit.*

When I asked my mother what *shit* meant she opened her mouth wide like she would scream, then put both hands over it. When she recovered she told me never to use that word again. Then she told me to go see Daddy about it. When I asked him, he called it trashy, vulgar language and even a fool could talk like that. It didn't prove anything he had said. When he asked me where I had heard it, I told him I had heard it yelled out at recess one day, but I wasn't sure who had said it. I was afraid to tattle on Benny, because I didn't want to be an outcast my first year at Boyduling. Daddy had told me not to use that word again.

Anyway, we had our last dinner for the school year. At least we had strawberry short cake for dessert.

I stopped by July's room on the way back. The door was locked. Even if July was off fixing something or mopping something, the door was always open. As I jiggled the doorknob over and over a voice called my name.

"Now, Charlie McCoy, are you supposed to be here or back in your room?"

"Well, in my room, I guess." I turned and saw Mrs. Thomas, the principal.

"You guess?" Her voice raised a bit.

"Yes, ma'am. But I was jus' gonna tell July good bye."

"Well, July is off today." Her voice lowered. But this time she didn't have the fierce gaze that could make a third grader pee in his pants. She seemed almost like my mother for a minute. "He had to be with his family. They have to make preparations for a funeral."

"Who died?"

"Well, it'll probably be in the newspapers but his cousin, Franklin, drowned in the Pearl River." She turned me around and gave me a gentle push in the back. "Now you run along to Miss Ashley's room."

The magic time of two-thirty arrived and it seemed like forever getting there. Finally, at two-twenty Miss Ashley announced with a big smile, "I am going to let y'all go ten minutes early on this last day. Class is excused until September, and y'all have a wonderful summer."

The stampede to the door exploded like one of those prison riots in a James Cagney picture show, except for me. I walked slowly. I hadn't completely absorbed what Mrs. Thomas had told me.

At supper I announced our janitor at school had been absent because he had to prepare for a funeral. I asked Daddy if the paper had anything about it.

"Well, the story I read didn't have much information. Just said a Negro man, known only as Franklin, had been found over in Rankin County in the river. No evidence of foul play. The sheriff said the best guess was maybe he had been fishing, maybe checkin' trot lines, and fell into the water. An eddy or whirlpool must've sucked him under."

"And he was your janitor's relative?" Mother asked.

"Yes, ma'am. A cousin or something."

"A lot of folks have heard about him," Daddy said. "Never seemed quite right in the head. Joe's redbone sired puppies for his little redbone female. I hope he sold or gave away all those pups. There were eight or nine, I believe They're all eight or nine months old by now. I believe Gifford up at the Tote-Sum has one."

Katy Jean didn't seem hungry.

The first day without any school to go to, I hopped on my bike and headed up to the Tote-Sum. I wanted to see Joe when he made his ice delivery. Gifford had several customers and I stayed back by the rear door drinking an R.C. I watched Lewis battling the bottles and waited for Joe.

About noon he drove up. With his leather serape pulled over his head and his Jersey Joe stance and strength, he pulled an enormous load of ice down the ramp. He turned as I came up. "Well, if you up here in de mornin' it must mean school's out."

"Friday was the last day."

The ice came down the ramp, his back and shoulders waiting to resist its weight as he pulled it with his tongs. "Gonna be workin' at yo daddy's warehouse dis summer?" He grunted as he hoisted the ice.

"Maybe, some, if he can use me," I said. "I wanna make some money." I paused, waiting before I finally asked: "Are you going to Franklin's funeral, Joe?"

He stopped, lowered the ice for a minute. "Well, I s'pose so, Mr. Charlie. I s'pose so."

"Wonder why he drowned? I mean, how come he fell in the water?"

"Jus' an ol' man out dere thinkin'. Thinkin' and not payin' attention to his bidness, prob'ly."

"Wonder what he was thinkin' 'bout?"

Joe took out his bandanna and wiped the sweat from his face. "Oh, child, dat's hard to say. Maybe he wuz jus' thinkin' 'bout how far a river could take a fellow."

"What about his dogs? He got any left?"

"Oh, I think he still had dat female. But de rest all sold off. I spec' somebody'll take care of her."

"What about you?" I asked.

"Aw, child, I got all I can do to feed me and Gumbo. And I ain't gonna be able to take him out much longer. As least not as close as a place up there off Old Canton."

"Why not?"

"Well, the gov'ment and right of way folks still rootin' 'round up there to see if dey c'n find any more skeletons— maybe thinkin' dere's some cemeteries or more buried people. Dey gonna tear down dat house."

"Who's going to?" I asked.

"The gov'ment and highway people. Dat house gonna go de same way of de land. Seems like folks don't want land for *being on* no more, jus' *goin' through*. Folks in Memphis gettin' paid for it and even if dey wanted to keep it, de gov'ment gonna git it. Could be dat's what Ol' Franklin wuz thinkin' 'bout. Wid no more land, he'd jus' take to de river. Kinda like crossin' o'er de river."

He turned to see if anybody was close, then pulled something from his shirt pocket. He took my hand and placed it in mine and closed my fingers around it. It felt hard and I squeezed it as I looked into his face.

"Mr. Franklin would want me to give you dis. Dere ain't many I s'pose."

I opened my fingers and looked down and saw the 1907 mint silver dollar. "What—?"

"Don't say nothing,' child. Don't say nothin'. I got to git down de road. I gotta take a block of ice to Miss Nettleton fer her icebox."

I looked at him. His eyes sparkled. And I was sure I saw, once again, a tiny rainbow in a bead of sweat rolling down his face.

Two weeks later we attended our own funeral. Katy Jean died. Complications of pneumonia or something as a result of her cerebral palsy had taken her life. She took her last breath at the Baptist Hospital on North State Street.

I never saw Daddy cry. I only saw his red eyes afterwards. He kept the tears away from us. The rest of us wept long and openly. I don't think Mary Hester ever stopped until the day she died. At church the day of the funeral service, we were standing with Minnie. Mother said the last thing, the last words, Katy Jean uttered were, "I love y'all."

"She whispered it," Mother said.

Daddy had his arm draped over Mother's shoulder. "It was her way," Daddy said. "It was all her strength allowed her to do."

"It was like when we watched the seagulls on the coast," I said.

Mother dabbed at her eyes with a tissue. "What do you mean?"

"We use to sit on the veranda of the hotel and watch the seagulls. She always wanted to give them names. She would hold out her hands hoping they would land and she could name them. But she said we had to whisper or we would scare them away."

Mother smiled and then she cried. Daddy kissed Mother on her temple. "It was a Mississippi whisper. That's what God gave Katy Jean: a Mississippi whisper."

Epilogue

KATY JEAN DIED AT THE AGE OF TWENTY. SHE WAS BEAUTI-
ful. Jackson was her home. It still is. Henry returned
after a sojourn here and there, and often takes flowers to the
family resting place just outside Jackson. I left, but never
have my roots been torn. Often when I visit, Henry and I and
whatever friends are available remember the days when we
could roam the wooded areas around Jackson and the times
when such things as hoodoo and voodoo were almost real
because somebody said they were; and an escaped convict
was real because he was real.

In April 1955, a month before I "graduated" from Boyduling, the event—the miracle—the answer to prayers,
North and South, exploded in the newspapers, radio and
television; Dr. Jonas Salk announced his research had developed a vaccine for polio. The plague had been chased.

Boyd Hasting died at Khe Sanh, a decorated hero.
Theron Couch became a Blackjack dealer in Reno, Nevada,
and died before he was forty, of lung cancer. Grover owns
two dealerships on the Gulf Coast. Billy Cohen who became
an attorney said Grover probably cleaned up on insurance
after Hurricane Katrina. Billy's firm, with a bit of childhood
irony, cashed in on the great tobacco lawsuits. Ronny Erl's

life carried him to South Carolina while Buck remained close by in Clinton with a landscaping business.

But the plum trees and blackberry bushes and access to Bobcat Creek are no longer available for children to pursue and cherish. The interstate and all it brought: traffic, shopping centers, suburbia has taken the land and brought expensive bridges across the Pearl River.

July died a few years ago, but lived long enough to see his son graduate from Jim Hill and sign a professional baseball contract. He moved up no farther than AA and lives in Jackson, a Federal Express driver. I never was sure whether Joe Washington would have been a better ballplayer than Willie Mays. He wouldn't be a fighter; he couldn't be a farmer. He died as the best iceman I ever saw. I still have the silver dollar. Sometimes I take it out and turn it between my fingers. I think about Joe and July and Franklin. And the memory of Chambers Gallagher is etched.

Eudora Welty once said: "Childhood's learning is made up of moments. It isn't steady. It's a pulse." One of my strongest beats happened three weeks after Katy Jean died.

The day Streety was killed: A truck driver speeding down one of the neighborhood streets hit him broadside. He lay there bleeding from the mouth, his crumpled body twitching. But I knew the twitching was not a sign of life but of the end. I cried as much for Daddy as for Streety, I think. Daddy strode slowly toward the street, his deliberate steps a sign he, too, knew Streety would never stand or run again. As he knelt beside Katy Jean's noble old friend, I saw him rub his eye with the back of his hand. I finally saw his tears for Katy Jean. It was his whisper.

About the Author

WITH BRIEF INTERRUPTIONS FOR U.S.M.C. DUTY AND A tour working for the Mississippi Highway Department, Paul Yarbrough has worked for two oil companies and been an independent consultant in the oil business mostly as a landman for the past forty years in Houston, Texas. He is married with one son, Douglas, who now lives in North Louisiana. Paul has published a handful of short stories, flash fiction and essays in a variety of forums. Learn more about Paul Yarbrough at his website: www.paulhyarbrough.com.

Special thanks to Natalie Maynor, of Jackson.

www.ingramcontent.com/pod-product-compliance
Lightning Source LLC
Chambersburg PA
CBHW020413260626
47156CB00007B/2367